Somewhere there was another little girl

One she'd carried in her womb. She'd made so many promises to that baby as she dreamed of the future. She'd sung to her and laughed and tickled her own belly whenever a tiny toe or elbow surfaced.

But, through no fault of her own, she hadn't kept those promises. Her baby had never heard her voice again. Someone else had taken her home. Did these other parents love her and sing to her and tickle her toes?

"If only..." Lynn breathed soundlessly. If only she could *know*. See that this other little girl was loved and cared for, read to and hugged, see that *her* artwork was on the refrigerator for all to admire.

But how could she ever find out, without contacting the hospital and telling them? Without taking the chance of losing Shelly?

That was the torment. Risk the little girl who was the center of her life for the one who couldn't possibly remember her voice?

Lynn closed her eyes on a soft agonized exhalation. Risk *her*? How could she?

But how could she not?

Dear Reader,

I'm sure it won't surprise you to hear that the idea for *Whose Baby?* came to me when I was reading about the recent case in which it was discovered that two little girls had been switched at birth. All of us, I'm sure, were transfixed when reading about this horrifying mistake. I'll bet every parent thought immediately *"What if…"* Perhaps our deepest instinct is to protect our children. And yet…which child? If I found out one of my daughters wasn't biologically mine, I'd feel no less fiercely protective, no less loving. And yet…I could so easily come to feel the same about the child I'd carried for nine months.

Any time I read or hear about something so emotional, the writer part of me kicks in and also wonders *"What if…"* What if the hero had lost his wife, and their biological child is all he has left of her? What if the heroine fears he wants *both* girls? Talk about conflict!

I don't know that I've ever written a story with so many layers of painful and exhilarating emotion. Sitting in front of the computer each day, I felt as if I were unwrapping a gift from someone I'd loved and lost. Each layer was poignant, making me grateful for my own family.

See if you don't feel the same!

Best,

Janice Kay Johnson

WHOSE BABY?
Janice Kay Johnson

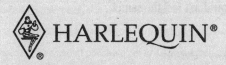

HARLEQUIN®

TORONTO • NEW YORK • LONDON
AMSTERDAM • PARIS • SYDNEY • HAMBURG
STOCKHOLM • ATHENS • TOKYO • MILAN • MADRID
PRAGUE • WARSAW • BUDAPEST • AUCKLAND

ISBN 0-373-70889-0

WHOSE BABY?

This edition published by arrangement with Harlequin Books S.A.

® and TM are trademarks of the publisher. Trademarks indicated with
® are registered in the United States Patent and Trademark Office, the
Canadian Trade Marks Office and in other countries.

Visit us at www.romance.net

Printed in U.S.A.

WHOSE BABY?

CHAPTER ONE

$O + O$ DOES NOT $= B$. So why was she even nervous?

Oblivious to the salt-scented breeze and the familiar whoosh of the broken surf, Lynn Chanak stared at the envelope in her hand. *Open it,* she told herself. *Then you can quit worrying about nothing.*

And nothing was just what it would prove to be.

That Portland lab had mixed up somebody else's blood with Shelly's. It was dumb to let the results shake her even for a minute. Poor Shelly had had to endure being stuck with a needle again, which still made Lynn mad, but it was done, over with, and now with the results from the new lab she'd be able to refute her ex-husband's ridiculous accusation.

There was no way a second lab would make the same kind of mistake. Lynn and Brian both had Type O blood; heaven help her, she'd once been foolish enough to think that meant they were made for each other.

With both parents having Type O blood, Shelly had to have the same.

So why not open the envelope?

"Mama!" Lynn's three-and-a-half-year-old daughter tugged at her sleeve. "See what I found?"

The small hand cupped a flame-red, wave-polished

chunk of agate that beachcombing tourists would have killed for.

Lynn smiled in delight and hugged her daughter. ''That's a pretty one! You've got sharp eyes!''

She sat on a gray, winter-tossed log on the beach, the pile of mail in her hand. This was a daily ritual for her and Shelly when the shop was closed. Wait for the mail, don sweatshirts against the sharp breeze, and then walk the two blocks from home to the rocky beach, famous for the sea stacks that reared offshore. Otter Beach had been a tiny lumber town until the Oregon coast became a favorite tourist destination. Now streets were lined with art galleries and antique shops, and prime beachfront real estate was taken by inns and bed-and-breakfasts.

Lynn's bookstore was one block over from the main street. The upstairs of the old house was home, the downstairs her business. During tourist season, she stayed open six days a week. By the time winter storms pounded the coast, she only bothered to open from Thursday through Sunday for locals and for the few hardy souls who came for romantic weekends and beachcombing after storms deposited Japanese floats and agates on the shore.

''I'll give this to Daddy next time he comes,'' Shelly announced. ''C'n you save it for him, Mommy?''

''You bet, sweetie,'' agreed Lynn, hiding her dismay. How was she going to explain to a three-year-old why Daddy wasn't visiting anymore?

Giggling, Shelly wormed her hand into the pocket of Lynn's faded, zip-front sweatshirt to deposit her find. The chunk of agate joined the crab claw and the mussel shell entwined with dried seaweed that she'd already collected.

For a moment Lynn watched as Shelly wandered away. She looked so cute in her denim overalls and rubber-toed sneakers, her mink-brown ponytail straight and sleek. Lynn tried hard to see what Brian did, but how could she? This was her *daughter*.

So what if her own hair was a warm, wavy chestnut-brown, if Brian was blond? So what if Shelly's eyes were brown, while Lynn's were green and Brian's blue? Kids didn't always look just like their parents. In fact, they hardly ever did. The genes that created a person were like…like the threads of color in a Persian carpet, thousands of bits of wool, woven together with a complexity that defied any ability to say that a certain blue came from such and such a sheep. Shelly might look like some forgotten great-grandmother. Did it *matter* that her face wasn't a reflection of her father's?

Apparently it did to Brian. He'd always been unreasonably jealous, both before they were married— when Lynn considered possessiveness romantic— and after. The marriage had been a mistake, a terrible mistake. Guilt ate at Lynn every time she thought about Brian, because she knew the failure was hers. She shouldn't have married him. He was right, when he had believed she didn't love him enough.

But she had never been unfaithful. There hadn't been another man; probably never would be, now that she knew she wasn't capable of the kind of passion a lifetime commitment required. She hadn't given Brian any reason to suspect she was seeing anyone, so it outraged her that now he should claim Shelly wasn't his.

Lynn bitterly resented having to put a three-year-old through the scary process of having blood drawn, but she'd done it. Not just because she needed Brian to keep paying the child support, but also because Shelly needed her dad.

So why wasn't she tearing open the envelope? Lynn wrenched her gaze from Shelly, crouched on her heels ten yards down the beach staring with intense fascination at something, and studied the return address on the envelope. McElvoy Laboratories, Seattle, Washington.

A different lab. Lynn hadn't taken Shelly back to their regular clinic for the second blood draw. She'd driven to Lincoln City. Of course she should have marched back into their doctor's office, waving that stupid piece of paper and proclaiming her indignation at the mistake. She shouldn't have had to pay for the second round of analysis. But she'd felt…cautious.

She made a face. Gun-shy. Brian had made her paranoid. She didn't want to give him any ammunition. If he knew about the first results, he wouldn't believe the second ones. He'd want more, instead of accepting the truth when she handed it to him.

Anyway, a voice whispered, *what if it* wasn't *a mistake? Shelly* doesn't *look like either parent.*

"Oh, right!" she said out loud. For Pete's sake, she'd been awake and present during her awful labor. Sure, because of the hemorrhaging, she hadn't seen her newborn daughter for the first hours, but then they'd laid the tiny red-faced baby at her breast, and she'd held her and loved her ever since. And, damn it, so had Brian! Only, now he had to get suspicious. Or cheap. He was late sometimes with the child-support check. Think what a good excuse this would be not to pay at all!

Lynn glanced up again; her daughter was in the exact same spot. A miniature tide pool, probably. Shelly had learned not to take living creatures from them, only to observe. She'd seen the difference between the rich color of a sea star clinging to a rock beneath the water and the dull hard body of a dead preserved one. She loved the scamper of tiny crabs, the dart of brown sandpipers, the hoarse roar of sea lions on the rocks offshore. This was home, magical and familiar at the same time.

Like having a child. For fleeting moments, Lynn saw through her daughter's eyes and became three years old again. Wondering, awed, frightened, reassured by simple comforts.

Other times, Lynn was perplexed by this complete, small person her daughter seemed to be. It was as if she'd been born whole, finished, and all Lynn could do was open the world to her. The idea that a parent could shape her child was as silly as believing the same blood type meant two people were mysteriously akin.

Open it.

Lynn couldn't understand her reluctance. She kept fingering that damned envelope. She'd peeked at all the bills, even flipped through a couple of publishers' catalogs as if their spring lists mattered more than the blood that traced pale blue lines beneath the translucent skin of her daughter's wrists, that beaded crimson when Shelly skinned her knee. Lifeblood.

Still Shelly crouched in the same spot, her attention span astonishing for a child her age. She didn't need her mom right now, except as home base. A pocket and a smile and a hug.

Lynn tore open the envelope and pulled out the single sheet of paper. Unfolded it, and stared down at the bald black letter *B*. There was more, but she didn't see it.

Her heart pounded so hard she wouldn't have heard Shelly scream. Her vision misted, and she had the eerie sensation of being alone on the beach after a late-afternoon fog had rolled in. Everything was gray, indistinct, abruptly looming in front of her and then swallowed behind her.

Oh God, oh God, oh God.

There had been no other man. Only Brian, ever. If Brian wasn't the father of Shelly Schoening, then she—Lynn—wasn't her mother, either.

How was that possible?

She moaned and hugged her knees. *How?*

She could think of only one answer. Somehow, two babies had been switched in the hospital. The little girl laid to nurse at her breast wasn't the one she'd carried for nine months. Her own baby had been given to another mother.

Somewhere, a toddler with bright blue eyes like Brian's or chestnut-brown hair like Lynn's called another woman Mommy.

Lynn whimpered again.

"Mommy?"

Swallowing her terror, Lynn looked into Shelly's frightened brown eyes. "Yes, honey?" She sounded only a little hoarse.

"Is Mommy sick?"

To death. Her whole world was her daughter. Not that unknown child somewhere, the one who might look like her, but *this* child—the one she'd nursed and diapered, whose toes she'd tickled and counted, the one who squeezed her hand and waited for an answer.

"No," she said. "Yes. Mommy's tummy felt funny for a minute. Like this." She burrowed her hand inside the OshKosh overalls and tickled until Shelly's elfin face crinkled with a giggle.

Shelly wrapped her arms around her mother's neck and pressed her cold, plump cheek against Lynn's. "I wanna cheeseburger," she confided. "And chocolate milk."

Lynn hugged back. Hugged until the toddler squeaked with alarm.

"You know what?" Lynn said. "A cheeseburger sounds good to me, too. *And* chocolate milk. What do you say we go home?"

Shelly nodded vigorously. Lynn rose from the log, feeling as stiff as an old woman. She collected her pile of mail and took her daughter's small hand. Feeling numb, she turned her back on the waves, her sneakered feet accustomed to the way the beach stones and sand gave with each step. One forward, half back. A struggle that strengthened the body.

Her daughter chattered. Lynn heard not a word, although she smiled and agreed.

She focused passionately on only one thought: Shelly was *hers*. Nobody must ever know that maybe, somehow, she wasn't.

After lunch, while Shelly napped, Lynn sat at the

kitchen table and convinced herself that Brian couldn't insist on this blood work. She'd give up the child-support money first, tell him he could think what he liked. Even agree that he was right, although she hated the idea of letting him believe she'd sneaked around and had sweaty sex with some man she hardly knew—because, after all, she had no real friends who were male.

It took until five o'clock for Lynn to get angry. She put water on to boil for macaroni and went to check on Shelly. She was curled at one end of the shabby velveteen couch watching Dumbo for the thousandth time. Her flowered flannel blanket was tucked under one arm and her thumb was in her mouth. On the dentist's advice, Lynn had been trying to break her of sucking her thumb, but tonight she didn't say anything, just kissed the silky top of Shelly's head and breathed in her essence before going back to the kitchen.

Things like babies getting switched in the hospital didn't happen! she thought incredulously, then more firmly. Parents were always afraid they would, but hospitals took such precautions these days. Lynn still had the plastic band that had been around Shelly's plump wrist when she was released from the hospital. It had exactly matched Lynn's.

No. There had to be some other explanation.

This lab was wrong, too?

She poured the macaroni into the boiling water and frowned.

Wait! Could Brian have lied about his blood type? She stirred the macaroni and tried to remember. Had she said what hers was first? It would be like him to try to create a fiction to make it sound as though they were destined for each other. He'd wanted her from the first time they'd met, in the bookstore where she'd worked after she graduated from college.

Closing her eyes, Lynn tried to replay the scene. A popular professor at the university had been in a car accident, and the English department had held a blood drive. She'd been resting after giving a pint, when the nurse pushed back the curtain and said, "If you've finished your juice, you're all set!"

And there Brian was, on the next gurney. Still lying down, he'd turned his head and grinned. "Hey, they've been sucking blood out of you, too, huh?"

He'd come into the bookstore for the first time just the previous weekend. Or, at least, she'd noticed him for the first time. And how could she not have noticed him? He was six feet two inches, with short sun-streaked blond hair and bright blue eyes. He was tanned from skiing at Mount Hood. She'd asked, because it was winter and most people in Portland were pale. He looked like a surfer, broad shouldered and athletic and golden.

"Well, it was voluntary," she'd said shyly.

"Yeah, so they say." He waved away the orange juice and sat up without taking it slowly. How like a man!

Somehow they ended up walking out together. And…yes! He'd asked, "What type blood do you have?"

She did volunteer the information first. She distinctly remembered the way he'd turned and said, so seriously, "That means the same blood runs through our veins. We must be meant for each other."

She'd made it a joke; they'd both laughed, but a small thrill had run through her at the idea, presented with the intensity and gravity of a marriage proposal.

The more fool her!

She dumped the macaroni into the waiting colander, jumping when the boiling water splashed her hand. She should have known better. The single, chipped porcelain sink was shallow, and she was always careful.

Tears sprang to her eyes. "Damn, damn, damn," she muttered, turning on the cold water and sticking her hand under it.

Why, that creep! All this anguish, and he'd lied!

She told herself she was furious, but really relief flooded her in a sweet tide. Such a simple explanation! And after she'd come up with such a convoluted one.

The relief lasted all evening. She played Chutes and Ladders with Shelly, then told silly stories and every knock-knock joke she could think of at bedtime, buoyed by that wash of exquisite release from fear.

She thought about calling him, the scumbag, and saying, "I might think about checking our daughter's blood type, if I knew what yours *really* is."

But, although she should be madder than she was, Lynn still thought she should cool down before she confronted him. Besides, she wanted to be sure of herself.

She could ask his mother. No, better yet, she could call the blood bank and say that he'd been in a car accident, and she didn't remember his blood type but she knew he'd donated.

That was the moment when she remembered. There she was, checking to be sure the bathroom door was open enough to cast light into the hall so Shelly wouldn't get scared if she woke up later. One part of Lynn's mind thought, six inches, that's perfect, and another part was wondering if she shouldn't add more books on tape to her stock downstairs—a man, a tourist, had asked for them Sunday, and left without buying anything after looking at what she did have—and oh yes, she had to pick up peanut butter at the store tomorrow, since Shelly practically lived on it.

Through all her other preoccupations, she felt the onset of fear and the prickle of goose bumps on her skin even before a memory came to her. A woman from the blood bank had called, not long after Lynn and Brian got married, and she'd asked Lynn to encourage her husband to donate blood again.

"He's got Type O, you know," she said, "and we're terribly short."

Lynn had said helpfully, "My blood is O, too," and she'd promised she would ask Brian, but she'd definitely come down to the blood bank herself. She had, and he must have, too, after work, not romantically together this time. That part didn't matter; what did was that the blood bank had specifically wanted him to come in because he had O.

Instead of going to bed, Lynn felt her way back along the narrow hall to the kitchen, with its tiny refrigerator so old she had to regularly defrost the freezer part, the linoleum with the pattern worn to a blur, the brand-new shiny white stove, bought when the old one gave up the ghost at the worst possible moment, the way it always went. In the brightness when she switched on the light, the cheery yellow she'd painted the cabinets looked garish, a disguise as obvious as a clown's red nose.

The living quarters of the house were crummy; she'd put all her money into the downstairs, the bookstore. She'd had to. She and Shelly could make do, Lynn had told herself. Until the store became really profitable. If bookstores ever did.

But now she couldn't help looking around and imagining what other people would think. If, for example, Shelly's real, biological parents were trying to take her back.

I wouldn't look very good, would I? Lynn thought. Her knees crumpled, and she sank onto one of the two mismatched chairs that went with the tiny, scarred Formica and metal kitchen table. *I don't have much to offer Shelly materially, and I'm divorced, and my ex-husband thinks I must have cheated on him.*

Those other parents, they could take Shelly away from her. She remembered a photo from some horrible child custody case, when the little boy was screaming and reaching for the only parents he'd ever known while the biological father carried him away. How painfully easy it was to transpose faces: she was the one trying to be brave, make this seem like the right thing, while Shelly was ripped away from her like one of the beautiful sea stars from a slick wet rock.

Oh God, oh God, oh God.

She drew up her knees and hugged herself and shook, panting for breaths. She could hear herself gasping. She must be in shock, she felt so strange. Cold, and frightened, as if an intruder had crept in and violated her, as if she would never feel safe again.

Nobody must ever know. That was her only hope. *Nobody. Ever.*

Eventually the shaking passed, and she saw again her kitchen, tidy and spotlessly clean, however shabby, and on the refrigerator Shelly's bright crayon drawings that were supposed to be sea stars or seals or horses, those inner imaginings that her short fingers were not yet capable of rendering. It was home: loving, safe, clean and ordered. What else mattered? Certainly not money.

Nor blood. She didn't care whose ran through Shelly's veins. She would never let it matter.

But first, she had to be sure.

The blue plastic clock on the wall said eight-thirty. Not too late to call Brian's mother.

Ruth Schoening's voice held caution, once she knew who was on the phone.

"Lynn. My, it's late in the evening to be calling."

Not: *Oh, gracious, Shelly is all right, isn't she?*

Lynn noticed the lack, and decided on honesty. "Brian's told you he doesn't think Shelly is his daughter, hasn't he?"

The pause resonated with awkwardness. "He did say something."

"I would never..." The automatic denial caught in Lynn's throat. Oh, God. She might someday have to claim she *had*. She took a breath. "You don't believe that, do you?"

Really, she was begging, *You* know *me*. Please say

that you have faith in me, that you love Shelly no matter what.

"It's not really my business," her ex-husband's mother said, the constraint in her voice obvious.

"She's your granddaughter."

"Is she?"

She had begun to shake again, Lynn noticed with peculiar detachment. "This is so ridiculous," she exclaimed, trying to laugh and failing.

"I hope so," Ruth said. "But, you know, he's right—Shelly doesn't look like anybody in the family."

"When my grandmother was a little girl…"

"Brian said he'd looked through your family album, and Shelly doesn't look like anybody on your side, either. She's so…so dark, and with that pointy chin she makes me think of, oh, a pixie from a fairy tale. *My* children were round and sturdy and blond. Like little Swedes."

She always said that as if Swedish children were fairer than any other kind. She never addressed the fact that Schoening was a German name, not Scandinavian.

Obviously, there would be no assurances of unfailing love no matter what. Shelly would lose her grandparents, too, if it came to that.

"Well," Lynn said, "the reason I'm calling is that I'm considering having Shelly tested so we can lay this foolishness to rest. It makes me mad to have to subject her to needles and all that scariness, but I might do it. So what I wondered is, do you remember what Brian's blood type is?"

"Oh, yes," his mother said promptly. "He's O

positive, just like me. What a good idea, Lynn! Doubts should always be laid to rest, don't you think?''

Fury kindled in her breast. Now that she'd gotten what she wanted, she let anger have its rein, sharpening her voice. ''What I think is that all this is incredibly insulting. I understand that Brian's still angry about our divorce, but you know me better than to believe this...this hogwash. You claim to love Shelly. You always say I should bring her for visits more often, that she's adorable, that I should send pictures so you can show all your friends, and now you talk about her as if she's tainted and you've always known something was wrong with her. She's...she's a bright, beautiful child whose eyes don't happen to be blue. Well, I'm not *Swedish,* and I don't expect my daughter to look like she is!'' Lynn ended with a snap. ''*That's* what I think.''

She didn't wait for a response. She hung up the telephone in a righteous rage that deserted her too quickly. How could she get mad, when Shelly *wasn't* Brian's daughter? Maybe she was the one who was blind! Maybe she should have realized immediately that something was wrong, that the baby the nurses handed her was a changeling.

But she hadn't, oh, she hadn't. Instead, the connection had been deep and instant, a mother's love for this child and only this one.

Well, the fierceness of her love hadn't diminished. She would tell Brian that she wasn't going to get Shelly tested, and if he cut his daughter off, so be it. She would let him live with a creeping feeling of shame. It would serve him right.

She stood up, as wearily as if she'd just overcome a violent bout of flu, and turned off the kitchen light, using the glow from the bathroom to find her way to her bedroom.

Life might get harder; Shelly would be hurt that her father didn't want her. *But no one must ever know.*

THE DREAM CAME EVERY NIGHT from then on. She was searching desperately for someone. For her little girl. First she was on the beach, and she'd been reading her mail, and the fog had rolled in, and she looked up suddenly and realized she couldn't see her.

"Shelly!" she began crying. "Shelly, where are you?" She leaped to her feet and spun in every direction, crying over and over, "Shelly!"

She began stumbling toward the water. Boulders reared from nowhere, tripping her. The roar of the surf filled her ears, and she knew with sickening certainty that Shelly had been caught by a wave.

But, no, she wasn't on the beach at all. She was in a city, although the fog still played tricks with her eyes. The sound was from traffic. Oh, no! How could she have looked away, even for a moment? The sea was merciless, but cars were deadly.

She searched the sidewalks frantically for a bright chestnut head. People passing ignored her. Then she saw her, out on the median, cars racing by without slowing at all for the toddler who teetered there. She wore rags; she looked like Cosette in *Les Misérables,* wretched and unwanted. Brimming with tears, her bright blue eyes met Lynn's momentarily through a break in the traffic, but without recognition.

My daughter doesn't know me, Lynn realized with horror.

"Stay where you are!" Lynn screamed. "Wait! I'm coming!"

But her voice meant nothing to this child, and with greater shock Lynn discovered she didn't know her own daughter's name.

Sobbing, the little girl stepped from the curb.

And Lynn awakened, as she did every night, her screamed "No!" trembling on her lips and tears running down her cheeks.

With a moan she curled into a ball and shuddered. At last she went into the bathroom and splashed cold water on her face, then stared hopelessly at herself in the mirror.

Of course she was having dreams; their content was hardly subtle.

Somewhere out there was another little girl, one she'd carried in her womb. How many promises she'd made to that baby as she dreamed of the future! She sang to her and laughed and tickled her own belly when a tiny toe or elbow surfaced. She played music and danced and read aloud, just so her child would know her voice, would know she was loved.

But, through no fault of her own, she hadn't kept those promises. Her baby had never heard her voice again. Someone else had taken her home. Did these other parents love her and sing to her and tickle her toes? Or had she gone home with a teenager who hadn't really wanted to get pregnant? Perhaps she was in a foster home, or had an angry father who shook her when she wouldn't quit crying. What if she was slow to develop, but nobody was patient?

Or what if they loved her, these parents, but they were raising her the only way they knew how, by spanking her when she got cranky or broke something, by screaming at her with the anger of their own childhoods in their voices?

"If only..." Lynn breathed soundlessly. If only she could *know*. See that this other little girl *was* loved and cared for, read to and hugged, that *her* artwork was on the refrigerator for all to admire.

If she knew, the dreams would go away.

But how could she ever find out, without contacting the hospital and telling them? Without taking the chance of losing Shelly?

That was the torment. Risk the little girl who was the center of her life, who meant everything to her, for the sake of one who couldn't possibly remember her voice. Who would have forgotten her songs and the stories she'd promised to finish someday, when they could giggle together.

She crept down the hall like a ghost to her daughter's room, hovering in the doorway because the bed nearly filled the space, which in a house of this era had probably been meant as a sewing room or a nursery. Sunny yellow and black cats frolicked among sunflowers on the wallpaper that climbed the slanted ceiling. Yellow curtains covered the tall sash window. Under a pale lemon-yellow and white comforter, Shelly slept peacefully. Lynn could just make out her face in the glow from the hall, and thought, Ruth is right. She looks like a Celt from old stories, a fairy child, with that small, pointy chin, that high curving forehead and glossy brown hair as straight as promises that were kept.

Risk her, for the dream child?

Lynn closed her eyes on a soft, agonized exhalation. How could she?

How could she not?

CHAPTER TWO

LATE AGAIN.

Adam Landry swore at the driver of the car in front of him, which hesitated just too long and missed the one and only opening to make a left turn before the light became red.

Damn, he thought bitterly. They'd both be sitting through another full light. And he was already—he snatched an edgy look at the clock on his dash—ten minutes past the closing of his daughter's preschool.

This was getting to be routine, and if he wasn't careful they'd ask him to make other arrangements for Rose. But the Cottage Path Preschool and Day Care was the best.

Oh, hell, why lie to himself? He didn't know if it was best. He didn't know a thing about it, except that Jennifer had chosen it, an eternity ago when she was pregnant and joyful, not planning to go back to work but figuring she'd need a place for drop-in sometimes.

Over dinner, she'd told him about it, her eyes sparkling with pleasure. "It's the Cottage Path Preschool. Isn't that perfect? Can you believe it? Our Rose will trip up the path to the cottage. Oh!" She shivered in delight, and he'd momentarily seen the vision that had become the center of her life: a little girl with the same mahogany brown hair as her mommy, her legs skinny, dimples flashing and her giggle a trill like a flute solo that reached for heaven and found it.

Their child.

And him? What had he said? A gruff, ''You're not letting the name of the place suck you in, are you?''

She'd only laughed at him, her joy undimmed. ''Don't be silly. It's a wonderful preschool! The director's written a book about early childhood development. They have animals—chickens and goats and this big lazy dog that lets kids climb all over him and only grunts. And puzzles and books and blocks and puppets! It's wonderland.''

Pain stabbed now and Adam rubbed his chest. He'd never considered any place else for Rose. He was trying to raise their daughter as Jennifer would have wanted to, which meant he scraped his memory for nuggets his wife might have dropped, perhaps in bed when he scanned the financial news a last time while she chattered on in her light voice as if oblivious to his lack of attention.

Adam took another savage look at the clock and swore. Was he screwing up one more thing Jennifer had wanted for Rose?

But maybe it wasn't the best choice now. Maybe he should go for a nanny.

He tensed when the light turned green and willed the driver of the Buick to make a dash before cross-traffic began. But, hell, no. The car didn't even inch forward. The heel of Adam's hand was on the horn when he clenched his teeth and made himself wrap his fingers around the wheel again. *Shit.* If he hadn't stayed for that last goddamn phone call, he wouldn't be in such a hurry he wanted other drivers to take their lives in their hands just to get out of his way. Why hadn't he walked out, ignored the ringing?

He couldn't do everything.

He had to try. He owed it to Rose. And to Jennifer.

An interminable five more minutes had passed before he barreled into the parking lot, yanked on the emergency brake and killed the engine, slamming his door before he strode in.

The director of the preschool, a woman of his own age named Melissa Gearhart, waited in the entry, eyes cool.

"Mr. Landry. Rose has been worried."

His intense anxiety made itself felt in a long huff of breath. "God, I'm sorry. I've done it again."

"I'm afraid I'm going to have to start charging you when staff has to stay late, like today."

"I understand." He swallowed. "Where's Rose?"

The dark-haired woman with tired smudges beneath her eyes turned. "Under the climber."

He stepped past her into the main activity room, where the floor was covered with bright mats to pad falls from the slide and wooden peg climber. He had to circle a playhouse before he saw his daughter, lying on the mat with her thumb in her mouth.

Wearing clothes he'd never seen before. Ill fitting and mismatched.

"She had an accident again," Melissa said softly behind him. "No big deal. I've got her clothes in a plastic bag for you. Just bring those back when you've washed them."

He closed his eyes for a moment, acknowledging

more failure. Or maybe not—he hadn't had the guts to ask the mothers who picked up their three-year-olds whether they had potty accidents still, too. Or the occasional father, none exclusive parents the way he was. Adam didn't even like to ask Melissa, because he didn't want to know something was wrong, that he'd already warped his beloved child.

If only he knew what the hell he was doing.

If only Jennifer were alive to help him do it.

"Hey, Rose Red," he said softly, crouching. "Ready to bloom?"

"Daddy!" She erupted to her feet and into his arms, her sky-blue eyes flooding with tears. "You're late, and I'm hungry, and I had a accident, an'…"

He stemmed the flow. "I'm sorry, I'm sorry. Here you were, all by yourself."

"Except for Lissa," Rose mumbled against his shoulder. She snuffled. "Lissa didn't leave me."

He felt the crushing addition, *Like you do*. Every day.

She'd taken lately to holding on to him and screaming when he tried to drop her off in the morning. He felt like the worst parent in the whole damned world when the day-care workers had to pry his daughter's fingers off him and haul her away, when the last thing he saw was Rose's round tear-streaked face. Those desperate, pleading eyes haunted his days, gave him a feeling of self-loathing.

But, goddamn it, he had to work!

Rationally he knew that other kids cried in the morning, too, that it was probably just a stage. Reason didn't quell the guilt that ate at his gut like too many cups of coffee.

She needed her daddy, and he wasn't there.

He hustled her out to the car, belatedly grabbing the white plastic garbage sack that held Rose's own clothes. That meant laundry tonight. He didn't want to leave these for Ann, their twenty-something housekeeper-cook. When Rose wet the bed, he always changed it, too. Three and a half wasn't so old, he tried to tell himself, but he hadn't seen those discreet plastic bags go home with Rose's friends Rainy and Sylvie, either. Not in months.

His daughter fell asleep during the drive home, worn out by a ten-hour day, and more guilt stabbed him. Poor Rosebud. How did a little girl grow into a woman without a mother to lead the way? What did he know about girlish secrets or adolescent crushes or makeup or menstrual cramps?

Well, he'd damn well learn. He was mommy and daddy both, determined not to foist his daughter's upbringing on a series of nannies. Jennifer wouldn't have wanted that.

I didn't mean it, he said silently, speaking to her as if she were listening. *No nanny.*

A nanny would be a replacement. A substitute mother. No one could be Jennifer, petite, quick moving, eternally optimistic, *alive.*

Dead, in every meaningful way, long before her daughter was cut from her belly.

He hadn't even looked at Rose when doctors performed the C-section. He'd been holding Jennifer's hand, although Jennifer didn't know it, would never know it, because she was brain-dead. He'd been saying goodbye, because the shell of her body had no purpose anymore, now that it wasn't needed to sustain her child. He had agreed that she would be unhooked from machines as soon as the baby could survive on her own.

"I'll do my best," he had whispered to the love of his life. One last promise, he thought, praying she didn't know how he had dreaded the birth because it meant severing any last wisp of hope that the doctors were wrong, that she would yet wake up.

How could she be gone? He had gripped her hand so hard it should have hurt, but she only lay there, eyes closed, breast rising and falling with the hissing push of the respirator, unaware of her daughter's birth, of his tears and whispered, wrenching, "Goodbye, Jenny." Unaware when he blundered from the room.

Unaware when her heart stopped, when the last breath caught in her throat.

His bright-faced, pretty, otherworldly wife was already dead when her daughter began life.

He named her Jenny Rose, and called her Rose, this little girl who showed no signs of looking like her mama, to his relief and disappointment both. Her hair had developed red tints and curls, and the deep blue of her eyes never changed, as everyone said it would.

Some days, Adam was intensely grateful that he didn't have to think about his lost Jenny every time he looked at his daughter. And yet, he'd wanted to hold on to a part of her, remember her, never lose sight of her pixie face, but sometimes now he had to pick up the photo that sat on his bedside table in a silver frame to remember her. Sometimes she faded to the point that he thought perhaps her face *was* round, like Rose's, or her nose solemnly straight; perhaps her hair had a forgotten wave, or she had moved or talked with a deliberateness that spoke of long thought.

But the sight of her face, even in the photograph, reminded him of her high cheekbones and pointy chin, turned-up nose and full yet delicate lips, always parted as she breathlessly waited for the chance to launch into speech. How often she'd had to crinkle her nose in apology, because she had been untactful or indiscreet, words flowing without thought. Even when she was hurtful, he'd found her spontaneity endearing, innocence to be treasured and guarded.

Adam had wanted the same for Rose, that she should grow up free to chatter. He wanted her to believe, always, that what she thought and felt was valued.

Instead his Rose was a quiet child, as thoughtful as her mother had been airy. Their daughter was in personality more his than Jennifer's, although she didn't look much like him, either.

He paused at the curb long enough to grab the mail from the box, then drove straight into the garage. Rose didn't stir when he turned off the engine. When he went around to unbuckle her car seat, he set the mail on the car roof. A card for her from Jennifer's parents, he noted with one corner of his attention. Good, Rose loved to get mail. A credit card statement, probably a demand for money from the utility company, the usual junk hoping he'd buy a new bedroom suite or refinance his house, and something from the hospital where Rose had been born.

The bills for Jennifer's protracted death and Rose's

birth had been horrendous. But paid, every last one of them. The insurance company, bless them, hadn't balked at a one.

The doctors and nursing staff had been compassionate, patient, gentle and kind. And he never wanted to see any of them again. Never wanted to walk those halls, smell cleansers and death. He'd go to any other hospital in the city in preference.

Unless perhaps, he thought, easing his sleepy, grumbling daughter from her car seat, Rose was seriously ill or hurt. Then he could endure the memories, for her.

In the house, Adam plopped her on the couch and put on a video. *Winnie the Pooh,* her current favorite. Hurrying to the kitchen, he took a casserole covered in plastic wrap from the refrigerator and put it straight into the microwave. High, twenty minutes, Ann had written on the sticky note attached to it. She was a gem. The kitchen sparkled, as always, and her cooking was damned good.

The one thing she didn't do was child care. She'd made that plain from the start. Her disinclination suited his reluctance to pass any part of his job as parent onto someone else, even though it would have been handy to have a housekeeper who would watch Rose when she was sick and couldn't go to day care, or to pick her up when Adam had to stay late in the office. But he'd known how easy it would be to slide from that into having Ann pick her up every day, feed her dinner, then perhaps make her breakfast and drive her to the Cottage Path Preschool, until in the end he wasn't doing much but kissing his daughter good-night.

So he and Ann had a deal: in return for weekly checks, she was like the shoemaker's elves, invisible and indispensable. Rose had scarcely even met her, and Adam and she communicated by sticky notes left on the fridge, but the house was clean and she always had dinner ready to go in the oven or microwave. Saturdays he cooked himself. Sundays, he and Rose usually went out for dinner, her choice, which meant McDonald's or Renny's Pizza Parlor, but he didn't mind.

While the microwave hummed, he thumbed through the mail and discarded three-quarters of it, setting aside the card for Rose when she was a little more alert. The envelope from the hospital Adam fingered. He was strangely reluctant to open it. Some kind of follow-up, he supposed, or maybe they wanted him on their board of governors, or…

Well, hell, find out.

He read the letter through the first time without understanding it. A distressing discovery had been made. At this point, hospital officials didn't know where to assign blame. He could be assured an investigation was under way. In the meantime, Jenny Rose Landry should undergo testing.

Testing for what?

He knew and wouldn't let himself see the sentence that began, ''Because of unusual circumstances, the mother of a girl born on the same day as your daughter in this hospital has found that she has been raising a child who is not a biological relation to her.'' The letter continued by raising the possibility that two of the six baby girls born that day had been switched in the nursery. Administrators were asking that parents agree to blood tests to determine whether this was, indeed, what had happened. He was particularly urged, because his child had been born within twenty minutes of the girl in question.

When Adam did, finally, make himself see, and when he grasped all that this could mean, anger roared through his veins, darkening his vision.

Could they really be so incompetent as to make a mistake of this magnitude? Babies were supposed to be tagged immediately so this wasn't possible! Hadn't they put a wristband on Jenny Rose while she was still bloody, still giving her first thin cry?

He hadn't seen. Adam bent his head suddenly and gripped the edge of the kitchen counter as panic whipped around the perimeter of his anger, as if it were only the eye of a hurricane.

They might not have followed the usual procedures, because the circumstances were so unusual. Respecting his grief, nurses might have carried the infant girl straight to the nursery before taking the Apgar and banding her wrist.

Even then—his anger revived—how could they screw up so royally? What did they do, leave babies lying around like Lego blocks in a preschool? Had the nurses wandered by sometime later and said, "Oh, yeah, this one must be the Landry kid?"

But the panic was more powerful than the anger, because his basic nature wouldn't let him be less than logical. If a mistake had been made that night, his daughter had all too likely been part of it. No mother or father had been hovering over her; she had never been placed at her mother's breast, and she wasn't held by her father until hours after her birth. Adam inhaled sharply, swearing. Hours? God. He hadn't thought about Jenny Rose until the next day, when his grief had dulled and he'd remembered that his wife had left a trust to him.

Only, by that time, the baby that had been lifted, blood-slick, from Jennifer's belly might have accidentally been switched with another little girl born the same hour.

Where had *her* parents been? he raged. How could they not have paid more attention? Why hadn't they noticed the switch?

He breathed heavily through his mouth. The microwave was beeping.

"Daddy?" Jenny Rose was saying from the kitchen doorway, the single word murmured around her thumb.

Think, he commanded himself. Then, *Don't think. Not now.*

"Yeah, Petunia?" He sounded almost normal.

She gave a hiccuping giggle. "Rose, Daddy! Not Petunia."

It was an old joke. "Oh, yeah," he agreed. "I knew you were some flower or other."

"Daddy, I'm hungry."

"Lucky for you, dinner's done." He hadn't put on a vegetable, but right now he didn't care.

He dished up the casserole in bowls and carried them out to the family room where he joined Rose in watching Tigger and Pooh Bear try to patch up Eeyore's problems, in their bumbling, well-meaning way.

Like the damned hospital officials.

Why contact me? Adam wondered. Was that

mother dissatisfied with the child she'd been given? Did she want to trade her in for another one? Fresh anger buffeted him. Wasn't his biological child good enough for her?

Not just his. Jennifer's.

That's when it hit him: In this other home, there might be a little girl who *did* have Jenny's pointed chin and quirky smile and ability to flit from idea to idea as if the last was forgotten as soon as the temptation of the next presented itself.

He groaned, barely muffling the sound in time to prevent Rose from wanting to know if Daddy hurt. Could she kiss it and make it better?

His Rose. By God, nobody was taking her from him.

But. Jennifer had left their baby in trust to him, and he might have lost her. He hadn't even looked at her. If only he'd seen her tiny features, he would have known, later, when they handed him Rose.

He made his decision then, as simply as that, although not without fear greater than any he'd felt since the phone call telling him his wife had been in a car accident.

Nobody would take his Jenny Rose from him. But he had to let her be tested, and if she wasn't his daughter, wasn't Jennifer's…

Well, he had to see the child who was. Find out what he could do to make her life right, from now on. Earn the trust he'd been given.

ADAM DIDN'T TAKE his Rosebud to that hospital. He didn't trust them, although he never defined the sins he thought them willing to commit. He only knew he had to protect Rose. So he took her to her own pediatrician for DNA testing. And then Adam went to the hospital with the results in his hand.

The results that had told him Jenny Rose was neither his daughter nor Jennifer's.

There, he listened to repeated expressions of regret, saw in their eyes the intense anxiety that meant officials had lawsuits dancing in their heads at night like poisonous sugarplums. He didn't quiet their fears. Hadn't made up his mind about a lawsuit. They deserved to pay until they hurt. But he didn't want or need blood money. And no justice he could exact on them would make up for what they had done to him and Rose. To his other daughter. And perhaps, to Rose's biological parents, although it wasn't yet clear to him whether they shared his agony, or were hoping to steal Jenny Rose.

They talked of an investigation. They were interviewing nurses, although it was taking time, they said, sweating. Several on duty that night no longer worked there, or even lived in Portland. But babies were always banded in the birthing room, that was hospital policy. Somebody would surely remember why, on this occasion, policy hadn't been followed.

Adam knew why it hadn't, in the case of his daughter. Although it should have been. How could the nurses and doctors not have realized how doubly precious his daughter would be to him, once the lines on the monitors flattened, once the machines were unplugged and the illusion of life was taken from his wife? Seeing his grief, how could they have been so careless?

And how the hell could two mistakes so monumental have been made on the same night?

The other mother—the hospital's representatives cleared their throats—Jenny Rose's biological mother, that is, had been hemorrhaging. Doctors had feared for her life. Had been concentrating on saving her. Thus, in this case, too, the baby had been an afterthought. Nurses had hustled her away, so she didn't distract the doctors. Neither parent had looked at her; the father had been intent on his wife, and she had been semiconscious. The mistake was inexcusable, but—ahem—they could understand how it had been made. Or, at least, how it had been set up, they said. Two bassinets next to each other in the nursery, two baby girls born within twenty minutes of each other, both brown haired. And newborns could look so much alike.

He vented his rage at this point and they quailed. But what good did his rage do? What satisfaction could he take in frightening a bunch of lawyers and administrators who hadn't been there that night, probably hardly knew what wing of the hospital housed the delivery rooms or the nursery?

None.

"The future," they suggested tentatively, and he bit back further rage even he recognized as naked fear. Nobody had said, *She's not your daughter. It won't do you any good to go to court and fight for custody. The biological parents* will *win, given that this situation is not their fault any more than it's yours.* But they were thinking it.

"All right," he said abruptly, voice harsh. "I'll meet with these other parents."

It would be only the mother, he was told. She was divorced, and the biological father was not at this point interested in custody. She was anxious to talk to him, they said. Could he please bring a photograph of Jenny Rose?

The hospital set it up for the next afternoon. Each parent could bring an attorney. Adam chose not to, although he knew it might be foolish. Right now, he just wanted to see what he was facing. He expected the worst.

The woman had begun this horror in a quest to find her natural daughter, apparently never minding the cost to the innocent child she had raised.

Adam fully expected to detest her.

A nearly sleepless night followed a half-a-dozen others. He'd forgotten how to sleep, except in nightmarish bursts from which he awakened to the sound of Rosebud screaming. But when he rolled from bed and stumbled into the hall, he invariably realized the sobs, the terror, were in his head. She slept peacefully, he would see, standing in the doorway to her room, able to make out her round, gentle face in the soft glow from her Pooh Bear night-light. He hadn't told her about any of this. She didn't know that a woman she'd never met wanted to tear her away from her home and her daddy. He might not be the best parent in the world, he thought in anguish, but she trusted him. He'd given her that much.

He left her that morning at the Cottage Path Preschool and let her cling longer than usual before he handed her, crying, to a day-care worker. Navigating Portland's old freeways like an automaton, Adam arrived at the hospital early. His eyes burned from lack of sleep, but he otherwise felt numb. He wanted to see her before she saw him, before she knew who he was. As he locked his Lexus and walked toward the entrance, he searched the parking lot for any woman who could possibly be the mother of a child the age of his daughter. Daughters. Of Jenny Rose and... Shelly. Shelly Schoening.

But of course he was denied any kind of anonymous entry. A receptionist was poised in wait to usher him onto an elevator with murmurs and more regrets and an "Oh, dear" when she got a good look at his face just before the elevator doors shut.

A lawyer took over when the doors sprang open on the third floor. "The conference room is just down this way."

They were so damned helpful, Adam was reminded of an old football trick: help your opponent up as fast as you knocked him down. Never let him rest.

The carpet up here was plush, the plants glossy, the artwork hanging on the papered walls elegant. This part of the hospital was completely divorced from the trenches, where babies were born and surgeries performed, where death happened. Up here they knew bills and statistics. He could have been in a law firm.

The conference room was smallish, holding one long table and eight chairs upholstered in an unobtrusive oatmeal. The air had that hushed quality that told him the room was well soundproofed. A place where grieving parents and spouses could be persuaded to sign away their loved ones' body parts. He might have been here, back then. He didn't remember.

Not even this air could muffle the anxiety crackling from his escort. It warned him before he saw her, sitting alone at the table, facing the door.

This slender woman with curly auburn hair had also wanted to be here early; wanted to see him before he saw her. She, too, clutched at any minor advantage.

This round, she'd won.

Poleaxed, he was barely aware of walking to the other side of the table and pulling out a chair. Sitting down, gripping the wooden arms, and looking a hungry, shocked fill.

She was Jenny Rose's mother. He would have recognized her in a crowd. A round, pleasant face, pretty rather than beautiful, a scattering of tiny freckles on a small nose, a curve of forehead and a way of tilting her head to one side...all were Rose. And that hair. God, that hair. Shiny, untamable waves, brown lit by a brushfire. He'd shampooed that hair, eased a brush through it, struggled to braid it. Kissed it.

"What," he asked hoarsely, "do you want?"

CHAPTER THREE

HE STRODE IN, just as she'd feared, a big angry man with a hard face. From the moment he sat down, she felt his hostility like porcupine quills jabbing and hooking her skin.

"What do you want?" he asked brusquely.

No preambles. No introductions. No "we're in a tough spot, aren't we?"

Through her exhaustion and dread, Lynn said, "I want this never to have happened."

His eyes narrowed a flicker.

Lynn had completely forgotten they weren't alone in the room until one of the lawyers cleared his throat. "Ms. Chanak, let me introduce Adam Landry. Mr. Landry, Lynn Chanak."

His mouth thinned, but he gave a brief, reluctant nod in acknowledgment of the formal introduction.

She swallowed. "Mr. Landry."

He looked past her. "I'd prefer to talk to Ms. Chanak alone. If—" the coldly commanding gaze touched her "—she doesn't mind."

In the flurry of objection, she caught only one phrase, which annoyed her unreasonably.

"The hospital's interest is in seeing us come up with an amicable future plan." She'd memorized that phrase: amicable future plan. Was there such a thing?

"Only we can decide on the future of our daughters. We need to get to know each other. Please."

She had hoped, heaven help her, for approval. He only waited.

The lawyers offered their intervention if it was needed. Adam Landry said nothing. Lynn stared at her hands. After a moment, the two men backed out, shutting the door behind them. The silence in their wake was as absolute as any she'd ever heard. The courage that had gotten her this far deserted her. She couldn't look up.

Her nerves had reached the screaming point when Adam Landry said at last, "Perhaps I phrased my question incorrectly. Why did you start this? Did you suspect your daughter..." he stumbled, "Shelly, wasn't yours?"

"No." At last she lifted her head, letting him see her tumult. "No. Never. It was my ex-husband. He...he didn't want to pay the child support anymore. He claimed I must have had an affair. That she wasn't *his* child. But it wasn't true! I never..." She bit her lip and said more quietly, "I wouldn't do something like that. So I took Shelly to have a blood test to prove to Brian that she was his. Only..."

"She wasn't."

"No. Which meant—" she took a deep breath "—that she wasn't mine, either. Unless you believe..."

"In immaculate conception?" His voice was dry.

"Yes. And...and I don't." She tried for a smile and failed. "I wasn't going to tell anybody. Only, then I started worrying about the other little girl. The one who was really my daughter."

The dreams wouldn't impress him, not this man. He reminded her too much of the lawyers. His gray suit cost more than she spent on food and mortgage in a month or more. His dark hair was clipped short, but by a stylist, not a barber. She could easily picture his big, capable hands gripping the leather-covered wheel of an expensive sedan, or resting on the keyboard of a laptop computer. Not changing diapers, or sifting through the sand for a seashell, or brushing away tears.

Who was raising Jenny Rose Landry? A grandmother? A nanny? Anxiety crimped her chest.

Softly she finished, "I wanted to be sure she was all right. Loved."

"And that's it. That's all you want." His tone said he didn't believe her for a second.

Lynn didn't blame him for his skepticism. Already, if she was being honest, she'd have to admit that she wouldn't be satisfied with that modest goal.

"I don't know." She held his gaze, although she quaked inside. "I'm not sure anymore. I suppose I'd like to meet her. And…perhaps get acquainted. Now that I know she doesn't have a mother."

"What makes you so sure she needs one?" Landry stood abruptly and shoved his chair back. Looming over her, hands planted on the table, he said tautly, "Is it so impossible to believe I'm an adequate parent?"

Her breath caught. She'd obviously struck a raw nerve. "No. Of course not. I'm a single parent myself, and I think I'm doing a fine job." Naturally she would say that; did she really expect him to believe her? More uncertainly, she continued, "It's just that…'' For all her rehearsing, she didn't know how to express these inchoate emotions, these wants, these needs, these fears. "She's my daughter," Lynn finished simply.

A muscle jerked in his cheek. "You suddenly want to be a mother to *my* daughter."

"Aren't you curious, too?" How timid she sounded! No, perhaps *hopeful* was the word. Could it be that he didn't want Shelly, wouldn't try to reclaim his birth daughter? That she'd never had to worry at all?

He swung away in a jerky motion and took two steps to the window. Gazing out at—what? the parking lot?—he killed her hopes in a flat, unrevealing voice. "Yes. I'm curious. Why do you think I'm here?"

Lynn whispered, "Is that all? You're just… curious?"

He faced her, anger blazing in his eyes. "My wife died and never held her baby. Now I find out that neither have I. Does 'curious' cover my reaction? Probably not. But we have to start somewhere."

He sounded reasonable and yet scared her to death. She'd hoped for a completely different kind of man. Perhaps a car mechanic, struggling to make ends meet, grease under his fingernails and kindness in his eyes. Or a small-business owner. Someone like her. Ordinary. Not a formidable, wealthy man used to having his way and able to pay to get it. Someone she could never beat, if it came to a fight.

Make sure it doesn't, she told herself, trying to quiet the renewed panic. *You can work something out. Go slowly. He may not be that interested in parenting even one girl, much less two.*

"I brought pictures," she said tentatively. "Of Shelly."

He closed his eyes for a moment and rubbed the back of his neck. Lynn could tell he was trying, too, when he said gruffly, "I brought some of Rose, too."

They stared at each other, neither moving. *I'll show you mine if you show me yours,* she thought, semihysterically. How absurd. Make the first move.

Lynn bent down and took the envelope from her purse, which sat on the floor by her feet. Slowly she opened it, her fingers stiff and reluctant. She felt as if she were sharing something incredibly private, pulling back a curtain on the small, sunny space that was her life.

He came back to the table and sat down. As she removed the pile of photos from the envelope, he pulled a matching one from the pocket of his suit jacket. When she pushed the photographs across the span of oak, he did the same with his.

Lynn reached for them, hesitated.

"She looks like you," he said, startling her.

"What?"

"Her hair." His gaze felt like a touch. "Her nose, and her freckles, and her chin. But her eyes are blue."

"Brian's…Brian's are blue."

Her hands were even more awkward now. Did she want to see the child's face? There might be no going back.

She turned the small pile of four-by-five photographs, peripherally aware that he was doing the

same. And then the fist drove into her belly, bringing
a small gasp from her, and Adam Landry vanished
from her awareness.

She saw only the little girl, grinning at the camera.
At *her*. My daughter, Lynn thought in astonishment.

He was right: Jenny Rose could have been Lynn
at that age, except for the pure crystal blue of her
eyes. The little girl's face was round, solemn in the
other pictures Lynn thumbed through. She was still
plump, not skinny and ever in motion like Shelly.
The freckles—Lynn touched them, almost startled by
the slick feel of photographic paper instead of the
crinkling, warm nose she saw. How like hers! Rose's
mouth was sweet, pursed as if she wanted to consider
deeply before she rendered a judgment.

There she was in another photo, on Santa's lap,
not crying, but not entirely happy, either. And
younger yet, a swimsuit over her diaper, the photograph taken as she stood knee-deep in a small back-
yard pool filled by a hose. Why wasn't she smiling
more often? Was she truly happy?

Lynn looked through the pictures over and over
again, beginning to resent the meager number, hun-
gering for more. What was she really like, this little
girl who had once been part of her? What made her
sad? What did she think was funny? Did she suck
her thumb? Have nightmares? Wish she had a
mommy?

At last, at last, she looked up, aware that tears were
raining down her cheeks, that Adam Landry had
made a sound. Like a blind man, he was touching
one of the photographs she'd given him. His fingers
shook as he traced, so delicately, her daughter's face.

She saw him swallow, saw the emotions akin to hers ravage his features.

"Jenny," he whispered.

"Does she look like your wife?"

His hand curled into a fist. "It's...uncanny."

For the first time, Lynn understood. "This must be almost worse for you, with your wife dead."

He looked up, but his eyes didn't focus; he might have been blind, or seeing something else. "Our daughter was all I had left."

She couldn't draw a breath, only sat paralyzed. He saw the wife he'd loved and lost in Shelly's face. *He would want her.* She could even sympathize with how he must feel. She had to meet Jenny Rose, answer the questions the photographs didn't, hold her, hug her, hear her voice, her laugh, feel her warm breath. She had to be part of her life.

As he would, somehow, have to be part of Shelly's life.

"I want to see her," he said, a demand not a request. "Where do you live?"

Her sympathy evaporated at his assumption that he could bulldoze her. She wanted suddenly to lie, or refuse to answer, or...but what was the point? People were easy to find, particularly one who hadn't been trying to hide. A few phone calls and he could be knocking on her door.

"Otter Beach. Over on the coast. I own a bookstore."

"Did you bring her with you?"

"No. She's...she's home. With a baby-sitter." Lynn lifted her chin. "What about Jenny Rose? Where's she?"

As impassive as his face was, still Lynn saw his initial reluctance give way to the same begrudging acceptance. "She goes to a preschool Monday through Friday. While I'm working."

"You don't have a nanny, or someone like that?"

"No." He caught on, and a flush traveled across his cheekbones. "Is that what I look like? A man who takes care of his personal life by writing a check?"

Yes. Oh, yes, that's exactly what he looked like.

But she couldn't say so, of course. "What do you do for a living?"

"I'm a stockbroker."

"It's just that it's hard to be a single parent. Most of us do everything because we have to. You don't."

"You assume I'm wealthy."

She raised her eyebrows. "Aren't you?"

"I make a decent living."

Ten or twenty times the one she made, if Lynn was any judge.

"Couldn't you afford a nanny?"

"I don't want someone else raising my child." He said it in a hard voice.

The words sliced like a switchblade between the ribs. *She* was someone else.

He swore. "I wasn't talking about you."

"No?"

"When you contacted the hospital, what did you have in mind? That we trade kids?"

Trade kids? Lynn stared at him in shock. Was that what he had in mind?

"You don't love your—" she corrected herself "—*my* daughter at all, do you?"

Neither his voice nor his expression softened an iota. "I wasn't talking about me. You're the one who started this. I'm asking what you thought you'd get out of it."

She squeezed her fingers on her lap. "What I'd get out of it? You think I'm using this mix-up to gain something?"

"Why not?" He sounded grim. "You know the hospital is prepared to pay a fortune to shut us up."

"I don't want money." Shaking, she gathered the pictures of the daughter she'd never met and pushed them heedlessly into her purse, then snatched it up and stood. "I told you what I wanted. That's all I have to say. My attorney will be contacting you about visitation rights."

"Stop," he snapped. "Sit down."

"Why?"

"We have to talk." He shut his eyes again for a moment, then opened them and let out a ragged breath. "Please."

Lynn bit her lip, then slowly sat again. "What is there to say?"

"I don't know, but these are our kids. Do we want the courts mandating their futures?"

"No." Lynn sagged. "I didn't bring a lawyer today. I hoped…"

"I hoped, too." After a long silence he sighed. "Where do you suggest we go from here?"

"I'd like to meet her. Jenny Rose. And I expect you'd like to meet Shelly." When he nodded, Lynn said fiercely, "You can't have her, you know. She's my daughter. I love her. I'm her world."

Adam Landry's hard mouth twisted. "It would

seem we have something in common. I'd fight to the death for Rose. Nobody is taking her. So you can put that right out of your mind.''

Had she imagined raising both girls? "Then what?" she asked in a low voice.

He shook his head. "Visitation. We can take it slow."

"Have you told Rose about me?" Lynn asked curiously. "About what happened?"

"No. You?"

"No." She made a face. "It's a hard thing to explain to a three-year-old."

"On Rose's nightstand is a picture of her mommy, who she knows is in heaven. How the hell do I introduce you?" Bafflement and anger filled his dark eyes, so like Shelly's.

"All we can do is our best." How prissy she sounded, Lynn thought in distaste.

He didn't react to her sugar pill, continuing as if she'd said nothing, "It's going to scare the hell out of her if I suddenly announce she isn't my daughter at all. And, oh yeah, here's your real mommy.''

Lynn had imagined the same conversation a million times. To a child this age, parents were the only security. They were the anchor that made exploring the world possible.

"Maybe we should meet first," she suggested. "Would it be less scary once they know us?"

"Maybe." He made a rough sound in his throat. "Yeah. All right. We'll all just be buddies at first."

She let his irony pass, giving a small nod. When he said nothing more, Lynn clutched her purse in her lap. "Shall I bring Shelly to Portland one day?"

"Why don't I come there instead? Rosebud would enjoy a day at the beach. It might seem more natural."

Rosebud. She liked that. She liked, too, what the gentle nickname suggested about this man. Perhaps he wasn't as tough as he seemed.

"Fine. Saturday?"

They agreed. He wrote down her address and phone number, then gave her a business card with his. It all felt so...mundane, a mere appointment, not the clock set ticking for an earthshaking event.

He escorted her out of the conference room and, with his hand on her elbow, hustled her past the cluster of lawyers and administrators lying in wait.

Over his shoulder, he told them brusquely, "We'll be in touch once we figure this out."

Lynn imagined the consternation brewing at their abrupt departure. Together.

She and Adam Landry rode down silently in the elevator, Lynn painfully conscious of his physical presence. She caught him glancing at her once or twice, but each time he looked quickly away, frowning at the lighted numbers over the door. Of course, he couldn't help being so imposing at his height, with broad shoulders and the build of a natural athlete. Nor could he help that face, with Slavic cheekbones and bullish jaw and high forehead that together made him handsome enough to displace Mel Gibson in a woman's fantasies.

She was glad that Shelly looked like her mother and not her father. It would have been too bizarre for words to see her daughter in this stranger's face. As though they must have had sex and she just didn't remember it, or else how could she have breast-fed his child, raised her, loved her?

Heat suddenly blossomed on her cheeks. Had he had the same thought, she wondered, about her? As though he must know her on a level deeper than he understood? No wonder he didn't want to look at her!

When the elevator doors opened, he gripped her arm again as if she wouldn't know where to go without his guidance. Habit, she gathered, when he was with a woman. "Where are you parked?"

"My car is right out in front."

He urged her forward, his stride so long she had to scuttle along like a tiny hermit crab just to avoid falling and being hauled ungracefully to her feet. Outside the hospital doors, Lynn balked.

Adam Landry looked so surprised when she pointedly removed her elbow from his bruising grip that she might have been amused under other circumstances.

"My car is right over there." She gestured. "I don't see a purse snatcher lurking. I can make it on my own, thank you, Mr. Landry."

"Adam."

"Adam," she acknowledged. "I'll see you Saturday."

The lines between his nose and mouth deepened. "We'll be there."

Neither moved for an awkward moment. Then he bent his head in a stiff goodbye and stalked away across the parking lot. With a sense of unreality she watched him go, wondering how she would have viewed him if they'd passed in the halls earlier, before she knew who he was.

I would have thought he must be a doctor, she decided. He had that air of money and command, as though he could make life and death decisions before breakfast and assume it was his right.

He would be a tough opponent, way out of her league.

Then she didn't dare let him become an opponent, Lynn thought again. Although she disliked the idea acutely, she must accommodate him, coax him, play friends—do whatever it took to stay out of court.

Her stomach roiled. It was bad enough that a divorced woman with a child had to spend the next twenty years somehow getting along with her ex-husband. Now she, Lynn Chanak, had gone one better: she had to get along with a man she hadn't chosen, even if foolishly. A man she'd never married, never made love with—a total stranger. All for the sake of the child they shared.

For better or worse, they were tied together until Shelly and Rose were grown.

How bizarre did it get?

LYNN MADE THE LONG, winding trip back over the coastal range to the Pacific Ocean and home. Her instinct was to collect Shelly right away, to reassure herself by her daughter's presence that nothing would ever change, that they were a family.

But there were things she didn't want Shelly to hear, and she should make some phone calls first.

She got Brian's answering machine and started to leave a halting message, feeling like an idiot. Why was she always taken aback when the beep sounded and she had to talk onto a tape? But this time she'd barely begun when he picked up the phone.

"Yeah, I'm here."

"I, um, I told you I'd found her."

"Our daughter."

"Yes." She took a breath. "Today I saw pictures of her. She has your eyes. And my hair."

Strangely, what flitted into her mind at that moment wasn't the photo, but rather the potent way Adam Landry's gaze had touched her and the grit in his voice when he said, "She looks like you."

"How do you know this is the right kid?" her ex-husband, the true stranger, said with an audible sneer.

Closing her eyes, Lynn said evenly, "We've had DNA testing done. And you'd know, if you saw her."

He grunted. "So what do you want from me?"

"Nothing." How glad she was to be able to say that! "I thought you should know. That's all."

"Uh-huh. Well, you do what you want." His tone changed. "Hey, my call-waiting beeped. Hold on." When he came back on a minute later, Brian said, "You don't have her there, right?"

"The man who has been raising her didn't hand her over to me, if that's what you mean."

Brian being Brian, he stayed focused on all that he cared about. "Well, I'm not paying any more child support. I mean, Shelly's not my responsibility. And I'm not paying this other guy, I can tell you that."

How could she ever have married this man? How

had she deceived herself, even for a while, into thinking she loved him?

"You held Shelly and kissed her and changed her diaper. She thinks you're her daddy. After all these years, don't you love her at all?" Lynn asked, trying to understand.

"She's not my kid," he explained, as though she was an idiot not to grasp the concept immediately. "Maybe it's different for a woman. But for a guy…hey, we want to pass on our own bloodlines. I mean, sure, Shelly's a sweet kid. But she's got a dad now, right?"

"That's lucky for her, isn't it?" Lynn carefully, gently, hung up the telephone receiver.

However much she feared Adam Landry, he had to be a better father than the man she'd married.

She picked up the phone again and dialed quickly. Her mother answered on the second ring.

"Mom, I saw her picture today."

"Oh, honey," her mother said, compassion brimming in her voice. "I wish we were there. I can hardly wait to meet her. And to cuddle Shelly and make sure she knows we'll always be Grandma and Grandpa."

Just like that, tears spilled hotly from Lynn's eyes. "Oh, Mom." She sniffed. "I wish you could be here, too."

Her mother had raised Lynn alone, but she'd remarried right after Lynn left home. Hal would never feel like "Dad" to Lynn, but he was a kind man who loved to be Grandpa. Lynn was grateful her mother had found him. She only wished his work hadn't taken them to Virginia.

"For Christmas," her mother said. "I promise we'll come for Christmas."

She gave a watery laugh. "I'll hold out until then. No, really we'll be fine."

"Do you need money? We can help more than we have been, you know. If we have to, we'll take out a loan."

Lynn's mother and stepfather had loaned her the seed money for the bookstore and her mortgage on this old house. She wasn't going to take another cent from them. She knew darn well they didn't really have it.

"No, money's not the problem," she said, meaning it. "It's just…everything."

"Then tell me everything," her mother said comfortingly. "And we'll see which parts of it really count."

Lynn saw herself suddenly, a child. What grade had she been in? Third or fourth? The teacher had accused her of cheating, and she hadn't been! Goody Two-shoes that she was, she never would. She'd been humiliated and hurt that Mrs. Sanders hadn't believed her. All the way home, she'd dragged her feet. What if Mom didn't believe her, either?

She found her mother in the kitchen. Unable to speak, she began crying. Funny how clearly she remembered every sensation of her mother's embrace, the soothing warmth of her voice. "Tell me what's wrong," Mom had murmured, "and we'll see which parts of it really count."

Mom had always said that, when troubles seemed overwhelming. And her analysis invariably did help. She brought problems down to size.

Well, not even Mom was going to be able to shrink this one.

But she told her mother everything anyway, the way she always did.

THIS WAS THE SECOND toughest phone call Adam had ever had to make. Both to his parents-in-law.

He probably should have told them these past weeks what was going on, so that they could absorb the shock slowly, as he apparently had.

But he hadn't wanted to alarm them. It might all come to nothing. Jenny Rose was all they had left of their Jennifer. They always called her Jenny, and sometimes he was sorry he'd named his daughter after her mother. He'd turn, half-expecting to see Jennifer. Besides, Rosebud shouldn't have to live up to such an intense emotional demand. She wasn't her mother, and shouldn't have to fill Jennifer's shoes. Her own were enough, right?

So he hadn't told them. Unfortunately, the time had come. Some things couldn't be avoided forever.

"Mom," he said carefully, when Angela McCloskey answered the phone.

"Adam, dear! Oh, I was just thinking about you. And Jenny, of course." She chuckled. "Christmas is coming, you know."

It was barely autumn. Adam was interested in how retailers did in November and December, but he didn't do his own shopping until the last week or two before Christmas. How hard was it to take a day and fill the trunk of his car?

He made a noncommittal sound. "Mom, something has happened." At her intake of breath, he regretted his choice of words. "Rose is fine. Nothing like that. The thing is…" Oh, hell. He didn't know how to be anything but blunt, but instinct told him he needed to edge into this.

"What?" His tone had given something away. His mother-in-law sounded scared.

"There was a mix-up at the hospital."

"Not Jenny's…Jenny's ashes."

"No," he said hastily, then closed his eyes and squeezed the bridge of his nose. "Not Jenny. Rose. We've, uh, had DNA testing done. Rose isn't my biological daughter. Or Jennifer's."

"Rose isn't…I don't understand." She was pleading with him.

How well he knew the feeling. He'd begged God himself. Some prayers weren't answered.

"The other mother and I met today. We… exchanged pictures."

"You've found her, then?" Angela latched on to the idea with frightening, pitiful eagerness. "Our Jenny's little girl?"

"Yes."

"You'll be bringing her home, won't you?"

He pinched his nose again. "Mom, we're taking it slowly. This mother…she loves Shelly. That's the girl's name. Shelly Schoening. And I love Rose."

"We do, too, of course," she agreed, but he heard no conviction in her voice. "But…but Jenny's daughter. You can't leave her to be raised by someone else."

"How can I not?" he said brutally. "I wouldn't trade Rose away, even if I could."

His mother-in-law was crying now, he could hear

hitches of breath, the salty pain in her voice. "No...but our granddaughter..."

"I hope you'll still think of Rose that way."

"Jennifer was all we had."

How well he knew!

Gently he said, "I'll try to arrange for you to meet Shelly as soon as possible. The, uh, mother seems like a decent woman." He still had his doubts, but he wasn't sharing them with Angela, reeling from one blow already. "I can't imagine that she won't be willing to involve you in Shelly's life."

"Shelly! That wasn't even on Jenny's list of possible names."

"No, but it's pretty, isn't it?" he soothed. Had she even heard him?

"Yes, I suppose. Adam..."

"We have to take it slow. For the girls' sake."

"Does she know?"

"She" wasn't Rose, he guessed, anger stirring. "Neither Rose nor Shelly has been told. They're really too young to understand. We've agreed to meet, get to know the other child, so it's less frightening when they have to be told."

"You're just going to leave her?" Fixated, his mother-in-law made it sound as if he was deserting his own flesh and blood.

"I am not going to wrench her from the only home she's ever known, if that's what you mean," Adam said evenly. "We'll see what happens. You've got to be patient."

"We want to meet her."

He suppressed a profanity. "I'll try."

But he saw suddenly that he couldn't let them near

Shelly too soon. They couldn't be trusted not to tell her they were Grandma and Grandpa. And, God! When they saw her resemblance to Jennifer...

He got off the phone after a dozen more promises he didn't mean. He paced his office, anger and pity and intense frustration churning in his belly. Rose had just lost her grandparents, he knew. Angela and Rob McCloskey would say the right things, but without meaning them. He wondered about the other grandparents. Would they be as desperate to meet Rose?

His own parents wouldn't be, he knew. Not especially warm with him, they were pleasant and remote with Rose. One or the other might become interested when Rose reached school age if she displayed a real spark of artistic ability—Mom—or a powerful interest in anatomy or oceanography— Dad.

Adam made the call nonetheless. For better or worse, they were his parents.

His mother listened without interrupting.

Only when he was done did she ask, "Why didn't you say something sooner?"

He couldn't believe he'd hurt her feelings. "I wanted to be sure."

"Is going further with this a good idea?" she asked unexpectedly. "Rose is a sweet child. I don't see how this can end happily for her."

Adam assured her that he wasn't going to let anybody take his Rosebud from him. But she'd stirred a different kind of uneasiness that ate at him from the moment he set the phone down in its cradle again.

Saturday seemed a century away and, at the same

time, too close. What would he feel when he saw her, that little girl with his eyes and Jennifer's face? Would there be some instant connection? In a way, he hoped not. He didn't want anything to affect his love for Rose. To lessen it. Emotions shouldn't be so insubstantial. They shouldn't be dependent on blood tests or facial features.

It had unnerved him, though, to see how much of Rose had come from her mother. That hair. On the ride down in the elevator, it had been all he could do not to touch it, see whether the texture was the same as Rose's.

The sweetness of her face had stunned him. He'd arrived certain he would hate her, but how could he hate someone who looked like his Rosebud?

Now he didn't know what to think of her. Her ex-husband had thought her capable of having an affair, which didn't speak very well for her morals. And yet, she'd defended her Shelly as fiercely as he had his Rose. Whatever her other flaws, she seemed genuinely to love the little girl she'd raised.

Or had it all been an act?

He sank into the leather chair behind his wide bird's-eye maple desk and cursed. How could he know? How could he trust her?

Did he have any choice?

CHAPTER FOUR

OTTER BEACH REMINDED ADAM of Cannon Beach, just up the coast: charming, but self-consciously so. Inns, bed-and-breakfasts, bakeries, restaurants and shops lined the brick main street. It was one of those towns that existed for visitors, not for the people who lived there. Where did they buy groceries? he wondered. Or get tune-ups for their cars, or their teeth cleaned?

On the other hand, this was a hell of a beautiful spot. Maybe, living with this view, you didn't mind having to drive an hour just to go to a hardware store. Between shingled cottages that were now shops and restaurants, he caught glimpses of the pebbly beach and the two famous sea stacks just offshore. Bright, tailed kites rose in a brisk breeze, and beachcombers wandered. Tendrils of smoke gave away the presence of small fires shielded by driftwood. He cracked his window and breathed in the scent of the ocean.

Rose was sound asleep in her car seat, he saw with a glance in the rearview mirror. Good. He wasn't in the mood for her excitement. He'd told her only that they were going to spend the day with a friend who had a daughter Rose's age. They'd go to the beach, he promised. Maybe out for lunch. The trunk of the car was full of plastic buckets and shovels, sand molds and towels, plus an ice chest with drinks and snacks. Rose was ready for anything.

Adam wasn't. He was doing his damnedest not to think about what lay ahead, about why they were here. He didn't care about Otter Beach. If he let the crack in his self-control open, his mind filled with images, people—Shelly, Lynn, Jennifer lying in the hospital pale as marble. Questions. What would he feel when he saw Shelly? Would Rose notice how much she looked like Lynn? What would they talk about? And after today, what?

How the hell could they pull this off?

Sheer willpower allowed him to slam the crack shut. Brooding would get him nowhere.

Per her directions, Adam turned down a side street. Then right one block. He heard stirring behind him. The tires on brick had woken Rose. On the corner was an antique store, the windows filled with bottles and knickknacks. Next door, espresso was being served on the canopied sidewalk, where half-a-dozen wrought-iron tables jostled for room. Finally, the bookstore.

A simple, old-fashioned wooden sign declared, Otter Beach Books. Beneath it dangled a smaller sign, Open. The old house was painted butter-yellow with the trim deep pink—rose colored, he supposed, with awareness of the irony. The white picket fence was a nice touch. Yellow and white roses, fading now, scrambled over a broad arch. He could only see partway up the brick walk, which led between tangles of asters and other flowers he didn't know to the porch steps. He did recognize the hollyhocks leaning drunkenly against the clapboard wall of the house. His grandmother had grown ones just like them.

Gravel crunched as he turned the Lexus into the driveway and joined one other car in the slot. Business didn't appear to be booming, or, come to think of it, most shoppers probably came on foot.

Ignoring the dread that sat like a heavy meal in his belly, he turned off the engine. "Hey, Rosebud, we're here."

She rubbed her eyes and swiveled her head. "Where's the beach? Is there sand?"

"I bet we can find some. In a few minutes. This is where my friend lives. She owns a bookstore."

"Oh." Rose momentarily gazed at the garden. "There's Tigger."

Good God, she was right. A garden statue of Pooh Bear's buddy Tigger looked ready to bound over a cluster of pansies.

"Hey, maybe Pooh's there, too."

She began to struggle. "I want to get out! I want to see!"

"Hold your bouquet, kiddo!"

He went around the car, aware of the house behind him and the small-paned windows. Was she looking out, even now? He was unsettled to realize that the *she* he imagined with such disquiet wasn't Shelly.

Well, that was natural, Adam told himself as he unbuckled his daughter. Lynn Chanak was the one who shared his emotional turmoil. The one who understood, the one who might turn out to be an enemy. He and she—Adam made a sound in his throat that brought a single curious glance from Rose before she scrambled under his arm and out of the car. His mouth twisted. He and Lynn Chanak were going to have one strange relationship.

Rose was quivering with eagerness, taking everything in, but she waited for him as she knew to do in a parking lot. When he slammed the car door, she snatched his hand. "Come *on,* Daddy."

A touch on Tigger's rough, concrete head, and Rose tugged her father under a second white-painted arch thick with huge blue saucer-shaped flowers— clematis?—and into the small front garden.

In its heart was a tiny brick-paved courtyard with a birdbath, a garden seat and Pooh Bear peeking shyly from a tangle of another bluish-purple-flowered perennial Adam didn't recognize. Rose squatted in front of Pooh.

Maintaining this garden must take time, but it was damn fine marketing, Adam decided. Any passerby would be seduced into stepping beneath the rose arch. Once that far, why not go in? The mood was set, the imagination captured. Lynn Chanak was a smart woman. It was a shame the store wasn't on the main drag.

"Let's go in," he said, suddenly impatient to have the first meeting over. Shelly would just be another little girl; he wouldn't feel anything but a sense of obligation and perhaps regret. Maybe he and Ms. Chanak would agree to leave things as they were. Stay in touch. He'd help out if she needed it. With her ex out of the picture, she wouldn't be able to put Shelly through college on the income from a bookstore, for example.

Someday Jennifer's parents would have to meet

Shelly, he remembered with a frown. But he could explain, refuse to tell them where she was.

"I like books," Rosebud told him slyly as they started up the steps. "I'm tired of all the ones I have."

Adam's mood lightened, even as that lump stayed, grew, in his stomach. "Then pick out a couple of new ones before we go to the beach. They'll give us something to remember the day by."

"Is...Shelly nice?" She stumbled over the name, although she'd asked the same question half-a-dozen times. "Will she like me?"

"What's not to like?" He scooped her up and settled her on his hip, liking the idea of walking in the door with her plainly claimed. *Mine.* "And I've never met Shelly."

A bell rang when he opened the door to a room filled with warmth and clutter and bright colors: a bookstore the way they were meant to be. Dark wood shelves, tables heaped with books, a comfy rocker in what had been a sunporch, a playhouse...and at least a couple of customers browsing, including a teenage boy with tattoos and a pierced eyebrow.

He heard her voice first. "Mary, can you help this gentleman find..."

They saw each other at the same moment. The words she'd intended to speak trailed off. He had a violent moment of reaction to that damned resemblance to Rose. After a moment, he recognized it as anger. He hated seeing his daughter all grown up in a woman he didn't know.

After that first shocked instance, Adam realized she was no longer looking at him. Her gaze devoured

Rose. The book she held slipped from her hand and slapped to the floor. Heads turned, but Lynn Chanak kept staring.

"Daddy?" Rose said uncertainly. "Is that lady your friend?"

Friend. The way she was looking at his daughter scared the hell out of him.

"Yeah." He swallowed. "This is my friend Lynn. Lynn, my daughter Rose."

"I..." Lynn couldn't seem to tear her eyes from the child. "I'm happy to meet you, Rose."

In a sudden bout of shyness, Rose buried her face in his neck. She whispered, "Why is she looking at me so funny?"

"Maybe," he whispered, too, "because your hair is the same color as hers. How many people have curls like my Rose?"

She giggled, but shakily, because even her three-year-old intuition knew something was up.

God, he thought with gritted teeth. They looked so much alike. Everyone in the store must notice. They probably all thought he was the proprietor's ex-husband, and this her daughter. How was she going to explain the resemblance?

"Rose is anxious to meet Shelly," he said, too loudly. He didn't so much want to meet his daughter, as he wanted this woman to quit staring at Rose as if she were royalty. Or, hell, a baboon. Something she might never see again.

"I..." Lynn blinked and turned her head, cheeks pale and her eyes unfocused. "I...I'm not sure..."

He glanced around and saw that the shoppers had gone about their business. A young woman behind the counter was ringing up a purchase. At the same moment, a giggle wafted from the sunporch.

"I'm here, Mommy! Remember?"

The playhouse. It must be two-story, because framed in an upper window of the fake castle was a little girl's face, flushed with delight because her presence had been a secret.

The rock that had been sitting in his stomach was suddenly a boulder, craggy and painful. It pressed his lungs until he couldn't breathe.

Rose was wriggling, so he set her down without tearing his gaze from the child. He felt his lips move, knew they formed a name: *Jennifer.*

Even the voice. Sounding confident and open, she invited Rose to come up. Shyly his daughter went, bending to crawl across the mock drawbridge and inside. As if Rose couldn't figure out how to climb a ladder, Shelly gave her directions and told her what she'd find up at the top and how Mom had said they'd go to the beach and did Rose like hot dogs 'cuz Mom said maybe that's what they could have for lunch. The words flowed like a stream over stones, making a kind of song, and all as inevitable as water finding its way downhill.

Jennifer, he thought in agony.

She peeked out the window at him, her face, alight with laughter, looking for all the world like a nineteenth-century children's book illustration of an elf perched on a flower stem. Shelly's ears stuck out just a little. Jennifer had hated hers, though he had thought them cute. Just like Jennifer's, Shelly's face narrowed from high cheekbones to a pointy chin, and just like Jennifer's, her eyes shimmered with amusement and devilment.

"It's worse than seeing the picture, isn't it?" the woman beside him said softly.

Taking a ragged breath, he turned his head and met Lynn Chanak's eyes. "God."

She nodded.

"Do you see yourself?" he asked, keeping his voice low.

"I suppose." Like him, she gazed toward the playhouse. Neither girl was visible in the window, although whispers and laughter drifted out. "She does look like pictures of me at that age, but I don't exactly remember my face in the mirror from when I was three, so it's not quite as big a shock as Shelly must be for you."

He fumbled for his wallet and, with shaking hands, took out a photo of his dead wife and handed it to Lynn.

She looked at it for a long moment. When she lifted her head, her gray-green eyes were misty. "She was beautiful."

"Shelly is going to look like her."

A tear dropped, shimmering, from her lash. She wiped it from her cheek. "Oh, I wish…"

"This hadn't happened?"

She squeezed her eyes shut, as if willing back further tears. "No," Lynn said finally. "Because then I wouldn't have Shelly, and she's my life. No, I was going to say, I wish we'd never found out. But now…" She gazed again toward the playhouse where first one girl's laughing face, then the other, popped up. "But now, I'm not so sure."

"Jennifer's parents want to meet her," he heard himself say.

Lynn squeezed her hands together without looking at him. "I thought they might. But how can we do that, without Shelly knowing who they are?"

"I told them they might have to wait."

She smiled with obvious difficulty. "Thank you."

"What about your parents? And your ex-husband's?"

"My mother and stepfather love Shelly, and I'm sure they'll love Rose, if you give them the chance. They'll support whatever we decide. Brian's parents…" She hesitated. "I don't know. At the moment, he's washed his hands of the whole thing. My pregnancy wasn't planned, and…" She swallowed whatever she had been going to say, perhaps suddenly aware that she had been going to reveal too much that was private to a relative stranger. "Well," she said, a little awkwardly. "Certainly there's no rush, where they're concerned. Right now, it's just Shelly and me."

"Not anymore," he murmured.

Her startled glance became troubled, but she said nothing, although the small creases stayed between her brows. He understood how she felt. They were both between a rock and a hard place.

"Does Rose want to go to the beach?"

Adam cooperated with her desire to put their visit on conventional ground. "She can't talk about anything else."

"Then shall we?" Lynn nodded toward the register. "I have someone to mind the shop for me."

Belatedly he noticed that she wore jeans, faded

canvas sneakers and a T-shirt the color of the Aegean Sea. Her hair was gathered into a ponytail, making her look absurdly young, with that round face and sprinkling of freckles. The fact that he couldn't help noticing her full breasts and flare of hip was a useful reminder that her husband had suspected her of infidelity. He couldn't let her resemblance to Rose disarm him.

"Rose wanted to pick out a couple of books first," he said. "Maybe I'll do it for her. Any suggestions?"

Lynn led him into the children's area and offered several of Shelly's favorites.

"We've read this about two hundred times," he said, setting one aside. "I liked it the first hundred."

She grinned, her nose crinkling. "Yeah, me, too. But, hey, most of them wear thin after five or ten repetitions."

Damn it, under other circumstances he'd have been attracted to her, Adam realized in dismay. *Don't,* he told himself sharply. Talk about messy.

He grunted and probably glowered, and pretended to concentrate on the book he was flipping through. After a moment Lynn turned away and began straightening a rack of paperbacks for middle-grade readers, but he didn't forget her presence. He'd never be able to forget her, he thought grimly. How could he? She was the mother of his daughter. Of both his daughters, one way or another.

How many men could say that about a woman they'd never touched?

Irritated with himself at a thought that nudged uncomfortably close to sexual awareness, Adam raised his voice. "Rosebud, you want to go to the beach?"

He heard whispers above his head. Then Rose said, "Okay, Daddy. If Shelly can go."

"You bet." Lynn smiled as if she hadn't noticed his withdrawal.

The sounds of scrambling within eventually produced both girls, his Rose in her pink flowered overalls with matching shirt, and Shelly in a bright red dress—he thought it was a dress, made out of T-shirt fabric—over purple leggings.

"I know, I know," Lynn murmured, evidently seeing his astonishment. "She wants to dress herself, and mostly I let her."

"Ah." Rose accepted what he laid out. A difference in temperament? Or was Rose, as he feared, immature for her age? God! What if there was even something wrong with her?

But her language was well developed, he reminded himself.

"Hey, kiddo," he said. "You still want some books?"

She approved his selection and added two more with scarcely a glance inside the covers. He carried the pile to the register and let Lynn ring it up, not even wincing at the total.

"Let me give them to you at cost," she offered.

He shook his head brusquely. "Don't be ridiculous. This is your business. If I weren't buying them here, it would be somewhere else."

"I thought..." Her expression closed. "Thank you. No, I don't need to see ID."

She was a stranger, he told himself. He hadn't hurt her feelings in some way he didn't understand. How could he? She didn't have the power to hurt his.

Lynn smiled brightly as she came out from behind the counter. "Shelly, Rose, let's go use the bathroom before we head off." She raised her eyebrows at him. "Adam?"

"No. If you don't mind taking Rose…"

Her sidelong glance reeked of irony. Oh, no. She wouldn't mind taking his daughter. He couldn't help a minor feeling of loss when Rose willingly took Lynn's hand and went without a look back.

They returned hand in hand, the pretty woman, his Rosebud and Shelly, so much like Jennifer that his heart spasmed again.

His face revealed too much once more, because Lynn said in an achingly gentle voice, "Shelly, this is Rose's daddy."

"Hi, Shelly." He sounded gruff to his own ears. "I see you have a sweatshirt. Rose had better get hers from the car."

"I have buckets, too," Rose confided. "An' shovels, an' everything."

"Wow." Lynn's smile was wide and unaffected for the girls, tentative for him. "Then how about we go make some sand castles? Or chase crabs, or hunt for shells and agates?"

She and Shelly had both tied sweatshirts around their waists. He grabbed sweaters from the car for Rose and himself, as well as the beach paraphernalia.

Rose took his hand and they walked behind Lynn and Shelly the two blocks to the public pass-through to the beach. Rose stared at the tourists and shop windows. A toy store brought her up on tiptoes as they passed. Adam watched the pair ahead, the woman's springy auburn ponytail, the child's sleek brown one just as familiar to him. The way Shelly danced instead of trudging obediently along as Rose did. He loved every placid, thoughtful bone in Rosebud's body, but something in him ached at the sight of Jennifer reincarnated, a sprite in constant movement.

All that distracted him from this child was the sway of Lynn Chanak's hips, her faded jeans snug, or the sight of her pale, slender nape when she bent her head to listen to the little girl.

Dressed like this, she seemed not so much young as vulnerable, Adam decided. Here was who she was, how she lived. In letting him come to her home, she had bared herself for him, in a way. Their meeting at the hospital had had an anonymity, a sense of the impersonal, that was lost now.

At the ocean, broad concrete steps led from a paved boardwalk down to the pebbly beach. Once at the bottom, Shelly let go of her mom's hand and spun eagerly.

"Come on! I'll show you the best places."

Rose's grip tightened on her dad's hand. "The birds won't hurt me, will they?" she asked uncertainly.

Seagulls gathered only feet away, their beady eyes searching for handouts.

"Nah." He waved his arm, and the nearest hopped backward. "See? They're not interested in you. They want a peanut butter sandwich."

She giggled a little weakly. Instead of prying her fingers loose, he walked with her and Shelly, Lynn trailing. The gulls stayed behind, hoping for bread thrown from the diners eating outside just above.

At a safe distance from the scary birds, Rose proved willing to let go and join Shelly. The adults strolled behind as the girls ran ahead, scrambling up a favorite driftwood log and jumping over and over again to the forgiving pebbles. Finally Shelly took Rose's hand and led her onto slick rocks where they crouched to stare into a tide pool.

As Adam looked over their shoulders, Shelly was saying earnestly, "We can't take anything out. Sometimes I touch. See?" She dipped her hand into the cold water and let a swaying anemone brush her fingers. Her face scrunched up. "But if you take them home, they get icky. They stink and stuff. So we leave 'em."

Rose nodded, not wanting to admit she didn't have a clue what her new friend was talking about. Not two minutes later, she slipped over to her father.

"Why do things get icky if we take 'em home, Daddy?" she asked, not bothering to hush her piercing voice.

Death and decomposition was not what he wanted to talk about.

"Because those are sea creatures. They can't live out of the sea. Just like we need air, they need water."

"But they could take a bath with me." Her mouth was pursed with perplexity.

Lynn stepped forward. "They need this *special* kind of water. See? Put a drop on your tongue?"

Rose stuck her tongue out, then made a horrible face at the taste. When she could speak, she exclaimed, "They want *that* kinda water?"

"Just that kind." Lynn smiled at her. "And no

matter how hard we try, we can't make the bathwater right for them.''

''Oh.'' Rose thought it over. After a moment, her forehead smoothed. She nodded and went back to her friend, squatting beside her to stare down into the tidepool.

Adam stayed near Rose as Shelly led the way next across mussel- and barnacle-encrusted rocks to a blowhole. Each incoming wave rushed beneath the rock in a froth of white, sending a thin jet shooting upward through the hole like a geyser. Here the roar of the surf surrounded them and spray hung in the air, dampening their hair and filling their nostrils and lungs with salty wet air.

''Ooh,'' breathed Rose, clutching Adam's hand and watching with wondering eyes.

Eventually they made their way to a tiny cove of gritty sand between arms of basalt worn by the pounding of the waves. Adam dropped to his knees and helped build a sand castle, grander than anything the girls could have done alone.

He wondered wryly whether he was trying to make points with Lynn by showing what a great parent he was, or whether he was just avoiding having to talk to her.

She gave no sign she noticed either way. Instead, under her daughter's orders Lynn willingly ferried water by the bright plastic bucketful from the foamy fingers of surf. At the sound of her laughter, Adam sank back on his heels and watched her squelch back toward the construction site, her sneakers and the hems of her jeans soaking wet.

Like Rose, she wasn't a chatterbox, and her face

didn't have Jennifer's animation, but it was bright and good-humored.

"The wave got me," she announced. "I think the tide is coming in."

Sure enough, each wave licked onto dry sand and inched toward the tide pools.

"Let's dig a moat," Adam declared. "We can watch the water rush around the castle."

"Good idea." Lynn dropped to her knees and began hollowing out a trench with her hands, sand flying.

"What's a moat?" Shelly asked.

Adam grinned at her. "It's filled with water to keep the invaders away from the castle walls."

"Oh. What's 'vaders?"

"Um." Almost unconsciously, he looked to Lynn for help.

"Invaders are the enemy," she said in mock growl. "Like Ian and Ron at your play group, when they want to grab the dolls and run over them with their trucks."

Shelly's chocolate-brown eyes widened. "I don't like *them*." She began scooping sand. "Come on, Rose. We don't want no 'vaders in *our* castle!"

They stayed long enough to see the water fill the moat but not long enough for the girls to watch their magnificent castle crumple. By that time, the girls were getting tired anyway. When Rose whimpered after her foot slipped in the loose pebbles, Adam swung her up onto his shoulders.

Her mood revived. "Giddap, Daddy!" Her heels drummed his chest. "You're my horsie, Daddy."

Shelly stopped in her tracks. "I want you to be my horsie, Mama."

"Only if I can take you piggyback, punkin." For a fleeting second, Lynn's eyes met Adam's, revealing a complex of emotions he didn't know how to read. "I'm not big enough to lift you onto my shoulders."

Had he somehow made her feel inadequate?

Shelly's mouth trembled. "But I wanna ride like *her*."

"Her daddy's bigger than I am."

Shelly's expression became calculating. "Maybe *he* could give me a ride."

"But he's already carrying Rose—"

"Tell you what," Adam interjected. "We'll switch back and forth. Okay, Daisy?"

"'kay, Daddy," Rose agreed. "But I'm not Daisy."

He bounced her a couple of times. "Nope. Guess not. You have too many petals."

She giggled.

Shelly climbed onto her mother's back. "Why'd he call her Daisy? That's not her name. Her name is Rose."

"Her daddy is just teasing," Lynn explained. "It's like me calling you Belly when I tickle you."

"Oh." She booted her heels into her mom's hips. "Giddap, horsie!"

Halfway up the beach, Adam stopped. "Okay, Shelly Belly, your turn."

"Daddy!" Rose whined.

"Nope. Fair's fair. Besides, you want to try out the other horse, don't you?"

Rose being Rose, she didn't say any more when

he lowered her to the sand, but she clutched his leg, the afternoon's acquaintance not enough to let her go to this lady. Shelly, on the other hand, had already taken a handful of his shirt and was demanding, "Up! You're my horsie, now."

Lynn's smile never wavered as she said, "Do you think we can beat them to the stairs, Rose?"

But, damn, she had to hurt, looking at her own daughter none too eager to trust her. Never mind that Rose had no idea. He knew how Lynn must feel, because something in him had soared at Shelly's eagerness to climb onto his shoulders.

"I'll tell you what," he said. "Let me lift you up, Rosebud."

He set her on Lynn's back, where she had no choice but to wrap her arms around Lynn's neck. In the breeze both had lost tendrils of hair from their ponytails, and the two auburn heads looked so much alike, his heart squeezed. They looked up, reminding him of an advertisement for a skin-care product, maybe, their complexions both creamy with the delicate scattering of freckles, the shape of their mouths so much alike, even their eyes, although Lynn's were green and Rose's blue. Mother and daughter.

For an instant, he couldn't breathe.

"Up!" Shelly demanded again.

And a hint of mischief sparkled in Lynn's eyes.

"Race you to the steps!" she announced, and took off.

"Hey!" Adam protested. "No fair!"

She had a good ten-yard head start by the time he'd swung his daughter—his heart cramped again—

onto his shoulders and grabbed Rose's bucket and shovel that he'd earlier set down.

"Go! Go!" Shelly screamed in delight.

She was so light, as fine of bone as her mother, a wiry little bundle of energy. She twined her fingers in his hair and bounced, urging him on the whole way, her shrieks happy and uninhibited.

Shelly wasn't his Rosebud, but she was his, too.

He almost caught them, but not quite. Rose was quietly pleased by the victory, Lynn's face was alight with laughter, and Shelly giggled as he swung her onto the boardwalk.

"Mommy's fast, huh?"

"Yep," he agreed. "You've trained her well."

Shelly thought that was hysterically funny.

Adam had a flash of memory. Jennifer in jeans and a white T-shirt, lying back on their bed with her arms flung above her head, laughing uncontrollably until tears came in her eyes. He didn't remember what was so funny. Only that he had followed her down onto the bed and kissed her until...

He almost groaned. To hold Jenny again. To touch her like that. To see her laugh. He hadn't recalled her so vividly in a long time.

He had needed her daughter—*their* daughter—to bring his Jennifer back to him.

Any thoughts of maintaining his distance after today were gone. He hoped Lynn saw it the same way. He didn't want to hurt her; damn it, he saw a reflection of his own chaotic emotions in her eyes. Worse yet, he saw Rose in her.

But he couldn't let Shelly go, any more than he could let Rosebud go.

He was going to be Daddy to both girls, whatever it took.

"How about if we go get that hot dog you were promised?" he said easily, and, with only a small pang, took Rose's small hand and let Shelly go to her mother.

CHAPTER FIVE

HOW LONG HAD IT BEEN since she had sat beside the phone waiting for a man to call? Years. Eons, Lynn thought wryly.

And this was more like being a teenager, when she'd desperately wanted to pick up the phone and hear *his* voice, and yet was terrified every time it rang that he might be on the other end of the line. She'd never felt at ease socially, never known the right thing to say. If the boy she had a crush on called, she'd blow it, Lynn had been certain during those difficult years. Her mother had said comfortably that she'd learn.

Lynn scowled at the silent telephone on the wall. *Yeah, Mom?* she demanded. *Then how come I haven't?*

This was different, of course. She wasn't interested in *him*. It was Rose, sweet, shy Rose, whose voice Lynn hankered to hear. But she couldn't see Rose without going through her daddy, which Lynn fiercely resented even as she felt as protective about Shelly.

Seeing her natural daughter once had seemed as if it might be enough, back when they planned the one-day visit. Just knowing that she was healthy and loved...

She made a sound in her throat and prowled the kitchen. Silence from the bedroom, where Shelly napped.

Enough? Sure. Like that first piece of chocolate would be enough. Like you could eat three potato chips and then put the bag away.

A taste was worse than never having.

Feeling Rose's chubby arms around her neck and hearing her throaty giggle in Lynn's ears had been heaven. Rose and Shelly had taken to each other immediately, and yet they were so different. Lynn had applauded but never understood Shelly's boldness and flamboyance. In Rose she saw herself, not because of the freckles or the hair, but because Rose hung back when a braver soul forged forward, because Rose's hand clung to Daddy's instead of letting go, because Rose wanted oh so desperately to be sure she would be safe before she leaped.

Lynn understood all of that. She had been—was— afraid. Her own mother had had to boot her gently out of the nest. When the time came, Shelly would fly without hesitation. Rose would wobble, come back, flap her wings and try again.

Lynn wanted to be there to coax and urge and comfort, just as her mother had been for her.

It wasn't as if Rose had another mother, she thought defensively. Then she might have made herself let go, though it would have hurt terribly. But Rose needed her. She was certain of that.

Oh, why didn't the man call?

When he hadn't on Sunday, she had figured he wanted to wait until Rose wasn't around. Or perhaps he needed to think. But now it was Monday, and

there wasn't a reason in the world that he couldn't
phone from his office. Why wait? Why not settle this
now?

Perhaps she should call him. The anxiety that immediately swelled at the very thought annoyed her
terribly. There she was, frightened of doing something straightforward. She wanted to talk to him.
Why *not* call?

She didn't reach for the phone. After buckling
Rose into her car seat and circling the car to where
Lynn and Shelly stood, Adam Landry had said, ''I'll
call.'' His eyes had met Lynn's; she had nodded. Of
course they had to talk. More than ever, they had to
talk.

I'll call.

Why should the ball be in his court? She had rights
equal to his.

But, oh, she didn't want to pick up the phone. She
didn't want to catch him at a bad moment, hear that
brusque, impatient note in his voice. She wanted him
to be the one calling, because he was eager. She
imagined him conciliatory, agreeable.

Was he ever, except with his daughter?

Lynn sighed and considered making blueberry
muffins as a surprise for Shelly when she woke from
her nap. It would give her something to do.

The telephone rang.

Lynn stared at it, a lump clogging her throat. On
the fourth ring, she snatched it up before her answering machine could do so.

''Hello?''

''Lynn, this is Adam.''

''Oh.'' Brilliant. ''Yes. Um, hello.''

No "how are you?" Or "we had a great day, didn't we?"

Instead, he said straight out, "I want to see Shelly again. I'd like to keep seeing her."

Relief washed over her even as worry began its familiar niggle. To see Rose, she needed him to want to visit Shelly. But how far would he go? What if he went to court for custody, claimed he would be the best parent for both girls?

She'd borrow the money from her parents and fight him, of course. Tooth and nail.

"I'd like to keep seeing Rose, too," she said.

A pause ensued. She wondered if he had the same mixed feelings. Or was he so confident of his ability to win that he didn't consider her a threat?

"It was awkward, all of us together," he said at last. "Maintaining a pretense."

"Yes," she agreed, but with a thrum of hurt she chose not to examine. "Do you have another suggestion?"

"That's why I called. What if we were to take turns dropping one of the girls off for the day? Maybe work our way up to weekends? For now, surely you could spend a Saturday shopping or seeing a movie or something in Portland?" The last was thrown out carelessly; why should he care what she did? "When I drop Rose off, I could take a drive up the coast, have lunch in Cannon Beach, maybe. Just to give you time with her."

"Won't they think it odd, after we said we were friends?"

"We'll make excuses." A hint of impatience

sounded in his voice. Obstacles weren't to be considered.

"Yes. All right," Lynn said. "We might have to make the visits short at first. Shelly has never played at a friend's house for more than a couple of hours at a time."

"Rose is used to day care."

He spoke arrogantly, and yet she heard something. Uncertainty? Did he remember Rose's clinging hand? Her reluctance to climb onto the strange lady's back, even after several hours spent building a sand castle together?

"Does it have to be a weekend?" Lynn asked.

"Does it have to be?" The surprise in Adam's voice cleared. "I suppose leaving the bookstore is difficult on weekends."

"Saturday and Sunday are my busiest days. And I have to pay someone else to be there when I'm gone. The store is closed anyway on Monday and Tuesday. Later in the winter, on Wednesday, too."

"I suppose I could take some Mondays off," he said thoughtfully. "Sure, why not? Rose would be thrilled to stay home from day care."

Aha. So Rose might be "used" to day care, but was not necessarily enthusiastic.

"Shall we say next Monday?" he continued. "Can you bring Shelly here?"

"Certainly." They might have been arranging a transfer of funds or the repair of an appliance. She reached for a notepad. "Tell me how to find your place."

A moment later, she hung up, the plans firmed, a map drawn. She would take Shelly to play at Rose's house. Go shopping herself for a few hours. It would give her a chance to see Rose briefly, and in return Adam would bring Rose here the next Monday.

It sounded simple enough, but a gnawing hole in her stomach told her simple didn't mean easy. She was going to hate leaving Shelly with her father. Not being there to see what he said and did.

What if, after a few visits, Shelly wasn't happy to see her mom after the day spent with Daddy? What if she wanted to stay, and he encouraged her? What if Shelly always had to go there, because Rose was too shy to be left here?

Lynn squeezed her eyes shut on a burning sensation and thought, *what if I die of loneliness, on one of those Mondays?*

"ARE WE ALMOST THERE?" Shelly's neck stretched as she tried to peer ahead.

"I think so." Lynn glanced again at the directions and address that lay on the seat beside her. The neighborhood was reinforcing her worst fears. Adam Landry had money. Plenty of money.

What chance would she have if he took her on?

"There," she said, spotting the numbers on the mailbox. A paved driveway led onto wooded grounds. Rhododendrons grew under mature cedars and hemlocks and firs. She caught a glimpse of a tumbling stream and an arched stone bridge.

Money.

Ahead, the house seemed to grow out of the hillside and the forested land, the cedar siding and shake roof blending in, the several levels and the rock work around the foundation somehow disguising the sheer size of the structure. Lynn suddenly imagined Rose wandering in the middle of the night, lost and scared, trying to find her daddy's bedroom.

Don't be silly, she told herself sharply. Rose seemed loved and secure. Her bedroom would be near his. Surely.

Lynn admired the flower beds filled with shade-loving plants like hostas and Solomon's seal that flowed into the natural landscape as if God himself was the gardener. She couldn't quite see Adam Landry on his knees in the dirt pulling weeds. Even if he had built a sand castle with gusto. No, he'd have a gardener, as well as a housekeeper.

The car rolled to a stop. "Well," she said, trying to sound hearty. "We're here."

"Oh." Shelly's enthusiasm seemed to have dwindled. She stared at the house, her voice small. "I don't see Rose."

"She doesn't know we're here yet." Lynn attempted a cheerful smile. "Did you see the bridge? I'll bet Rose will show you around her woods."

"Like I showed her my beach."

"Right." Except, these woods really *were* Rose's.

Shelly unbuckled her own car seat and inched forward. "Can we go see Rose?"

"You betcha."

They didn't reach the front door before Adam came out with Rose holding his hand. Today he wore crisp khaki slacks and a polo shirt with a tiny—and probably expensive—emblem on the pocket. What he looked was handsome, unapproachable and not quite real: the wealthy professional pretending to relax.

Lynn had felt more comfortable with him when he wore jeans and a T-shirt.

The two girls murmured, "Hi," and hung their heads.

Adam's dark gaze met hers. "Come on in."

She wondered if he would have invited her at all if their daughters had gone racing right off to play.

Inside the carved-wood door, a slate entry led to a large living room with a wall of windows, pale nubby carpet and warm, comfortable leather furniture. A few antiques lent character to a room that might have been too colorless and modern for Lynn's tastes. She loved the wool tapestry that hung on one wall, a dark African mask on another.

The elegance of the room made her confidence plummet another inch.

"What a beautiful room."

"Thank you." He barely glanced at her. "How are you, Shelly?"

"Fine," she whispered.

"Rose has been excited about having you come."

Shelly peeked at her friend but said nothing. Rose hid behind Daddy's leg.

He tried again. "Would you like Rose to show you her room?"

Shelly didn't let go of Lynn's hand. In her piercing voice, she asked, "Mommy, are you gonna go?"

"That's the plan." She sounded as bright and fake as a dinner-plate dahlia, Lynn thought ruefully. "Remember? We talked about it. I'm going to do some mom things. Shop, and call a friend. I'll bet you won't miss me for a second."

"Yes, I will," Shelly said clearly.

"Not once you start to play—"

"*I* like to shop, too."

Out of the corner of her eye, Lynn saw Rose's face start to crumple. A crease deepened between Adam's brows.

"Honey," she said gently, "I know you'll have fun with Rose. We don't want to disappoint her."

Shelly held her hand in a death grip. This time she whispered, "Can't you stay, Mommy?"

God help her, she was pleased that Shelly *hadn't* dashed off without caring whether her mother left. How petty could you get? These visits *had* to work! Darn it. She was an adult. She owed it to both children to be selfless.

Crouching, Lynn looked her daughter in the eye. "Honey," she began.

Adam interrupted, "Maybe I can talk your mom into staying for a while. Rose and I planned a nice lunch. You'll join us, won't you, Lynn?"

Oh, right, she thought. *Now* be cordial. Pretend this "dumping her daughter for the day" thing was her idea. His easy, "of course you're welcome" voice made her the villain.

Torn between her daughter's pleading brown eyes and her own flash of anger, she couldn't speak for a moment. Just as well, because the pause gave her time to realize that he was right: they had to pretend. And, by God, she could do it as well as he could!

"I'd love to," she said, smiling. "Maybe first Rose would show me her bedroom."

Her gaze met his briefly, with a chill on both sides that neither of their voices revealed. *You don't want me in your house,* her eyes said, *but she's my child.*

I'll sit on her bed and admire her toys and coax her into friendship, whether you like it or not.

Sure you can, his said in return. *Today. Because the girls have left me no choice. But don't get your hopes up, lady. We're not setting a precedent here.*

"Good idea," he said with the same charm he'd show a new client. "Rosebud, I'll bet Lynn will enjoy seeing your dolls."

The floors were hardwood beyond the living room, the halls spacious. She caught glimpses into other rooms: one that held a dark big-screen television and a bank of stereo equipment, a formal dining room, an office with a huge leather chair and a state-of-the-art computer and a fax machine that hummed as it rolled out pages. Rose led the way, Shelly gaining enough confidence to peer through doorways and finally let go of her mom's hand when Rose said, "My bedroom is that one."

All the way, Lynn felt Adam behind her with a prickling, disquieting awareness. *In the presence of mine enemy.*

What she hated most was the knowledge that her reaction was partly sexual. Adam Landry would have been the kind of boy she'd watched from afar in middle school and high school and college. With that build, he must have been an athlete. With his confidence, he was probably the student body president. Petite, sparkly blondes would have hung on his arm, not quiet, shy girls with difficult hair.

This man was that boy all grown up, and she was no more capable of exchanging snappy repartee or sultry looks than she'd been then.

Worst of all, the man he'd grown into was obviously capable of kindness and restraint and intense love. *Then,* she had told herself the popular boys were shallow. Her mother had agreed, hugged her and told her to look for a late-bloomer, they were the best kind.

How disconcerting to discover that she still secretly wished he would notice her. Not as if she really truly wanted him, but because his attention would mean she had arrived. She could be one of those girls who casually slipped an arm around any boy's waist, who laughed with him and boldly asked him to dance and assumed she would have a date on Friday night.

No, it wasn't that she wanted Adam Landry to share her unnerving awareness. Heaven forbid. He was the enemy. He only represented something to her. He awakened inchoate girlish longings she'd thought long dead. He was a symbol.

She grimaced when the girls weren't looking her way and wondered for the forty-second time: Why couldn't Shelly's birth father have been a nice plumber with a tub of his own?

"See? This is my room," Rose said shyly.

"Ooh," Shelly breathed, and Lynn's heart sank anew.

Right behind her daughter, she stepped into a young girl's fantasy kingdom, all pink and purple, with shelves and shelves of dolls, some porcelain, some meant for play. And horses—Breyer's statues of the Black Stallion and Misty of Chincoteague and a unicorn with a glittering horn. The gleaming mahogany rocking horse was an objet d'art, not a child's plaything. Rose had her very own cushioned window seat heaped with stuffed animals, and a small Ferrari parked in front of a huge pink plastic Barbie house, completely furnished.

Lynn stood there with her mouth open. Her worst fear had come true. Rose would never want to visit her. Shelly would never want to come home.

He had bought his victory.

SHE'D TRIED. Adam had to give her that. She clearly didn't want to stay any more than he wanted her to.

Or so he told himself. If he were being brutally honest, he'd admit that he had sweated all week over this visit. He felt inadequate enough with Rose. What in hell would he do if Shelly skinned her knee and cried or got homesick and wanted her mommy?

His mother wasn't a feminine woman. A potter, she had most often worn denim overalls and rubber boots she could hose off. Barb Landry was a creative, passionate, intelligent woman, and not for a moment even in his childhood would he have traded her in for any of his friends' mothers, but she hadn't been terribly interested in her son's childish problems, either. She wanted nothing more than to be back in her studio, as if the spinning of her potter's wheel had mesmerized her so that she could never wander far from it. He'd always known, when she made him lunch or looked at his artwork or helped with homework, that she would have preferred to be footing a bowl or delicately incising a pattern in a vase or experimenting with firing temperatures.

From her he'd learned to focus with an intensity most people couldn't manage. A single-minded commitment to work brought success. He'd learned the power of words and books and ideas. He'd grown up to be self-sufficient.

He hadn't learned a damned thing about parenting. Especially, about parenting a little girl.

Adam envied and resented Lynn Chanak's ease with both Shelly and Rose. He doubted she ever wondered whether she was doing everything wrong. Her ability to talk warmly and directly to a child without patronizing was exactly why he didn't want her here. In comparison, he felt wooden, even less capable of appearing to be the perfect father-figure than usual.

Her same ability explained his relief when she'd graciously agreed to stay.

It didn't explain why he couldn't seem to take his gaze from her nicely rounded hips and tiny waist as he followed her down the hall. Today she wore a little black miniskirt that exposed plenty of leg and fit her bottom like...

He swallowed an expletive. The completion of that sentence was a figure of speech. His hands had no business on her butt.

When she paused in Rose's bedroom doorway, his gaze moved upward to the generous swell of breasts barely disguised by a plum-colored silky shirt loose over a white tank top. He wondered if she knew the lace of her bra showed through the thin ribbed knit tank.

Then there was her hair, gathered into a high po- nytail that spilled thick auburn curls to the middle of her back. The wanton disorder of those curls was an intriguing contrast to her slender, pale neck and firm chin. Her hair would be glorious tumbled across a pillow.

Adam almost groaned at the lurch of sexual desire. Unlike many men, he didn't make a habit of seeing every woman as a sexual object. He couldn't remember the last time he'd pictured a woman in his bed.

This was sure as hell not the one to start with.

Think of Rose, he told himself. *Think of Shelly, and the god-awful mess all their lives already had become.*

His mouth twisted. Add even a flirtation, and he and Lynn wouldn't have a hope of achieving the friendly, flexible, rational relationship they would need to make this bizarre attempt to share their daughters work.

Through his preoccupation Adam finally became aware that Lynn had been silent for too long. Still on the threshold of Rose's bedroom, Lynn studied every shelf, every corner, with a care that made him nervous. What was wrong? Had he tried too hard?

"Does she know how lucky she is?" Lynn asked.

He plumbed her tone for sarcasm and came up with sadness. Because she'd never be able to buy as much for Shelly?

"I wanted everything to be perfect for her." He took a step closer, looking over her shoulder into his daughter's room, where both girls crouched in front of the Barbie house and talked animatedly. "I wasn't trying to spoil her."

"I didn't say you were."

"But you don't like her room."

She gave him an anguished look. "It's fairyland. What little girl wouldn't be thrilled?"

He still didn't get it. "You think Shelly will be jealous?"

Her smile trembled. "I think she won't want to come home."

Adam felt stupid for not understanding. "You can't buy love." Although Rose's room looked as if he'd tried, he saw suddenly.

The next instant, he squashed his chagrin. Damn it, he'd worked hard for his success! He sure as hell wasn't going to be ashamed of his ability to buy his daughter what she wanted.

"No. You can't buy love." But she didn't sound certain. "It's all so neat. Did you clean specially for Shelly's visit?"

His grunt held little amusement. Here was the kicker. "Rose doesn't play with most of this stuff. She doesn't want to be up here by herself. She has friends over once in a while, but otherwise..." He shrugged.

Rose still cried at night, too. A couple of times a week she crept down the hall, whimpering, and slipped into bed with him. The books he'd read said parents should never let their children sleep with them, but sometimes he weakened. He'd never been good at listening to his Rosebud cry herself to sleep.

One more thing he wished he could ask other parents, but didn't have the nerve. Did other three-year-olds need a diaper at night? Did they wake with nightmares, fear the shadows in the closet?

He had done everything he could to make Rose's bedroom beautiful and friendly. Obviously he lacked the knack. If Jennifer had been here...

But she wasn't. All he could do was his best.

"I'd better go work on lunch," he said abruptly.

Lynn gave him a distracted glance. "Can I help you?"

"It's a one-man job."

As he turned away, she went into Rose's bedroom. All the way back to the kitchen he could hear her voice, sweetly feminine and bubbling with delight, as she chattered with the girls. He had no doubt she would admire everything Rose most loved and succeed in entrancing his daughter. She would know exactly what to say, would feel perfectly comfortable sitting cross-legged on the floor joining in their games.

He'd expected Rose to talk about Shelly this past week, and she had. What he hadn't anticipated was that she'd also keep bringing up Lynn's name.

Tuesday, on the way home from day care, she had pulled her thumb from her mouth and said out of the blue, "Lynn is prettier than Amanda's mommy."

Amanda's mommy was sensational, all legs and cleavage and pouty mouth, but as it happened he agreed with Rose. Lynn was prettier.

Wednesday, in the middle of Ann's dinner, Rose had said shyly, "Lynn is funny, isn't she?"

Lynn had freckles, Rose had also told him another day, as if he hadn't noticed. And she ran fast, didn't she?

Lynn, it appeared, had acquired a fan club. And he was jealous. Adam swore under his breath and savagely chopped a green pepper, then scraped it into a bowl.

He'd moved on to whacking an onion when he realized he was no longer alone.

She stood hesitantly just inside the kitchen. "You could use help."

"I can chop. It's one of my few kitchen skills."

Her smile looked too damn much like Rose's. "Are you sure you have enough for me? Shelly is more comfortable now. I could probably get away."

"No. I should have suggested this in the first place."

She nodded seriously, her ponytail bobbing. "Why don't we do the same next week? You join us for lunch, then slip away for a bit. There's no reason not to take it slowly."

He resented her wisdom, as well as the implicit truth: they had years to get to know their respective daughters. This relationship was damn near as permanent as marriage.

"You're right," he said curtly.

She bit her lip. "I'm sorry."

"For what?" He looked up, jaw muscles locked.

Antagonism flared to life in Lynn's eyes. "No. I have nothing to be sorry for, except that this happened in the first place. I won't apologize again."

Adam swore and shoved the cutting board away, setting down the knife. "Well, I will. I'm being a jackass. I just... Oh, hell. I had visions of my two daughters and I having a carefree day. The truth is, I have no idea how to talk to Shelly. I'm not exactly a natural parent. Not the way you are."

Shock replaced the hostility. "But Rose obviously adores you. Why on earth would you think..."

He immediately regretted having opened his big mouth. "Forget it. I'm just not used to kids. You think when you have your first baby that the two of you will learn together.''

"Yes," Lynn said softly, that indefinable sadness creeping over her. "You do."

He wasn't the only one raising a daughter alone, he belatedly remembered. "How long ago were you divorced?"

"Six months after Shelly was born—" She stopped abruptly. Shelly, of course, was not the baby born to her that day. "Three years ago," Lynn amended.

"What happened?" None of his business, of course, but he found himself unexpectedly curious about her, not just Shelly.

"Oh, it was a mistake from the beginning," she said vaguely. "Having a baby didn't help. It wasn't his idea."

He made a sound and reached for the fresh mushrooms. "Jennifer wanted a baby so badly. She had a couple of miscarriages." Now why had he told her that? "When she got past four months with her pregnancy, she was so happy." His throat closed.

"And then she never knew…" Lynn pressed her lips together. "That must haunt you."

"You could say so." He cleared his throat. "I want you to understand why I need to be part of Shelly's life."

"I do," she said so quietly he just heard her. Lynn had bowed her head and was staring down at the pattern she was tracing on the tile counter. Her face was colorless and vulnerable when she looked up. "But I still won't let you have her."

Was that what he'd hoped? If so, he'd been a fool.

"We're stuck with each other," he said.

"It would seem so." She sounded as conflicted as he felt.

Adam set down the knife for the second time. He held out his hand across the kitchen island. "Well, Ms. Chanak, I suggest we make the best of it."

This smile, a twist of her lips, didn't produce dimples or the tiny crinkle of lines on the bridge of her nose. Her gray-green eyes remained grave as she took his hand, her own small and fragile in his stronger grip. "You have a deal."

Somehow her hand lingered in his; somehow he was reluctant to let her go. Solidarity, he told himself. Relief. Maybe they could be friends.

"Tell you what," he said. "Why don't you call the girls? This is a do-it-yourself pizza lunch, and I'm ready for everybody to make some hard decisions."

This smile was more natural, dimples and a curve of cheek as she started from the kitchen. "That kind of decision," she agreed, "I can make."

He didn't have to wonder what she meant.

CHAPTER SIX

DESPITE THEIR LITTLE TALK, the next couple of visits were no easier. Rose definitely didn't want Daddy to leave her, although she and Shelly had a grand time together so long as he stayed near. When he did leave, she cried inconsolably. Brave Shelly did somewhat better after that first time at the Landrys' house, but the third time Lynn came back, after an absence of five hours, only to be met at the door by a grim Adam.

His formerly pristine shirt was rumpled, rolled up at the sleeves and wet. His hair stood on end and an unpleasant odor wafted from him.

"Shelly's throwing up," he said bluntly. "I was about ready to call the doctor."

"Oh, Lord." Panic, well out of proportion, surged through her. Lynn whisked past him. "Where is she?"

"Lying down in Rose's bed." Although she moved fast, he was right behind her. "She has a big bowl next to her. For what good it does."

Lynn paused in the hall a few steps from Rose's open bedroom door. "She missed?"

He made a sound in his throat. "She's puked on the floor, Rose's bed and me. Rose is crying because she's scared. I think Shelly has a fever, but she doesn't want me taking her temperature. I couldn't give her anything to lower her temp anyway. It would just come right back up.''

The panic had begun to subside. Or, more accurately, she had recognized it for what it was: guilt. Her little girl had needed her, and she wasn't here.

''I wondered why she was so tired this morning,'' Lynn said, remembering. ''Her friend Laura has been sick.''

''Now you tell me,'' Adam muttered.

She ignored him and went in to see her daughter. The girls had done some damage, she saw on the way. Puzzle pieces were jumbled on the floor and unkempt Barbies strewn as if a tornado had swept through the room. It almost looked normal for a child's bedroom.

Rose curled, teary eyed, on the window seat. Face wan, Shelly lay in bed, looking so small and fragile and miserable that Lynn's own eyes burned.

''Oh, sweetie!'' She detoured to give Rose a quick kiss on the head and murmured, ''Shelly will be okay. Don't worry.'' Then she sat on the edge of the bed and laid the back of her hand on Shelly's forehead. ''You're toaster hot. Gracious, you've had an awful day, haven't you?''

Her daughter's face crumpled. ''Where were you?'' she wailed. ''I wanted you!''

Gathering Shelly into her arms, Lynn whispered, ''I know, I know. But Adam has taken good care of you, hasn't he?''

The three-year-old shook her head hard. ''I wanna go home!''

Lynn glanced toward the doorway and saw the

hurt in Adam's eyes before he shuttered his expression.

Hugging and swaying, Lynn said softly, "I don't know, sweet pea. The drive would be awful if you're throwing up."

"Don't go!" Her daughter latched convulsively onto her.

In a friendly voice that gave away nothing of what he must be feeling, Adam said, "Why don't you two spend the night? Your mom can have a room down the hall, and you can either stay here in Rose's bed, or share with Mom."

Lynn hated the alternatives. How could she say no and subject poor Shelly to the long, winding drive home over the Coast Range? But to stay, when she at least must be unwelcome...

Of course, she had no choice. As, she thought grimly, she so rarely did these days. Of course, it was unreasonable to blame Adam, who must be chafing as much as she was at losing control over such a hunk of his life.

As much? Who was she kidding? He was a man. Men wanted and expected to be in charge. Oh, yeah. If she resented him sometimes, he was probably angry enough to hire a hit man to rid himself of her.

"Thank you." She was just as capable as he was at putting on a good front. "I think we'd probably better stay."

She carried Shelly down the hall, helped her into a borrowed nightgown and bathed her forehead while he changed the bedding. Rose shyly came to visit Shelly while Daddy took a shower.

"Are you gonna pook again?" she asked.

Shelly nodded vigorously and shot to a half-sitting position. "Mama?" she begged in a strangled voice.

Lynn positioned the bowl in the nick of time. Rose watched wide-eyed. Heaven help them if this flu bug was a two-week affair instead of a twenty-four-hour quickie! Especially if—or should she say, when—Rose caught it.

Lynn was helping Shelly rinse out her mouth when Adam appeared in the doorway. In faded sweatpants and T-shirt, hair wet and finger-combed, he was breathtakingly sexy and a world more human than he usually seemed to Lynn.

"Do you want me to call the doctor?" he asked.

Lynn shook her head. "Not unless she keeps heaving once she's emptied her stomach. I take it they had lunch before she got sick?" Unfortunately, she could have itemized the menu.

"Yeah." His expression was sheepish. "They had macaroni and cheese, and hot dogs. Ice-cream bars. Oh, yeah. And Kool-Aid. Lots of lime Kool-Aid."

"I noticed," she said dryly.

Poor Shelly's face was flushed, but her eyes had become heavy. Lynn clicked on a bedside lamp at its lowest setting and motioned to him to switch off the overhead light. When she glanced back, he and Rose were gone.

She sang softly, smoothing Shelly's hair back from her hot forehead, until her daughter slept. Even then she sat there, just touched by lamplight in the dim room, thinking in despair, *How can we keep doing this?* What if she told him it just wasn't working?

Yes, but how could she? She saw Rose, scared and sad, hugging herself on the window seat in that gorgeous bedroom that was still strangely sterile. Her face, always so serious. Her need to hold on tight to Daddy, because who else did she have?

Me. She has me, Lynn's heart cried.

So, of course, she had no solution to the dilemma. They *had* to keep doing this. It was no worse, she told herself, than what many parents subjected their children to after a divorce. As long as those children grew up knowing they were loved, they forgot about the weekends when they didn't want to go to Daddy's, or the summers when they were packed off to Mom's. Love was what counted.

Lynn slipped out of the room, surprised, when she checked her watch, to find that it was seven-thirty. Shelly's usual bedtime was eight, so no wonder after her wretched and exhausting afternoon that she was already sound asleep! Muffled by a wall, Lynn heard splashes of water, a giggle followed by a deeper voice. Bath time. Maybe Rose had been "pooked on," too.

She left the door open a crack. Two steps down the hall, Lynn turned back for another look. Shelly hadn't stirred. Fingers crossed that she stayed that way, Lynn went into Rose's room and sat cross-legged on the floor, putting puzzles back together. How helpful, she mocked herself, and felt like a thirteen-year-old girl who just happened to be hanging out in front of a cute boy's house. *Oh, do you live here?*

Well, damn it, she wanted just once to tuck her daughter into bed! She closed her eyes briefly, imagining herself smoothing back Rose's curls, kissing the freckles on her nose, whispering, "Sleep tight, don't let the bedbugs bite,'' seeing a soft, sleepy smile light the face of this child she had carried for nine months.

Was that too much to ask?

Adam appeared with Rose in flowered flannel pajamas. For a moment, he hesitated, then nodded stiffly. ''Thank you.''

''No problem.'' Keeping her voice low, Lynn set the last completed puzzle on the pile.

''For some mysterious reason, Pansy here lost her appetite. She doesn't think she wants any dinner.''

A sleepy chuckle as Adam settled her into bed. ''Rose, Daddy! Not Pansy.''

Lynn made a face. ''I think I lost my appetite, too.''

''And you didn't eat the same things Shel—'' With a harrumph, he stopped. ''Never mind. Rosebud, I'll bet Lynn would like to say good-night, too.''

Oh, bless him! Instantly feeling kindlier, Lynn said, ''I'd love to.''

''Sleep well, honey.'' He kissed his daughter tenderly, carefully tucked blankets around her, and quietly left the room.

Lynn asked, ''Do you have a night-light?''

''Daddy forgot to turn it on.'' Rose sounded puzzled. ''Daddy never forgets.''

Daddy had left her something useful to do. Grateful, Lynn turned on the bright porcelain light and then sat on the edge of the bed. ''Sleep tight,'' she said softly. ''Don't let the bedbugs bite.''

A small giggle rewarded her. '''kay.''

Lynn let herself feel the intense pain and delight she usually denied, the bone-deep connection to *this* child. She hungrily looked, and saw herself as she never would in Shelly, who might be prettier and who she loved unshakably, but who did not look back sleepily with Brian's eyes, whose forehead didn't have a curve as familiar as the ache in her heart.

Oh, God, she wondered, *Am I as bad as Brian? Is passing on my genes so important to me?*

But, no, of course it wasn't. She felt the same as she ever had about Shelly. What she had to accept was that she could so quickly also love a child she hadn't known a month ago.

On a shaky breath, she bent and kissed her daughter's forehead.

Rose accepted the kiss with equanimity. "Are you gonna sleep with Shelly?"

"Yep."

"Sometimes I sleep with Daddy," Rose confided.

"When Shelly gets scared, she sneaks into bed with me, too."

"Oh." Rose pondered. "Daddy says big girls sleep in their own beds."

"Well, I guess big girls do, but you're not so big yet, are you? And even grown-ups get scared sometimes at night, if they hear a funny noise."

"Daddy doesn't get scared."

Lynn knew for a fact that wasn't true—the idea of losing his Rosebud was enough to scare Daddy to death. But she only smiled and said, "I wish I didn't." Then she kissed Rose again, this time on that small freckled nose. "Now, you go to sleep. Maybe Shelly will feel better in the morning and you two can play."

Rose smiled, sweet and shy. "'kay," she said again. "Night, Lynn."

Lynn's heart swelled and her sinuses burned with the effort not to cry, but she kept smiling through them. "Good night," she murmured.

She left the door open six inches and the hall light on. Thank God, Adam wasn't lurking outside the door. She needed a minute alone to wipe away the tears and convince herself that it could be worse: she might never have known, never have found Rose.

A peek in the guest room assured her that Shelly still slept, her face flushed but her breathing even. Then, nerving herself, Lynn went downstairs.

She found Adam in the kitchen. He glanced up, taking in far more than she wanted him to see with one sweep of his sharp gaze. But he only asked, "Shelly still asleep?"

She nodded.

"It's getting a little late to start the dinner I'd intended. How would French toast grab you? Or an omelette?"

"Either would be good."

His brows stayed up and he waited.

"French toast." She didn't care.

He'd already had the eggs out on the counter. She watched as he put a pan on to heat and started cracking eggs into a shallow bowl.

"Thank you for letting me tuck her in."

His jaw bunched. "Not much of a gift."

"You could have shooed me out."

"I hope I'm not that selfish."

He whisked the eggs efficiently but with latent violence. Wishing she could be whipped into an acceptable, smooth form as easily?

"Adam…"

"Do you like syrup?"

Frustration infused her voice. "Yes, but…"

"Let's eat and then talk. Okay?"

Lynn let out a gusty sigh. "Yes. Fine."

Not at all to her surprise, the French toast was thick, golden brown and crusty. Butter—real butter—pooled like sunlight. He'd even sprinkled the top with powdered sugar.

They took their plates to the kitchen table set in an alcove surrounded by windows that looked out at the dark garden. It must be a perfect spot in the morning.

She took her first bite. "This is wonderful! Do you buy your bread at a bakery?"

"Bread machine."

Lynn murmured with pleasure again. She must have been starved, she realized. She'd gone to a sandwich shop for lunch only to give herself something to do, one more way to kill the hours while she was exiled, but the sandwich had been dry and the turkey the kind that tasted fake. She'd had only a few bites.

"We hardly know each other," Adam said suddenly. "I think that's my fault."

Lynn set down her fork. "Yes. It is."

He acknowledged the hit with a grimace. "I'd like to change that. Tell me something about yourself. Where did you grow up? How'd you end up with a bookstore?"

"Eugene." She sounded rusty. She had the

sweaty-palmed feel of a fifth-grader standing up in front of the class to give a presentation. "I grew up in Eugene." That sounded bald all by itself, so words kept coming. "My mother was the secretary for the History department at the university. I never met my father. I think my mother had an affair, which isn't at all like her, but she wasn't married and didn't like to talk about him. 'It was just one of those things,' she always says."

Adam listened to her with the same concentration he probably gave to stock quotes on the Internet. He didn't interrupt, didn't look away, gave no sign of being bored. Lynn couldn't remember the last time anyone had really wanted to hear about *her*.

Which might have explained why even then she didn't shut up.

"I don't know. Maybe that's not the truth, either. Maybe Mom went to a sperm bank and just didn't want me to know my father was nothing but a few statistics in a catalog. You know—gray eyes, 130 IQ, five foot eleven, red hair." Oh, God, she thought belatedly. Why was she telling him this private suspicion?

"I do know my father," Adam said unexpectedly, "and I couldn't tell you a hell of a lot more than that about him. He and my mother suit each other, but he's not a warm man."

"What's he do?"

His grunt must have been a laugh. "He's a pathologist. Appropriate, isn't it? He's very, very smart, and cold as a morgue."

"But your mother..."

"Is an artist. A potter. She doesn't do dinner plates

or pitchers. These strange shapes connect..." His hands tried to form one of his mother's creations out of thin air, but he shrugged and gave up. "Ugly as hell, some of what she does, but the critics don't see it that way. It 'speaks to the heart.'" He fell silent.

Beginning to be puzzled, Lynn asked tentatively, "Are you proud of her?"

"Mmm?" He looked startled. "Sure. I have one of her pieces in the living room. Remind me to show you. The thing is...she's pretty distant, too. If I hadn't seen her working at her wheel, I'd have a hell of a time imagining her and Dad tangled in bed together."

Lynn blinked.

He closed his eyes briefly and rotated his neck. "I shouldn't have said that. Sorry."

"No. That's okay. I shouldn't have said what I did about the sperm bank, either." He'd offered her a trade, she realized. A glimpse into his privacy in exchange for one into hers. Whatever else Adam Landry might be, he wasn't selfish. His generosity compelled Lynn to continue, "But you're right, we should get to know each other. Warts and all."

Adam met her eyes, his breathtakingly intense. "What I'm trying to say is, ever since I brought Rose home I've been parenting by guess and by God. I'm the one browsing the parenting section in the bookstore. I can't call Mom and ask how to handle a two-year-old whose only word is 'no.'" Adam made another of those rough sounds meant to be a laugh. "Mom says, 'Why ask me?'"

"Why ask her?" Lynn echoed incredulously.

His mouth curved into something more closely approximating genuine amusement. "See, she handled it when she had to, but…absently. I guess that's the best way to put it. She was always focused on her art. I'll bet she doesn't remember me at two or three."

"But…that's appalling!" And terribly sad.

He ran a hand over a chin bristly with the day's growth of dark beard. "No, that's Mom. She's a cool lady in her own way. Brilliant, passionate about her art, smart about the business side of it. Just not all that interested in wiping snotty noses or leading pre-schoolers around the zoo."

Fascinated, Lynn pushed her plate back and crossed her forearms on the table. "Why did she have children, then?"

"An accident?" One cheek creased. "I've never had the guts to ask her."

Lynn sat there absorbing what he'd told her. Finally, she mused, "At least I had my mother. She might have been a little mysterious about my father, but, you know, I never really cared. She was always enough. Maybe that's why being a single parent hasn't been that hard for me." She smiled crookedly. "You might say, that's the pattern I know. But you…" She started to reach out to touch his hand, but stopped herself. "You've done an amazing job. Rose adores you."

"We've done okay," he said gruffly.

"Better than okay."

He shifted. "Maybe you'd better save the accolades for a few months. I screw up. Sometimes I think Rose is babyish for her age, and that's my fault."

"Babyish?" Why did she keep having this urge to take his hand, as if he needed comfort?

"Didn't you notice she went to bed with a diaper on? Three-and-a-half years old, and she still wets her bed."

"Lots of kids do," Lynn said, puzzled at his perturbation. "Maybe she's an extra sound sleeper. She seems to do fine during the day."

He shoved himself to his feet and grabbed their empty plates. "She has accidents."

"So does Shelly."

At the sink, Adam stood with his back to her. "Not when she's with me."

"Rose hasn't had one with me, either."

He stayed completely still for a moment. "I figured I was doing something wrong."

What could she say? Lynn fumbled for the right words. "Children, um, aren't like a product you assemble. They aren't perfect, any more than we are." Then she flushed. "I'm sorry. That was patronizing."

"I deserved it." When he turned, he was actually smiling. The fact that one corner of his mouth crooked higher than the other lent charm to a face that was usually too austere. "Anyway, funny thing. You've hit the nail on the head. *I* was expected to be perfect. I didn't want to lay that burden on Rose, but apparently my expectations weren't buried very far under. As you said, patterns."

Lynn didn't want to feel sympathy or liking or even understanding. She couldn't afford to. *Stop,* she told herself. *Now.*

"This isn't working," she said abruptly. "These visits. I hate them."

Between one blink and the next, he became a stranger again. "We agreed to take it slowly."

"I don't like to shop. The movies are all made for teenagers. I dread these days." She sounded peevish instead of firm. *Me, me, me.* "No," she argued with herself. "It's not me. If the girls were happy...but they're not. They're too young to be bounced back and forth like this."

"Then what do you suggest?" His voice was harsh. "Shall we just stay in touch? Send each other photos at Christmas?"

"No."

"Goddamn it!" he shouted. "Then what?"

"I don't know," she yelled back, suddenly furious. "But something different!"

"Different."

Lynn swallowed, moderated her tone. "Maybe... maybe less often. Maybe, for now, we need to put up with each other instead of pretending we can each have both of them."

Adam swore and massaged the back of his neck. "We are pretending, aren't we?"

"Yes." She pressed her hand to her chest, which inexplicably burned. "That's exactly what we're doing. Shelly and Rose don't understand."

"Today, all she wanted was you."

"Rose cries when you leave her."

"She cries at her day care, too. Sometimes I have to pry her hands off me."

Lynn hated that picture, but she couldn't blame

him. He was a good father; Rose loved him. He had to work.

"What shall we do?" she asked miserably.

"Maybe you're right. Maybe we went at this in too big a hurry."

She didn't want him to agree, Lynn was shocked to realize. She didn't want to go back to before, however serene it seemed in memory. To not see Rose as often. To not see him as often.

Now, what did *that* mean? she wondered, jarred. Had she come to have some kind of fellow feeling for Adam, because he was the only one who truly understood what she was going through? Was it self-defense, to bond with him?

Or—dear God—had she developed some kind of adolescent crush on the man? Was some of her Monday morning anticipation because she would see him, not just Rose? Did that explain some of the hurt and letdown, when he didn't invite her past the doorstep?

"Even the days I have both girls aren't that great, because Rose wants you. And because, oh, because it's like this special event. It's not *life*. I want Rose to feel at home with me," she struggled to explain.

He watched her with understanding that delved beneath her breastbone. "Question is, do you want Shelly to feel at home with me?"

Lynn gave a small, twisted smile. "Probably not. How do you feel about the idea of Rose happy with me?"

"Oh, I'm jealous as hell."

"I guess we can't help how we feel. Just what we do about it."

"You're not suggesting a change because you're jealous, too?"

He was asking for honesty. Lynn tried to give it. "I don't think so. I hope not. Tell me the truth. Do you look forward to Mondays?"

"No. Hell." He scrubbed a hand over his face. "The drive is getting damned old, and I don't like wasting a day over there any better than you do here. Okay. We can do better."

"How about fewer but longer visits? Overnight stays?"

"Rose has never even spent the night at her grand-parents'."

"Would you, um, consider staying over the first few times?"

The austerity was back as he frowned, and she quailed a little at her boldness.

"On your couch?"

"You can have my bed," she said, too quickly. *Why so eager to persuade him?* she asked herself. "I'm shorter. I'll take the couch."

"I do have the extra bedroom here." He was still thinking. "They have more fun when you're around, too."

"I know it's awkward."

"At first it was awkward." He contemplated her, but she couldn't tell what he was thinking. "I'm not so sure it is anymore."

"Maybe we could be friends." *Only friends?*

"All right." The lines between his dark brows cleared. "I'm game. How about if we make it the weekend after next? I'll come Sunday and Monday.

That way I can entertain the girls while your shop's open on Sunday.''

"It's not too long for you to take off?''

A shrug. "I can bring my laptop. Put in a little time Monday. I can be flexible.''

"Okay.'' Two weeks. How would she wait two weeks to see them again? "Um…'' she began apologetically. "My place is pretty tiny. I've put my money into the business. Maybe we can eat out,'' she decided with quick relief. But, oh God, he'd still have to use her shabby bathroom, see the chips in the porcelain sink and tub, bump his head on the too-low lintel.

She had a suspicion he read her shame and anxiety as if her face were the open screen of his laptop.

"Real life, remember?''

"Yes. All right.'' She was taking a risk in baring her life for his scrutiny. In court, he could use her poverty against her. But he could have done that anyway, she reminded herself. It wasn't any secret.

And she was beginning to believe, to hope, that he wouldn't. If she was wrong, heaven help her.

"I'd better go check on Shelly.'' She picked up her silverware and glass. "Unless you need help cleaning up…''

Adam crossed the kitchen and took them from her, his fingers bumping hers. "Don't be ridiculous. Go.''

Foolish that her pulse bumped in sync.

"Thank you, Adam. For listening.''

His eyes softened. "We should have talked sooner.''

"No one said this would be easy.''

"Has anyone else ever had to figure it out?'' He

released a breath. "Good night, Lynn. Make yourself at home if you wake up before I do in the morning."

She edged backward. "Right." At home. "Sure."

"I left Rose's shampoo in the shower. I'll put out clean towels."

"Thank you." Why was she still standing here? Why was she wondering, hoping, at the way his eyes seemed to darken, at the step he took forward?

"Rose needs a mother's touch."

Rose. Not him. Of course not him.

She was being foolish. He looked at her oddly sometimes because of her resemblance to his Rosebud. Not because she was a woman and he was a man.

This new plan wouldn't work, either, if she started suffering delusions. *So don't,* Lynn told herself sharply.

With a cool nod and another good-night, she went.

CHAPTER SEVEN

ADAM TRIED TO ROLL OVER and had to muffle a groan. The damned couch was not only a foot too short for his big frame, but it was about as comfortable as squatting against a driftwood log on a rocky beach: okay for a while when the sun was hot and the beat of the surf steady and lulling, but nowhere you'd want to snooze for eight hours.

Lynn had offered, four or five times, to sleep out here and let him have her bedroom. Offered, hell, she'd tried to insist. But, no, he was too chivalrous to accept.

He still didn't regret his refusal, and not just because he liked to think he was a gentleman. It would have made sense for her to sleep on the couch instead of him. She probably could have stretched out. She might have even rested more easily on the lumps and bumps. Along with being a good ten inches shorter than he was, she must weight fifty pounds less.

What Adam hadn't liked was the idea of invading her private space. Of being surrounded by her scent and her most intimate possessions. Oh, she'd have cleaned up for him. No sexy bras would be draped across the Lincoln rocker he'd glimpsed from the hall, and she wouldn't leave a diary open to yesterday's entry, but her makeup decorated a dresser, her books covered a bedside table, the prints on the walls were her favorites, the contents of her drawers...well, he'd bet homemade bags of dried lavender and rose petals perfumed her lingerie.

That one glimpse into her sanctum was enough, thank you. The bed was an old-fashioned double with a mahogany spooled head and footboard. It was heaped with pillows in lacy cases and covered by a fluffy chenille spread the color of butter. The makeup was arranged on embroidered linen darkened to old ivory. Late roses spilled languorously from a cream-colored stoneware pitcher.

The room was utterly feminine and graceful. Pretty, but in a womanly way rather than a girlish one. The fact that Lynn Chanak was a woman, and a sexy one at that, was something he tried hard not to think about.

He'd become good at blocking out that kind of awareness. Living like a monk, a man had to build some defenses.

Oh, he'd tried dating after the first year of mourning. Rhonda McIntyre, a commodities broker, had cornered him in the elevator and flirted with so little subtlety even he'd noticed. Why not? he'd figured.

The evening was a flop. She made plain her disinterest in children. They talked trading and the bull market for lack of any other topic. He kissed her on her doorstep and declined her invitation to go in.

A couple of months later, he'd dated another woman a few times—a single mother he'd met at the preschool. She was struggling to make ends meet as a secretary, and she had a hungry, desperate quality that scared him. She wanted marriage, and she wanted it soon.

Since then, he hadn't bothered. Now and again, a woman would turn his head on the street. Maybe her leggy stride, or the lush curve of a bottom in a tight miniskirt. A cleavage, or the smooth line of a stranger's throat as she laughed.

He was tempted sometimes to call Rhonda or another woman like her, just because his body ached for release. He'd never imagined being celibate for over three years. Nights, Adam stayed up later than he should, because climbing into bed alone was when he felt the loss. Jenny came to him most readily then, with an airy laugh or a teasing tickle of her fingers, and he would almost roll to gather her into his arms when he'd remember with a painful stab that she was gone for good.

Her death had come so damned fast. No time to prepare, to say goodbye.

The afternoon it happened, he'd talked to her quickly from the office, half his attention on the notes he'd been making on a new software company. He had dropped his car off for new brakes that morning, and the mechanic had let him know they had to wait for a part. "No problem," Jenny had declared. They chose one of their favorite restaurants in downtown Portland and arranged to meet there. He'd walk over, they'd go home together.

"If you're *sure* you don't mind being seen with a woman shaped like a gray whale," she'd said, so blithely he could smile into the telephone knowing she was only fishing for a compliment. She was well aware of her beauty, body swollen with his child, her breasts heavier in his hands at night, the mystery making her gaze remote often enough to tantalize any man. Jennifer had never lacked in confidence, during her pregnancy least of all.

Grinning, the last thing he said to her was, "Just make sure they seat you before I arrive," and she'd told him he was a rat.

Neither of them said goodbye or "I love you."

He was ten minutes late. Jenny wasn't there, hadn't been seated. He had a drink while he waited. Punctuality never had been one of her virtues. When she was half an hour late, he tried her at home. No answer. She had a way of forgetting to turn on her cell phone, but he tried it, too.

A police officer had answered, told him his wife had been hit head-on by a drunk driver. She had been transported to the hospital with a potential head injury.

She was already gone, his Jenny. Dead in every way that mattered, except that the beat of her heart and the soft machine-induced breaths sustained their baby. For lack of a brake cylinder in stock at the garage.

But cursing fate didn't change a thing.

From that day forward, he looked at other women, and he saw Jenny. He couldn't bed one and close his eyes. She would move wrong, sigh wrong, be too patient.

So he stayed celibate even when his body protested.

Like tonight.

Thinking about Lynn Chanak's bed had more to do with his restlessness than the lumpy cushions did.

Hell, maybe he'd have been better off between her sheets than imagining her there.

At bedtime she'd used the bathroom first. Thinking he'd heard her door shut, Adam went down the hall with his toothbrush just in time to meet her face-to-face outside the bathroom. Her faded flannel bathrobe gaped enough to expose a fine white cotton nightgown edged with lace as pretty as that on her sheets. Brushed until it crackled with energy, her hair tumbled over her shoulders and breasts. She smelled like soap and woman, her cheeks pink from scrubbing.

God help him, he'd looked down to see her bare feet peeking out beneath the ragged hem of her robe. Her toes, curled on the cold floorboards, were a hell of a lot sexier than Rhonda McIntyre's musk-scented cleavage as she deliberately bent to pick something up right in front of him.

Blushing, murmuring that the bathroom was all his, Lynn had fled, leaving him with an ache that kept him awake with a vengeance.

His sexual fantasies these days weren't specific. He imagined burying himself in a woman's body without thinking too much about her voice or her face or her cold feet sneaking to warm themselves against him in bed. Now, being tormented on Lynn Chanak's ancient couch, every time he closed his eyes, he saw himself tangling his fingers in that mass of glorious hair. He imagined her pretty, virginal nightgown. The smell of her soap and the lavender and roses drifting from her bureau.

She was the mother of his daughter. *Her* body had once swelled with another man's seed, but it was his

Rosebud she'd carried. Knowing that muddled his thoughts. When he tried to see his Jenny pregnant, he imagined Lynn instead.

It didn't help to tell himself that she'd be horrified if she knew he was lying out here on her couch lusting after her.

What if he acted on it? What if he kissed her? What if she didn't slap him?

Would he long for Jenny when he bedded Lynn?

Swearing, Adam rolled over again and stared up at the dark ceiling.

Even if he didn't think about Jenny, what he felt wasn't love. It was celibacy butting up against involuntary intimacy with a woman. It was encountering her barefooted in her nightie with her teeth freshly brushed and her cheeks rosy. It was seeing her as his child's mother.

And it could not be. The inevitable hurt feelings and anger would destroy any hope of sharing their daughters.

Grimly Adam tried to shut off the show his imagination was directing. Obviously, it was time—past time—he found a woman with whom he could laugh and enjoy sex, if nothing else.

Any woman but Lynn Chanak.

OF COURSE, BY MONDAY morning, rain dripped dismally from a gray sky, killing his hope of taking the girls to the beach. The kitchen table didn't seat four, so Adam sat wedged between Rose and Shelly while Lynn munched toast and served them.

"No movie theater in town," he remembered.

"Nope. Lincoln City is the closest. And I don't think anything is playing that they'd enjoy."

"Any ideas?" he asked without hope.

"We could hang around here." Whisking back and forth between stove and table, she barely glanced at him. "The girls'll be happy playing. You can do whatever it is brokers do. Use your laptop to check what prices are going up or down. That terrorist bombing in Rome probably panicked a few stock-holders."

He didn't give a damn whether Intel had dropped a point and a half because some zealot had blown up himself and half an office building just outside the Vatican. He didn't want to spend the day with her. But he'd had the girls yesterday. Today was, in a sense, her turn. He couldn't decide to leave until mid-afternoon at least.

"Sure," he said without enthusiasm. "Sounds good."

"You girls could dress up," Lynn suggested. "I'll get the box down if you want."

"Dress up?" Rose brightened. "We could have a parade. Like we do at preschool."

"Yeah!" Shelly bounced. "And maybe sing!"

"And dance."

"You could put on a performance for us." Lynn set more bacon on the table.

"Let's go practice." The girls were gone in a flurry, Lynn behind them to get down "the box."

Adam usually avoided cholesterol-laden foods like bacon, but he gloomily began crunching a strip. When Lynn reappeared, he asked, "What's in the box?"

"Oh..." She smiled and took a tea bag from a canister. "Dress-up clothes. I'm always adding new stuff from the thrift store. I have feather boas and gaudy jewelry and high heels and scarves. Lots of sequins. You'll see." Pouring hot water into her mug, she added over her shoulder, "But what makes it magic is, I only let Shelly into it every once in a while. On a day when she's really bored. Or like today, when she and a friend can put on a production."

Magic. Adam guessed he did okay as a parent, but he didn't know how to make magic. This woman did.

"What are you thinking about?" she asked.

Surprising himself, he told her.

"Nonsense." She joined him at the table. "A dress-up box is a girl thing. Why would you think of it?"

Jennifer would have, he knew.

"That doesn't mean you don't come up with your own ideas. Or at least provide Rose with the opportunity to find them elsewhere."

"Preschool."

"Sure. Why not?"

"If she loved it there, she wouldn't hate going."

Lynn lifted out the tea bag, squeezed it and set it on the edge of a breakfast plate. The rich scent of orange and cinnamon overrode the greasier flavor of bacon.

"I don't know about that," she said calmly. "Just because Rose cries when she has to say goodbye to you doesn't mean she has a terrible time. Doesn't she tell you about her day?"

"Sure she does." He ate another strip of bacon,

simply because it was there. "They're teaching the kids sign language. She shows me new signs every day. The goat tries to eat her hair, which means we have to wash it that night. I catch her sometimes giggling with a bunch of other girls when I get there early."

"I rest my case."

He took a last swallow of coffee and tried not to notice that her knees were bumping his under the small table. "Since you're so wise, tell me this— why do I worry constantly about whether I'm screwing up, while you know instinctively what to do? Is it the difference between a woman and a man?"

That difference was exactly what he *didn't* want to think about. So why throw it out on the table for discussion?

Because it was on his mind, he concluded.

"I know women who are terrible with their kids and men who are great. No." She shook her head, and her braid flopped over her shoulder. "I suspect it has more to do with the fact that my mother was an affectionate woman and yours wasn't. Parenting is a learned skill. Maybe it *is* easier to learn as a child, like a second language. You're having to work a little harder. That's all."

How simple. He felt like an idiot to be so comforted by an answer as obvious as this one.

"What would you normally do today?" he asked, more abruptly than was polite.

"Clean the kitchen." Lynn nodded toward the sink. "Do a little housework. Pay bills. Thumb through publishers' catalogs."

"Don't let me distract you."

Her clear-eyed gaze saw right through him. He wanted them not to spend the day together.

"Sure," she said agreeably. "The phone is here. Do you want to spread out on the table? I'll have it cleared in a minute."

"Let me help."

She'd already pushed back her chair. "This is a one-cook kitchen. We'd be tripping over each other."

Instead of going to the living room for his briefcase and laptop computer, Adam watched as she ran hot water into the sink. No dishwasher. He'd vaguely thought everybody had one.

In the past twenty-four hours, he had become shockingly aware of how near to the bone Lynn Chanak must live. The furniture was all secondhand. No, third- or fourth-hand. The linoleum in the bathroom and kitchen were both worn to the point where the pattern had become a memory and seams were peeling. She and Shelly had two bedrooms—if you could call Shelly's eight-by-eight feet with a slanting ceiling a room. Crummy bathroom. Creaky plumbing. A small eating space in the kitchen and a living room no bigger than his den. Woodwork and floors needed stripping or replacing, windows were single pane, and he wondered about the building's wiring.

It appalled him to think about the reaction of Jennifer's parents, if they could see where their granddaughter was growing up.

Funny thing was, the only uncomfortable part of this apartment was the couch. The place was tiny, too small for two adults and two children, but probably fine for just a mom and toddler. With the same imagination she'd used in creating the dress-up box, Lynn had managed to give the old house charm on a shoestring.

She'd rag-rolled paint on plaster walls to subtle effect and used bright enamel on wood furniture. Posters of far-off places and wreaths of dried flowers brightened bare spots. The tiny hall was hung with family photos. He'd lingered that morning to study them. Bright pillows were probably hand-sewn rather than bought; he'd bet she had crocheted the afghan, as well. She had an eye for color, he thought, an ability to bring cheer to the drabbest room.

His own house could use a little.

"I'm done," she said briskly, whisking a dishcloth across the table. "It's all yours."

"Thanks."

He tried to concentrate after that, but it was hard when the girls kept popping out for an opinion on the latest ensemble or to ask the words to a song. And he remained conscious of Lynn, who murmured apologetically when she slipped into the kitchen for stamps or a cold drink, who eventually heated soup and made sandwiches for everyone. When the girls at last teetered through their dances in gowns worthy of Vanna White and heels high enough to do a swan dive from, it was Lynn he noticed most. Her delight was so genuine, her laughs in the right place, her clapping endearingly enthusiastic.

She had that magical ability to see through a child's eyes. In that, she reminded him of Jenny, who had never seemed quite grown-up to him.

But unlike Jenny, who had never worked, Lynn successfully ran a small business and coped with a young child. On the way to the bathroom this morning, he'd seen her worry as she wrote checks, sighed, laid an envelope aside, then changed her mind and opened it again. She must have nothing put away. What kind of health insurance did she carry? he wondered, when he should have been thinking about the alarming, precipitate drop in the price per share of a small software company that had recently gone public and which he'd recommended to his clients.

Did he have a right to ask Lynn about her finances? If she was anxious now, what would her checking account look like in March after the winter slowdown in the tourist trade? Would she take help from him?

Instead of suggesting that he and Rose leave right after lunch, Adam let Lynn put both girls down for a nap. Maybe he'd take them all out to dinner.

Lynn came into the kitchen. "Well, they're giggling in there, so I can't guarantee they'll actually get any sleep, but it seems worth a try."

"Rose can catch up on the way home," he said indifferently.

"I'll leave you to work." She had some bright catalogs in her hand.

"Publishers' lists?" he asked, nodding at them.

"Yeah. I enjoy choosing what books we'll carry as much as I do selling them. Of course the reps try to push certain ones, but a bookseller needs to know her own market."

"What do you look for?" he asked with real curiosity.

"Um…" She was still hovering in the doorway.

"Why don't you sit down?"

"Can I get you something to drink?"

"I'll take a cup of coffee." He couldn't remember the last time he'd had instant, but it wasn't bad stuff. The caffeine kick was the same.

While she boiled water, he thumbed through spring catalogs from Little, Brown, Simon & Schuster and Scholastic. Every single book looked bright and appealing.

As they drank coffee, Lynn talked about what she found did well for her: local history and flora and fauna, of course, fiction set in the Northwest, a few paperback bestsellers, children's books. "When it rains," she said with a quick grin, "the kids suddenly need indoor entertainment." Gardening books, she continued; something about going on vacation in an ambience like Otter Beach inspired people to think they'd go home and transform their yards into cottage or Japanese gardens.

"I have some sidelines, too, including a few needlework and latch-hook rug kits. Vacation makes people dream."

"And you don't have to worry about a Barnes & Noble opening in the next block."

"Right." Her pretty, round face looked rueful. "Of course, the reason I don't have to worry is that there isn't enough volume of business here to attract one. Which also limits any possibility of expansion or growth for me, too."

"How about a second store? Say in Cannon Beach or Lincoln City?"

"I've thought about it. They each have independents now, and it doesn't make sense for two of us to compete. And with Shelly a preschooler, the travel and headaches don't seem very appealing. But maybe someday..." She shrugged. "If one of those stores should come up for sale..."

Adam drummed his fingers on his thigh. "What do you do about health insurance?"

"I have coverage." Her formerly artless tone became wary. "Were you worried about Shelly?"

"I want her well taken care of." Even he recognized how tactless that sounded, but too late.

Gentle green eyes became fiery. "Are you suggesting I *don't* take adequate care of her?"

"No." He grimaced. "I'm sorry. I don't always express myself well. I know you're doing the best you can. It's probably better than I do. I just got to worrying about whether you make enough to manage."

"Well, don't," she said stiffly. "I'll let you know before Shelly and I are out on the street."

Irked, he said, "I was trying to offer help."

Brows lifted, she said coolly, "Were you?"

"Clumsily."

"Then thank you." She gathered up her catalogs. "But we're doing just fine. I happen to believe that luxurious surroundings aren't essential to emotional well-being."

"I won't argue." Although he'd never forgive himself if he left Shelly with her and they both died some night in a fire started by antique wiring.

She stood, tiny curls escaping the severe braid to frame her face. Instead of leaving the kitchen immediately, Lynn hesitated. "I know today wasn't what you had in mind."

"Actually," he said, "I didn't have anything in particular in mind."

"You would have preferred a movie or a day at the beach."

"I thought the girls might," he corrected her, knowing he was lying.

"Real life, remember?"

"What about you?" he challenged. "Was this a good visit?"

"Yes." She sounded surprised. "I'm not totally comfortable with you sometimes, but otherwise... yes."

"Will things get better between us?"

"I'm sure they will." But she wasn't meeting his eyes. "Once I'm sure you won't try to take Shelly from me."

Adam felt an instant of disappointment that irritated him like hell when he realized its source: he'd wanted her to admit she felt an attraction to him that was a problem. Either she was being less than honest, or she didn't feel any of that edgy awareness that had him concentrating on her face so he didn't stare at her breasts under a tight T-shirt or imagine wrapping his hands around her small waist.

"We have an agreement, don't we?" he said.

"We have nothing in writing. Nothing that will keep us out of court."

"Goodwill."

"I don't trust it. I want to trust you, but I don't completely. How can I?"

He did trust her, he realized somewhat to his shock. Lynn Chanak didn't have a deceitful bone in her body.

"We could do a written parenting plan."

She sighed. "No. I just need time. And...and a routine. I'm happiest when I know what's coming."

"Like a child."

"I suppose." She tried to smile. "Living on the edge is not for me."

"And yet," he said softly, "you must feel as if you are all the time."

"Financially, maybe."

"Is your ex-husband helping?"

"He was. Until this happened." She gestured toward the bedroom, where silence had finally settled.

Adam frowned. "He quit paying child support?"

"I'm okay without it."

"The bastard."

"Took the words out of my mouth." Another of her almost-smiles hid a world of hurt. "He figured you wouldn't want his child-support checks."

"I'd shove 'em down his throat," Adam growled.

"Obviously, I made a mistake there. Except..."

"For Rose."

"Yes. I wouldn't change things if I could."

"Do you have a picture of him?"

"Sure. There's one in the hall. After all, he's Shelly's dad. Or she thinks he is."

Adam wanted, violently, for his daughter to know *he* was Daddy. Always and forever. Patience, he counseled himself.

Lynn came back in a moment with a framed photograph of a handsome young man with a confident grin, Nordic blond hair and vivid blue eyes. Although he had noticed it earlier, Adam took it from her and studied it closely.

"Not much of him in Rose," he decided, glad.

"Except his eyes. No," Lynn agreed, "there's even less of his personality in her. I always thought Shelly took after him. He mountain climbs and does that dangerous freestyle skiing and rides motocross. Unlike me, he enjoys taking his life in his hands. Shelly can be so reckless. At eighteen months old, I heard her sobbing in her bedroom. When I raced in there, I found she'd managed to climb out of her crib and scale her dresser. She was perched on top, finally scared."

"Rose never did get out of her crib. After I bought her a twin bed, I had to sit next to her until she'd gone to sleep the first few nights, because she was sure she'd fall out." He had tried to hide his impatience, not understanding her timidity. He'd tried to justify it by the loss of her mother. She hadn't gotten it from either him or Jenny.

"She sounds so much like me," Lynn said quietly. "Finding our daughters the way we have, I keep being hit by how much is innate instead of environmental. Rose is mine and Shelly yours, no matter how much we want it otherwise."

A clamp squeezed his chest. He couldn't deny a word she'd said, however desperately he would have liked to. *Rose is mine and Shelly yours.* He adored his Rosebud. He wouldn't let her be someone else's.

"We'd better go as soon as Rose wakes up," he said with brusqueness calculated to hide his disquiet. Staying was no longer an option. He needed distance to think about this. To figure out whether he really did trust this woman.

"Sure," Lynn said, with a faint ironic smile. "I assumed you would."

"But you'll bring her over in two weeks? And stay?"

"Of course I will."

"We have each other over a barrel, don't we?"

Their eyes met, stark honesty between them for once. "You could say that." Was it bitterness or fright that made her voice momentarily tremulous. "You have Rose, and I have Shelly."

"A balance of power."

"I don't feel balanced." She pressed her lips together. "You and I both know, I could never come up with the money to fight you."

"But I'd never hurt Shelly by destroying you."

"I have to believe that. Don't I?" She backed away. "Now, I'll leave you to…to do whatever…" Whirling, she was gone, and Adam was left to wonder whether those were tears clogging her throat.

CHAPTER EIGHT

ALTHOUGH NOT MORE THAN a few months old, this library book was already well read, the pages opening easily to the beginning.

"Not all princesses are beautiful," Lynn read. "In fact, some are plain. A few are even ugly."

A child curled on each side of her. Rose sucked her thumb; Shelly held tight to her flannel blankie. Both were rapt on the simple watercolor drawing of a truly ugly princess whose tiara crowned a head of lank brown hair.

She read on, their small bodies warm, their giggles sweet to her ears. Both girls smelled of soap and minty toothpaste. They wore nighties and fluffy socks to keep their toes warm. When she finished and asked if they wanted another story, two vigorous nods were her answer.

Since they'd visited the library just that afternoon and chosen twenty books, she imagined story time would go on for a cozy half hour or more. It was her idea of bliss.

The only mildly discomfiting note was Adam's presence, and she didn't find it nearly as disturbing as she would have a month before. Familiarity bred...well, not indifference, unfortunately, but something almost as good: near trust. Even liking.

This was the fourth visit since they'd agreed on these overnight stays. Counting, Lynn realized in amazement that over three months had passed since that first time when Adam had walked into her bookstore with Rose holding his hand.

Tonight he was reading in what she'd learned was his favorite chair, brown distressed leather with wide arms and a big ottoman for his feet. The newspaper rustled as he turned pages. Once, when the girls got a good belly laugh from the story, Lynn glanced up and saw him smiling as he watched them over the paper. A month ago, his smile would have died. Now their gazes met in mutual understanding and even a degree of warmth before she turned the page and continued the story.

The third book told of a boy's relationship with a beloved uncle who was a navy captain. It was about the celebration of homecoming and the sadness of goodbyes. When Lynn closed the book, Rose took her thumb from her mouth.

"I don't want you to go tomorrow."

Lynn wrapped an arm around her and squeezed. "Oh, sweetie, I'm going to miss you, too."

"How come you have to go?"

The newspaper had quit rustling. Aware of Adam listening, Lynn said, "We live in Otter Beach. If I'm not there, who will open the bookstore?"

"Can't we stay longer, Mommy?" Shelly asked from her other side.

Lynn let the book slide to the floor and put her other arm around her daughter. "You know we can't, sweetie."

"But why?" Shelly pleaded.

"These are just visits. Rose and Adam will be coming to see us soon. Maybe we can all make a sand castle again. Remember the first time?"

"Can we go tomorrow, Daddy?" Rose begged.

Adam lowered the *Oregonian*. "No, Rosebud, we can't. You know I have to work. Grown-ups have responsibilities."

She cried passionately, "I hate 'sponsibil…bil…'"

"Let's enjoy the visit while we can," he suggested. "We have fun when Lynn and Shelly come to stay. Don't spoil it by being sad. The boy in the story Lynn just read to you wasn't always sad when he was with his uncle, even though he knew he'd have to say goodbye, was he?"

She pouted, teardrops trembling on her lashes. "No," she finally whispered, tremulously.

The telephone rang and Adam groaned.

Picking it up, he said, "Yeah? Oh, Mom. Hi, how are you?" After a moment, he nodded. "I'll put Rose on for a second."

He crossed the room and handed Rose the cordless phone. "Say hi to Grandma McCloskey."

Not his mother, then, but Jennifer's.

Rose whispered a shy hello. After a moment she said, "I have a friend here. We're listening to stories."

Adam's hand shot out. "Okay, say bye now."

"Daddy says I gotta go. Bye," she managed to say, before he whipped the phone out of her hand.

Covering the mouthpiece, he said, "I'll go talk out in the kitchen."

"My grandma calls, too," Shelly told her friend. "She's comin' to see us."

"At Christmas," Lynn agreed. "In fact, she'll be here in only seven days."

"My grandma comes at Christmas, too. She says she's gonna bring lots of presents." Rose sounded satisfied if not excited.

"My grandma, too!"

From the kitchen, Adam's voice rose in an angry rumble. "What are you saying? Are you threatening me?"

To cover it, Lynn said brightly, "I'll tell you what. Why don't we take the books up and read some more stories in Rose's bed?"

"Okeydoke," Shelly said, hopping up with alacrity.

"But maybe Daddy wanted to listen," Rose said more doubtfully.

Lynn wrinkled her nose. "It sounds like your daddy is talking to someone else now. He's kind of mad, huh? Does business make him that way? He can come upstairs when he's done."

He did appear eventually, after ten or twelve more books. Both girls were getting sleepy, and when Lynn saw him in the doorway she set down the book. "Bedtime."

"Read another one!" Shelly protested, but the words slurred.

"Dream a story," Lynn murmured. "About an ugly princess and…"

"No, a beautiful one," Shelly interrupted. "'Cuz I'm beautiful, aren't I?"

Rose took her thumb from her mouth. "Me, too."

"You're both beautiful." She kissed them and stood up, passing Adam mid-room.

She went downstairs without pausing, leaving Adam to tuck their daughters in. *Trade about,* she thought, even as she missed the quiet ritual of turning on the night-light, smoothing the sheet over the blankets, breathing in the sleepy essence of two small girls as she touched her lips to smooth foreheads. She'd had all evening. From the rage she'd heard in his voice and the tension in the set of his shoulders, he needed any comfort they could give him.

They'd had dinner earlier with Rose and Shelly, but she poured two cups of coffee and helped herself to a second, sinful slice of lemon meringue pie from the bakery. When Adam came into the kitchen, she waved the knife at the pie. "Would you like a piece, too?"

"What? Oh. No."

She put the pie in the refrigerator. He was leaning against the island, frowning into space.

"Is something wrong?" Lynn asked.

His glower turned her way. "Wrong?"

"You were…um, yelling."

His eyes seemed to clear as if he were noticing her for the first time. "Oh, my God. Could you hear everything?"

"Just something about a threat. I don't think the girls did."

His head bowed suddenly and he pinched the bridge of his nose. "That was my mother-in-law. As you probably gathered. They figured out that Shelly must be visiting, and they wanted to come over. If not tonight, tomorrow."

"You said no."

Adam swore. "They'd swarm over her like yellow

jackets on jam. I can't make them understand why we should move slowly. They only know one thing—they want their granddaughter. Jenny is gone, and Shelly is all they have left, Angela keeps saying. She's like a goddamn broken record.'' He breathed out heavily.

Pie and coffee forgotten, apprehension rising, Lynn asked, ''What did you mean about her threatening?''

His gaze met hers, and she read in it both apology and anger. ''She says they're considering filing for a court order giving them visitation rights if not custody.''

''Custody?'' Lynn sagged back a step.

''They wouldn't get it.'' His face looked haggard, but his voice was strong. ''We're the parents. I'm behind you. Their lawyer will tell them to forget it.''

''But they might get visitation.''

''I don't know.'' He hammered his fist on the tile countertop. ''Damn them!''

''No. Don't say that.'' Perhaps the time was coming, Lynn thought, when they would have to tell Rose and Shelly the truth. Would it really be so hurtful now? If they were assured that nothing would change? ''I understand how they must feel. It's not so different than what we've both gone through.''

''They're a complication we don't need.''

''No.'' Lynn managed a smile of sorts. ''I poured you some coffee.''

She took her own to the table in the nook, and after a moment Adam followed her. This was only the third night she'd spent in this house, and yet these few minutes after the girls had gone to bed already felt familiar. They couldn't talk in front of Rose and Shelly. This was their time.

They sat in silence for a moment, Lynn making a production of stirring sugar into her coffee. Then unexpectedly, Adam said, "I wish you weren't going tomorrow, too."

She quashed a momentary thrill. He didn't mean her, he meant Shelly. "These visits have been nice, haven't they?"

"You're good with them."

She sneaked a look. The lines still between his brows, he was staring down into his coffee as if waiting for pictures of the future to form.

"Thank you."

"You ever considered opening a bookstore in Portland?"

"And competing with Powell's?" The famous bookstore filled a whole city block. "I don't think so."

He frowned at her. "If you lived closer, we could see our daughters more often."

"You could move to Otter Beach."

"You know that's impossible," Adam said impatiently.

What was this all about? "I have an established business," she said reasonably. "Moving wouldn't be any easier for me."

"What if you could find a bookstore for sale over here? Or a good location to start one up?"

She set down her fork. "You're serious."

"Damn straight." He took a swallow of coffee with the air of a man tossing back a shot of whiskey.

"Aren't you getting tired of these teary goodbyes, too?"

"Of course I am, but…"

"But what?" He leaned forward, his expression persuasive. "Think about it. Will you do that?"

"Do you have any idea how tough it was to start up a small business?"

Adam opened his mouth, but she overrode him.

"Without my parents' help, Shelly and I would have starved," Lynn said fiercely. "Ninety percent of small businesses don't make it. I did. And you want me to throw that away. Start all over. It's just not that easy!"

He wasn't ready to give up yet, she could see. He still leaned forward, intent on his perfect plan. "What if you found a going concern that's for sale? Portland has plenty of suburbs that support bookstores."

"Sure it does. Some of those stores are a lot bigger than mine. I couldn't afford them, even assuming I could conveniently find a buyer for my store at the snap of my fingers. Others…well, independents are being driven out of business by the hundreds. Thousands. On-line booksellers like Amazon.com are taking some business. That's bad enough, but as you pointed out yourself, in a metropolitan area like this I'd have to worry about a Barnes & Noble going in on the next block. Heck, B. Dalton and Waldenbooks are already at the mall. And you've got malls around here." She pushed away her half-eaten pie, her appetite gone. "Take a look. Either the independents are big enough to compete, and are therefore out of my league, or they're on the verge of bankruptcy. Trust me.''

Adam sat back, his dark eyes not wavering from her face. After a moment, he said, ''You could get a job.''

''Sure I could. Working for someone else. Hey, maybe if I was lucky B. Dalton would hire me to be a manager! Golly. That would be a thrill after owning my own store.''

His mouth twisted. ''All right. You've convinced me. Bad idea.''

''I *am* tired of saying goodbye. It'll get worse once Rose knows I'm really Mommy and Shelly thinks of you as Daddy. But what can we do?'' Now she was pleading with him. ''We do have responsibilities.''

''Sure we do,'' Adam said flatly. ''One of mine is going to be pacifying Jennifer's parents, convincing them to be patient.''

She'd almost forgotten. ''If you talked to them first, wouldn't they be satisfied just meeting Shelly? For now?''

He closed his eyes wearily. ''If only she didn't look so damned much like Jenny.''

''I'm sorry.'' She bit her lip. ''I forget.''

A razor edge of pain showed in his brown eyes. ''I don't.''

Had his wife known how much she was loved? Once upon a time, Lynn had fooled herself into believing she and Brian were in love, but even then she had known they weren't soul mates, meant for each other through the centuries. But he was handsome, and he wanted her, and he made her laugh. Love was supposed to grow, wasn't it? The grandest kind, she had always believed, was in the quiet clasp of gnarled hands that had known each other's touch for sixty years or more. Why couldn't she and Brian have that, if they worked at it?

Now she knew better. Perhaps the grandest love *was* the kind ripened by half a century or more together, but people couldn't endure each other that long, didn't care enough to hold on through hard times, if what they started with wasn't more heartfelt than "he wanted me" and "he was handsome."

Adam, she guessed, had been lucky enough to know real love.

"You still miss her." Lynn touched the back of his hand.

"When I let myself."

His hand turned over, slowly, giving her time to withdraw. She didn't. He gripped her hand gently, his so much larger, browner. Lynn lifted her gaze to see that he, too, was studying their hands.

"Tell me about your husband," Adam said unexpectedly. "Why did he think you'd been unfaithful?"

A sting of hurt cured her of any drift toward a romantic mood. She tried to yank her hand back, but he held on.

"I know you weren't," he said. "Even I can see that you're not the kind of woman who'd lie to her husband. So why couldn't he?"

You're not the kind of woman who would lie. A barrier of wariness inside her sagged and finally collapsed. Was it possible that her newfound trust was a two-way street? That they really could be friends?

"He never completely trusted me." Her fingers

curled into a fist and Adam let her go. She tucked her hand on her lap, under the table. It seemed to tingle, as if he were still touching her. ''Brian would accuse me of not loving him.'' She made a face. ''I'd feel so guilty. I couldn't figure out what I was doing wrong. My mother and I love each other, but we're not...not physically demonstrative. You know?''

Adam nodded.

''Maybe that was it, I'd think, and I'd force myself to hug and kiss even when it embarrassed me in public. But no matter how hard I tried, it was never enough. He'd come into the bookstore where I worked, and be mad because I was laughing with some customer. He'd decide we hadn't really been talking about books, and accuse me of sneaking around behind his back. It was a nightmare.''

''Was he abusive?'' Adam asked quietly, but with a flat, dangerous note in his voice.

''No. Oh, no.'' She sneaked a look at his face, set in hard lines. Her nails bit into her palms. ''Brian's not that bad a guy. I just...lacked whatever it took to make him feel secure.''

''*You* lacked?'' Adam growled in the back of his throat. ''Seems to me, he's the one with the problem.''

''I tried to tell myself that. Our marriage got harder and harder, the more I had to think constantly about what I was really feeling and how he'd interpret the way I was acting. Only, then one day I realized—'' here was the hard part ''—he was right. I didn't really love him. Not heart and soul. The way he claimed to love me.'' Lynn shrugged with difficulty, the next words hurting her throat. ''I shouldn't have married him. I remember getting cold feet the night before the wedding, but how could I tell him I'd made a mistake then? And my friends all laughed and said everyone chickens out at the last minute, so I decided it was normal. But I think I'd been pretending from the very beginning. He'd say, 'I can't live without you,' and I'd tell him the same, but because he expected me to, not because I had any understanding of what that meant. Until I had Shelly, I couldn't imagine how it would feel to fear losing the one person in the world who was essential to me.'' Lynn met Adam's gaze again in appeal. ''I should have felt that way about him, too, shouldn't I?''

''How old were you when you got married?''

Taken by surprise, she had to think. ''Um… twenty-two. It was the summer after I graduated from college.''

''That's pretty young,'' Adam said conversationally. ''Maybe too young to feel something so profound.''

Unwilling to grasp such an easy excuse, Lynn challenged, ''How old were you and Jennifer?''

''I was twenty-five, she was twenty-two like you.''

''Did you know, deep inside, that she was the one person for you?''

Adam moved in the obvious discomfiture of a man put on the spot. He rubbed his hands on his thighs, and the chair scraped on the vinyl floor. ''I'm not sure men put things in such poetic terms,'' he finally said. ''I wanted her to be my wife. To me, that was a commitment. Once you're in it, you make it work.''

Did that mean he disapproved of her because she was divorced? ''I thought that, too. Brian was the one who moved out. I wasn't giving him what he needed. I think," she said a little wryly, "he'd found someone who could. Although he hasn't remarried."

"The bastard."

"But it was my fault."

Adam uttered an obscenity that shocked her eyes wide-open. "Get real," he said bluntly. "If the jerk had really loved you, he'd have worked to earn your love, not tried to extract it by whining. He'd have been there with you through thick and thin, not hunting for what he 'needed' elsewhere. And he sure as hell wouldn't have abandoned you financially now, whatever came before. That's not love, even past tense."

Lynn blinked, then smiled tentatively. "Thank you. I think."

"You're welcome." The frown that had begun to seem perpetual had returned to his brow. He stood. "I'm going to call it a night."

Her gaze found the copper wall clock. Barely nine? What he really meant was, he'd had enough of their tête à tête.

"Good idea." She sounded as repulsively chirpy as a morning talk show host. "I'm in the middle of a book I'm enjoying. Here, just let me rinse this plate off..."

"I'll finish cleaning up." His tone allowed no argument. In the confines of the kitchen, his sheer size unnerved her. Except for the three years with Brian, she had never lived with a man, much less one as large and imposing as Adam Landry.

Murmuring disjointed thank-yous and good-nights, Lynn fled. Somehow, she feared, she'd blown this conversation, either disgusting him or boring him, she didn't know which. What had possessed her to go on and on about her marriage? Why not just say, *Brian was the jealous type and I could never satisfy him?* Why admit that her ex-husband's suspicions had been right? Why bare her soul and confess her sense of inadequacy? And this to a daunting man who held a power near to life and death over her?

She peeked in at the girls and saw that Rose had scooted over to cuddle with Shelly. Both heads shared a single pillow. Tears stung her eyes at the sight of her two daughters, as close as the sisters they weren't. Lynn went on to the bathroom and brushed her teeth with unnecessary force. In the guest room, she stripped quickly and pulled her nightgown over her head. Even between flannel sheets with a comforter pulled high, she felt cold.

And lonely, although she and Shelly wouldn't drive away until tomorrow afternoon.

"MERRY CHRISTMAS, HONEY." Lynn's mother heaped the last wrapped gift under the small Douglas fir that just fit in the corner by the window. Downstairs in the bookstore was another, more elegantly decorated tree, a Noble fir wrapped in gold and mauve. This one had tiny lights, a string of popcorn and handmade ornaments interspersed with a few red and green glass balls. Because Shelly had helped trim the tree, the ornaments were clustered where a three-year-old could most easily reach, but Lynn didn't care.

"I'm so glad you're here." She sat at one end of the couch and curled her feet under her, contentedly watching her mother. She began a wistful "I wish…" before thinking better of it.

But mothers had a way of finishing sentences. "Rose were here, too?"

Yes. Oh, yes, her heart cried. She said only, "I'd like you to meet her."

Irene Miller had her daughter's hair without the red highlights, in her case cut short into a curly cap shot with a few gray hairs she ignored. A little plump, she was a placid, quiet woman who had seemed satisfied with her life as a single mother and secretary when Lynn was growing up. Lynn didn't remember her ever even dating, so it had been a shock when she called, during Lynn's sophomore year at the University of Oregon, to announce that she was engaged to be married. Hal Miller had been a guest lecturer at the university where she was a departmental secretary.

"He absolutely insisted I have dinner with him," she had said with a breathless laugh, as though still surprised at either his determination or her own willingness to be swept away, Lynn never knew which. "We've seen each other often since then."

Lynn had grown very fond of her stepfather, who had insisted this afternoon that Shelly was going to take him to the beach. He had winked conspiratorially over her head; today was Christmas Eve, and Shelly was beside herself with excitement. Wasn't Grandma going to put presents under the tree? she'd asked twenty or thirty times. Mama had *promised* she could open one this evening. *When* could she open it? Now?

But she was young enough to be diverted, and the

two had gone off very happily into a misty, chilly day, both so bundled up they looked as if they were heading for the Arctic.

Hearing other mothers whining about how their husbands never took over the child care and gave them a break, Lynn usually wondered why they wanted one. She enjoyed Shelly's company. Shelly's naps gave her a little time to herself. When she absolutely had to run errands without her daughter, baby-sitting was available. But she had to admit, in the week since her mother and stepfather had arrived, she was discovering how nice it was to have someone else cheerfully offer to go to the grocery store, whip up dinner or take Shelly away for an hour here or there. She could get spoiled.

Her mother rose easily, smoothing her slacks as she admired the Christmas tree. Then she came and sat on the arm of the couch beside Lynn. Although Lynn had told Adam the truth—Irene Miller's warmth was in her smile and words more than in her rarely bestowed hugs—this time her mother put out a gentle hand and smoothed her daughter's hair from her face.

"You said he might bring her for a visit next week."

"Yes." Lynn smiled with difficulty. "Of course."

Her mother studied her worriedly. "Will you get used to seeing her only sometimes? Or are you always going to regret that you didn't share more of her life?"

"I don't know." Lynn had wondered the same thing, but it wasn't as if she had a choice. "What can we do?"

"You're lucky that he wants only the best for both girls, too."

"I know I am," Lynn said on a sigh. "I was so sure at first that he'd try to take Shelly from me. But he really does adore Rose. He calls her his Rosebud, did I tell you that?" Of course she had. She'd talked of little *but* her newly discovered daughter this past week. Her mother must be getting sick of hearing her go on and on! But she couldn't seem to help herself. "I think he really, truly does want the same thing as I do for the girls."

"Whatever that is," Mrs. Miller said softly.

Trust her mother to figure out how muddled Lynn's dreams still were. But what could she and Adam do other than experiment until one day the routine was right?

"Do you think Shelly is ready to find out Adam is her father?" Lynn asked, as much for reassurance as in the belief her mother really had the answers.

Mrs. Miller made a face. "Is anyone ever ready to find out something like that?"

"I wouldn't have been," Lynn admitted. "In fact…"

"In fact?"

She was sorry she'd begun. Or was she? Now that she had a child of her own, she wondered more than ever about her own father.

"Do you know, I used to imagine all kinds of things about who my father was."

Her mother stood and went to the tree, moving an ornament from one branch to another as if she'd suddenly noticed a lack of balance. Her back to Lynn, she said almost casually, "Oh? Who was he? A movie star?"

"That crossed my mind, along with a cowboy or a spy or Roberta's dad. Do you remember him? He was…oh, a TV repairman, I think."

Mrs. Miller didn't laugh at the very idea as Lynn had expected. In fact, she said nothing.

Twining her fingers on her lap, Lynn continued steadily, "But what I finally decided was that you'd gone to a sperm bank."

That one did get a reaction. Her mother spun around. "What?"

"Women do it." Lynn watched her carefully. "I thought maybe you were single and decided to have a baby. And that, well, you chose what qualities you wanted and didn't know anything else about the donor. Which is why you never talked about him. My father."

Her mother's laugh was semihysterical. "Oh, dear! Oh, I should have guessed that you might think of something like that." She seemed to sag, still standing there in the middle of Lynn's tiny living room. "Do you want to know the truth?"

"Yes," Lynn said quietly. "I always have, you know."

But never so much as lately, she realized. Ties of blood weren't necessary to love, she had discovered, but they did exert a pull she had never understood.

"He was a married man." Shame crept over Irene Miller's cheeks, although she met Lynn's gaze. "Not your friend Roberta's father, although he might as well have been. It was…it was something that should never have happened. I suppose I was lonely, and…if it had been just a one-night stand, a case of being swept away, I could excuse myself. But actually I...I slept with him several times.''

''Oh, Mom,'' Lynn whispered. ''Things like that happen. *He* was the one who was married!''

Her mother's chin lifted with conscious dignity. ''I can only be responsible for my own decisions, and I knew better. I despised myself, but I was lonely and he was such a kind man! I thought his marriage must be in trouble.'' Her smile was faint and tinged with remembered bitterness. ''But after a couple of weeks, when he'd said nothing about leaving his wife or our future, I realized that he had no such thing in mind. I was the one with foolish dreams. I quit my job—he was my boss. He probably started a...a fling with the next secretary. Very likely he made a habit of them.''

''And you found out you were pregnant.''

A single woman with no great job skills and distant parents who were unlikely to help, she must have been terrified.

This smile was more genuine, but her mother's eyes were misty. ''I never regretted what happened, not the way I should have, because out of it I had you. Please believe that.''

''Oh, Mom!'' Lynn catapulted off the sofa and wrapped her arms around her mother, who hugged her back although such embraces weren't commonplace for them. ''I do believe you, because I feel the same about Shelly. It scares me sometimes. I think that I should have realized I didn't love Brian enough. I shouldn't have married him. But if I hadn't...'' She shivered and pulled back a little. ''Then I wouldn't have Shelly.''

An odd thought sifted into her mind. No, *she* wouldn't have Shelly, but Adam would. The mix-up would never have happened that night at the hospital. *Rose* was the child who wouldn't have been born. Quiet, sweet-faced Rose.

The very idea was equally unendurable.

A thunder of feet on the stairs gave warning before the door burst open and Shelly called, ''Me and Grampa are home! Did Grandma...oooh,'' she breathed, when she saw the bright packages spilling out from under the tree. Puzzlement replaced the dazed joy in her eyes when she saw her mother's face. ''Why is Mommy crying?''

''Oh.'' Lynn dashed at her cheeks. ''Happiness. I'm just being silly, punkin.'' And feeling dizzily as if she had been remade in a new form. She had a father. She would never meet him, but now she knew, which seemed to matter.

Her daughter frowned. ''But Grandma's crying, too.''

Hal Miller laid hands on his small step-granddaughter's shoulders. ''I think she's crying from happiness, too.''

''But I cry when I'm hurt. Or scared. Not when I'm happy,'' Shelly objected.

''Grown-ups do sometimes,'' Irene said. She gave Lynn another quick, spontaneous hug. ''When they realize how lucky they are.''

''Right.'' Lynn blinked back more tears that threatened despite her smile. ''You know what, sweetheart? I think this might be a good time for you to open that present.''

Shelly squealed and flung herself to her knees in front of the tree. ''I want the *best* present!''

Hal, gentle, balding man that he was, ignored the undercurrents of emotion and settled onto the sofa with a smile. Lynn's mother went down on her knees and joined her granddaughter in a colloquy about which present would be the most satisfying, considering she got only one tonight.

Lynn stood back and watched, fighting a strange desire to cry. She had a successful business, a home, her parents, and Shelly. It wasn't as if her real daughter was abandoned in an orphanage or lived in a home without warmth and love. There would be a beautiful tree in Rose's living room with ten times the presents under it that Shelly had. Her grandparents—perhaps both sets of grandparents—would be there tonight, and, best of all, her daddy would do everything in his power to insure that her Christmas was joyous.

Once upon a time, Lynn had only wanted to be certain her child was happy and loved. Why, oh why, was that knowledge no longer enough?

Why did grief swathe her in gray that took the glory out of the bright sparkling lights on the tree and the wondering ''ooh'' in her daughter's voice as the wrappings gave way to her still-clumsy fingers? Why did she mourn, only because Rose was not here?

CHAPTER NINE

ROSE'S SMALL HAND CREPT into Adam's. "Do you think Shelly got good presents, too?"

"I bet she did," Adam said heartily, although he felt sick looking at the torrent of ripped paper and bows and ribbon covering the floor. Toys and new clothes and books formed islands in the midst of the chaos. No, he knew damn well Shelly didn't get as much.

But then, Rose didn't need any of it. He'd bought less this Christmas and had made a point of taking Rose shopping to choose gifts for children whose parents couldn't. Somewhat to his surprise, given her egocentric age, she had helped him, earnestly debating which Barbie would be the most fun if you could only have one, which remote control car was the coolest. She'd learned that word lately from bigger kids at the preschool, piping up in her little girl voice, "Cool."

Adam's relative restraint in the gift department was meaningless, however. Her two sets of grandparents had come bearing carloads of goodies. On the one hand, he was glad: even Jennifer's parents weren't turning their backs on Rose. Although Angela had given him a couple of wrapped gifts to set aside for Shelly, she hadn't stinted where Rose was concerned.

On the other hand, he wished they had more time for Rose instead of so much money. Rose would have loved to go to their house one day a week instead of to preschool. But no, they were too busy. Visits instead were special occasions that usually cost a hell of a lot and took the place of something deeper.

He'd begun to realize that the McCloskeys must have raised their only child in much the same way. If Jenny had had a flaw, it was her liking for luxuries and for her own way. She pouted with such charm, somehow he'd never minded, but just lately he had begun to wonder whether that might not have changed. He felt disloyal that the thought had even edged into his mind but couldn't dislodge it.

Would Jenny have had the patience to be a good mother? Or had she looked forward to having a baby like a child wanting a doll? Of course she was going to do it all herself; she'd read a million books and planned every glorious moment. What she hadn't foreseen was that having a sobbing baby waking you every couple of hours all night long, night after exhausting night, was not glorious. Those parenting books hadn't showcased a photo of a three-year-old's stinky diaper. The whining of a tired child was mentioned, certainly, but the boy in the picture was so cute the reader couldn't imagine how explosively tired and angry and tense a parent could get.

Sometimes—God help him—his imagination balked at the idea of his Jenny coping. If she'd lived, by now they might have a nanny who would present a sweet-mannered, clean child for a good-night kiss.

He tried to convince himself he was doing Jenny an injustice.

Once again, he shoved the disloyal thoughts under a pile of mental garbage that he hoped would keep them from surfacing again.

"We'll see Shelly next week," he reminded Rose. "You can show each other your new stuff. And exchange presents."

Rosebud's fingers tightened and her eyes pleaded. "I wish we could see her today."

So did he.

He wanted to spend Christmas with both daughters. And with Lynn, who was inescapably part of their peculiar mixed family. The day stretched bleakly before Adam and Rose. Both sets of parents had come last night. He'd cooked a huge ham and all the trimmings then. The two mismatched couples had made polite conversation and avoided inflammatory subjects like politics. His parents had left as soon as possible with their usual excuses. He imagined that today his father had gone to the hospital and his mother was working at her wheel and keeping an eye on the red-hot kiln.

Angela and Rob had wanted him to bring Rose to their house today, but he'd demurred. The past week, they'd dropped talk of lawyers and court—the Christmas spirit must have gotten to them—but the threat wasn't removed, only in abeyance. It tainted his affection for them. Just lately he'd noticed, too, that Rose was nice to them, but not comfortable. She didn't run into their arms for a hug, or go to Grandma when she bumped herself on the coffee table, or confide in her shy voice to Grandpa.

Not the way she did with Lynn.

"Don't you want to play with your new toys?" he asked Rose now, as they stood looking at the aftermath of last night's and this morning's whirlwind of gift opening.

"Will you play with me?" she pleaded.

Not dolls. Please, not dolls. "Did you get any games?" he asked hopefully.

"Uh-huh." Her mood lifted. "Chutes 'n Ladders. I've played that one at school. And Grandma 'Closkey gave me a clown game. Only, I don't know where it is."

Oh, God. He supposed he should clean up. Where was *his* Christmas spirit?

In Otter Beach. The answer came swiftly, certainly.

"Lily," he said, "let me make a quick phone call."

"Okay." She didn't correct her name, a barometer of how spirited *she* was feeling. "Then can you help me find my new games?"

He crushed her into a hug. "You betcha, Violet."

A giggle rewarded him. "Daddy! I'm *Rose.*"

In the kitchen, Adam dialed and drummed his fingers while the phone rang once, twice, four times. When someone picked it up, "Jingle Bells" was playing in the background. "Hello?" said an unfamiliar woman.

Rose's grandmother. "Uh...merry Christmas to you. May I speak to Lynn?"

"Of course." The voice was warm and friendly. "And the same to you."

Lynn came on a moment later, sounding breathless. "Adam!" she exclaimed, when he'd identified himself. "Did Santa visit?"

Thinking about his living room, he said ruefully, "Big time. Did he touch down there, too?"

"Oh, yeah. Did you want to talk to Shelly?"

"Actually..." Unconsciously he squared his shoulders. "I was wondering. Do you have anything special planned for today?"

Stupid question. It was *Christmas,* for Pete's sake. But he didn't retract it.

"No," Lynn said quietly. "Except, my parents are here."

"So you said. Um, what I was thinking is..." Damned good thing he didn't stumble and fumble like this all the time. He finished more strongly, "That maybe Rose and I could drive over today. She wants to play with Shelly, and your parents could meet her."

"Today." Lynn sounded dazed.

"If it's not convenient..."

"No," she said quickly. "No, I'd love to have you. I just thought...aren't you getting together with your parents? Or Jennifer's?"

"We did that last night."

"Oh." He could hear a dawning smile in her voice. "Please. Come. We'd love to have you. Can you stay the night?"

"Your parents..."

"Have a room at an inn." She laughed. "That sounds fitting, doesn't it?"

"Rose and I'll pack up and be on our way as soon as we can."

"I'm so glad you called."

He was, too. Suddenly Christmas Day had become joyous.

LYNN CHANAK'S HOME at Christmas was everything he'd imagined it would be. Everything, despite the poverty of her possessions, that his wasn't.

Her mother and stepfather were warm, uncritical and present not just in a corporeal way, like his own parents. The Millers seemed delighted to meet him and they swept Rose into an affectionate circle of games and stories that soon had her chattering as naturally as she did with him.

Carols played in the background, the delicious smell of turkey and stuffing in the oven drifted from the kitchen, the decorations were more affecting for being modest and homemade. If Shelly hadn't gotten as many gifts as Rose, she hadn't suffered. She and Rose would have plenty to do today.

A cold rain fell outside, but the early darkness pressing at the windows suited the season and made him all the gladder for the golden glow of life and liking in here. With four adults and two children, there were hardly enough places to sit; except for the girls and Grandma, who insisted on joining them at the kitchen table, they ate with plates on their laps and drinks carefully set on the floor at their feet. He and Hal Miller, Lynn's stepfather, talked about the economy and the stock market. Miller had enough investments to be interested and to have some intelligent questions and observations about the recent, unexpected drop in the prime rate. The feds had everyone puzzled.

"I've bought shares in several of the more solid Internet companies, even though they're not making much of a profit yet," he commented. "It's got to be the future."

Lynn made a face. "Don't tell me you've invested in my competition?"

"'fraid so." He grinned. "Figured we'd better have a cushion in case the independent book business crashes."

She rolled her eyes, but grinned. "Oh, thank you. I'll have you know we had a fabulous Christmas season!"

"Weather was good this fall," Adam said. "Did that keep tourists coming?"

"It didn't hurt, but tourism is booming over here no matter what the weather," she answered. "Off-season rates entice people to get away for a few days. I guess an ocean storm sounds exotic and wonderful compared to a Portland or Seattle drizzle. Everyone hopes to find a treasure washed up on the beach afterward. In the meantime, they get here and it's rainy and cold and they didn't bring enough to do in their hotel rooms." She sounded smug. "They come and see me."

"Ah." Her stepfather nodded seriously. "Not hard to find something to read in your place. I browsed yesterday." He glanced at Adam. "Good section on money and investing."

"I noticed." Adam had browsed, too. Wanting— *well, hell, admit it,* he thought—to find out how smart Lynn Chanak was.

Very, he had concluded. She knew her business, which a surprising number of people who hung out a shingle didn't.

Lynn excused herself to dish up apple pie, à la mode, for those who wanted it. The pie was warm and obviously homemade. Flaky crust, the apples spicy, tart and melt-on-the-tongue soft.

Taking a sip of coffee followed by a mouthful of pie, Adam almost groaned in pleasure. Without a drop of alcohol, he felt as if he'd imbibed a snifter of fine cognac, not enough to get fuzzy, just enough to make him relaxed, benevolent.

In one corner of the living room, Rosebud and Shelly squealed happily over a game that seemed to involve contorting their bodies into absurd positions to put hand or foot on big bright colored circles on a mat. Grandma Miller spun a dial and announced, "Right hand, blue!" and the girls both collapsed in an attempt to move their hands.

The next round, they spun the dial while Grandma and Mom played. Adam savored the sight of Lynn, her nicely rounded bottom sticking up in the air as she struggled to keep left foot on yellow, right on blue, and her hands on two different colors. Her legs, he couldn't help thinking, were deliciously long, her hair a glorious tousle that tumbled to the mat and exposed a pale, delicate nape. Her cheeks were flushed with laughter, her eyes bright, her groans throaty.

Damn it, he was *happy,* Adam realized in some astonishment. He and Rose had good times, but it wasn't the same. He *liked* being here, or having Lynn—and Shelly, of course—staying at his place.

He wished they could do it more often. He was amazingly comfortable with Lynn. As far as he was concerned, she could just move in with Shelly…

Bang. He might as well have walked into a sliding glass door. Dazed, head pounding, Adam saw the answer to everything through the clarity of the glass.

A marriage of convenience. Miraculous convenience. They could share the girls, each have a legal claim on the other one. The grandparent problem would be solved. He could help Shelly and Lynn financially. He didn't have to miss them. Rose and Shelly would be sisters in truth.

He hardly saw Lynn fall amid giggles, leaving Grandma triumphant but needing a hand to straighten up and unkink her back. Adam was too busy examining his incredible idea.

Yeah, okay, he argued with himself out of habit, he wasn't in love with her. Presumably she wasn't with him. But he wasn't seeing anyone else, and he hadn't heard even a hint that she was. He liked her. They could talk about things he usually stayed close-mouthed about, and he had an idea she felt the same about him. God knows, they had something profound in common: their daughters.

He wasn't looking for a love match. Once was enough. But he missed having a woman in his bed and at the breakfast table. He'd been disconcerted by his attraction to Lynn, but what had formerly been a problem now was a bonus. Despite the peculiar beginning, they might make a comfortable, affectionate marriage out of it. It didn't have to be temporary. He could see himself growing old with her.

Assuming she saw the logic of his proposal.

Damn, he thought in astonishment. Proposal? Did he mean it?

"Is something wrong?"

Adam swung his head around sharply enough to crack a vertebra. Lynn had sat down on the couch beside him and was gazing at him with soft concern.

"Wrong?" he croaked. "No. Nothing's wrong."

It was right. He wanted to shout and seize her hand. Go to his knees.

Now? Her parents were making leaving motions. He could let her tuck the girls into bed, and then ask.

But he wasn't a man of impulse. No. Wait until the chill gray light of morning and see whether his idea seemed as brilliant. Maybe he'd be dying to escape back to his big solitary house after a look at Lynn Chanak in her bathrobe before a cup of coffee.

Of course, he'd seen her that way before, and she'd looked cute.

Wait. Don't be an idiot, he told himself. *Be sure before you jump.*

Morning was soon enough.

ADAM AWAKENED at the damned crack of dawn after another wretched, chivalrous night on Lynn's too-short couch. He felt as if he'd had more than a snifter or two of that nonexistent cognac. His head pounded, his mouth was dry, and his joints ached. He dreaded the drive home.

Christmas was gone, and with it his cheer.

He couldn't stand under the hot spray in a shower, because that might wake everyone else up. Disgruntled, he rooted in his overnight bag and got dressed in clean clothes. After gulping a couple of painkillers in the bathroom, Adam went to the kitchen, put water on to boil and dumped two teaspoons of instant coffee into a mug. Then he braced his hands on the edge of the counter and stared at the kettle, waiting for steam and gurgling.

What if she walked into the kitchen right now? Smiled shyly, offered to make breakfast? Adam asked himself. Would he wish her to Hades, or feel his mood lift?

The kettle stayed still. The force of his stare didn't heat the water.

His thoughts stumbled back into a rut worn by a night's worth of brooding.

Was he insane to think of marrying a woman he didn't love, didn't even know all that well except as the mother of his three-year-old daughter?

No.

The answer stayed the same. It made sense. So much sense, he couldn't believe he hadn't thought of the possibility before. He wondered if Lynn had.

Maybe it would have occurred to him before if he didn't find the idea of a temporary marriage abhorrent. He was old-fashioned in believing that a wedding vow should be kept. No matter how convenient it would be to take Lynn and Shelly into his household, he wouldn't have considered proposing if he didn't think they could make the marriage work for the long haul.

The teakettle whispered and gave a little hop.

He heard a footstep a second before Lynn said, "Good morning."

There she was in a new, nubby cotton bathrobe and fuzzy slippers, with her tousled hair, sleepy eyes and sweet smile reminding him sharply of his—no, *her*—daughter on early weekday mornings. Yet there was nothing childlike about her. The bathrobe sagged open above a loosely knotted tie, giving him a glimpse of flowery flannel and creamy throat and chest with a sprinkling of cinnamon freckles. He had to tear his gaze from the first swell of breasts beneath a lacy edging on her nightgown.

"Good morning." After hearing his scratchy voice, he cleared his throat. "Did I wake you?"

"No, I just didn't sleep well." Her gaze flew to his. "Oh, dear. There's no way you did, either. I wish you'd let me take the couch."

"Maybe next time."

"I'll hold you to that." Lynn advanced hesitantly into the kitchen. "Your water's boiling."

"It is?" The kettle was rattling on the burner, steam bursting out. "Oh. Right. Can I get you something?"

"I'll make a cup of tea." She stood on tiptoe and took down a copper canister that held tea bags.

Adam wanted to take a step across the tiny kitchen, wrap his hands around her waist and bury his face in her wild, soft curls.

Hands fisting, he managed to stay put as she murmured under her breath and got out a mug, adding sugar and one of those tea bags that brought the scent of oranges and spice into the kitchen. With an apology, she took the step to him, but reached past him for the kettle. Adam stood frozen as she poured boiling water into first her own cup and then his.

"Are you hungry yet?" she asked.

"Um? Oh." The grit was in his throat again.

"No." Still he didn't move, watching as she took her mug to the table. "Were the girls still asleep?"

Her smile was fond. "Rose was giving little snorts. Shelly has her head under her pillow."

She'd momentarily distracted him. "Rose sounds like a little pig when she's deep under. I've wondered if her tonsils will need taking out."

"Well, snoring is not hereditary," she said in amusement. "Brian didn't, and I'm pretty sure I don't."

So she slept quietly. Would she burrow like Rosebud did when she slept with him? Would she murmur under her breath, the way she did when she was puttering around the house? Would he wake to find her head on his shoulder?

He grabbed his mug and took a scalding gulp. The burst of caffeine failed to clear his head.

"I'm not looking forward to going home," he said abruptly. *Okay, it was a beginning.*

Lynn looked up in surprise. "You're welcome to stay another day if you'd like. I know Shelly would be pleased. In fact, stay as long as you'd like. Are you taking the week until New Year's off?"

"No, I wasn't planning to."

Actually, a generally disappointing Christmas retail season was playing hell with the stock market. Right now, he didn't give a flying you-know-what.

He took another gulp of coffee, then tried a new tack. "I was thinking."

"Yes?" Her eyes were wide and clear, a gray as luminous as the dawn sky.

"I've thought of a solution to this back-and-forth business."

Her lips parted and he imagined that her expression became wary, but she said nothing.

"Will you marry me?"

She stared at him for the longest time. Adam shifted uneasily.

"Say something." He sounded gruff. Defensive.

"I..." Lynn swallowed. "You mean as a...a sort of convenience?"

"At first." He rubbed his hands on his thighs. "For the girls. We can take it slowly." Dimly he realized that this wasn't coming out the way he'd intended it to. He sounded as though he was proposing a cold-blooded legal contract, not a flesh-and-blood marriage. "I'm not saying we'll get divorced. Down the line, I mean." Oh, yeah, that was coherent. "I thought maybe we could make it work," he stumbled on. "You and me."

He'd have sworn she hadn't blinked in two minutes. The owl-like stare had him twitching like a second-grader in trouble with Teacher.

"Is this another way of convincing me to sell the bookstore and move to Portland?" she finally asked.

"No." Yes. Of course he wanted her to. She'd no longer need the income.

No, he realized in confusion, he didn't want her to give up something she loved. Besides, he liked this house, its creaks, the sound of the ocean always throbbing in the background.

"I thought," he tried again, "that for now we could commute. I could come over here two or three days a week, and you could bring Shelly to Portland on the days when the bookstore is closed. We could

be together most of the time without changing anything.''

Who was he kidding?

But she didn't call him on it. Instead she continued
to study him with grave eyes. ''You're serious,'' she
said at last.

''Damn straight I am.'' He was getting irritated.
''It would let you be Rose's mother, me be Shelly's
father. It would solve all our problems.''

''But...marriage.''

She *hadn't* considered the possibility, he could
see. She was too shocked.

''We get along well. We want the best for Shelly
and Rose.'' They had to talk about sex. ''I won't
push you into the marriage bed, but I thought, down
the line...'' He'd said that already. Spit it out, he
told himself. ''I find you attractive. I can wait, but I
don't, uh, find the idea unappealing.'' The palms he
rubbed on his thighs were sweaty now. ''If you
do...''

''I...'' Suddenly she wasn't looking at him. ''No,
I suppose not. I just hadn't...'' Her voice died away.

''I hadn't, either.''

''Marriage.''

He wished she'd quit saying the word in that incredulous way. ''I think we can pull it off.''

Her pretty greenish-gray eyes flashed with annoyance. ''Pull it off? We're not talking about a corpo-
rate merger. Or...or a buyout.''

He went to her at last, sitting across the tiny Formica table. ''Lynn, I won't pretend to be in love with
you. I haven't thought of you that way. But I like
you, and I do love my daughters. Both of them. I

know you do, too. Can't we learn to love each other, too?''

Her soft exhalation sounded as if he'd landed a blow to her body. She seemed to sag inside that thick chenille robe. "I need to keep the bookstore."

"That's fine."

She looked fiercely at him. "It'll mean compromises for you, too."

Hardly daring to breath, he agreed, "Of course."

"Then—" her eyes closed briefly, and when she met his gaze again, hers was dazed "—yes. I'll marry you."

He was shaken by a surge of exhilaration out of proportion to the deal they'd just struck. Disquieted, he hid a response that was partly sexual. Instead, he stood, took a step and kissed her cheek.

"Good," he said inadequately. "When?"

"I...I suppose there's no reason to wait." She still sounded shell-shocked. "My parents are here."

He kept a tight rein on his gratification. "We can apply for a license today."

A tremor passed through her. "All right."

"You won't regret this," he said quietly.

This time she visibly shuddered. "I hope and pray you're right. But for Rose and Shelly..."

She'd do anything. He'd counted on it. And it scared the hell out of him to think of what they were going to do for the sake of two toddlers.

THEIR WEDDING DAY DAWNED clear and cold, with a wind that sliced through overcoats. Lynn's minister had agreed to marry them when he heard the details of their situation, although he had expressed reservations about marriage as a solution.

So there they were, gathered in the small white church two blocks from the oceanfront, a tiny cluster at the altar. Lynn's mother and stepfather had come, of course. A friend of Lynn's was maid of honor; likewise, Adam had asked Ron Chainey, his closest friend, who was also his business partner, to drive over from Portland to stand as best man. He told his own parents about the wedding but didn't expect them to come and wasn't surprised by their absence. Jennifer's parents he hadn't invited. Their shock was too evident, their fear that he would forget their Jenny.

Lynn wore a navy-blue sheath with creamy pearls, her hair in a loose roll. With him in a dark suit and white shirt, the two of them looked as ready to attend a funeral as a wedding.

The brightest note was provided by the two flower girls in matching white dresses with frothy full skirts—Grandma Miller had outfitted them. Each carried a small basket filled with dried rose petals that the girls scattered in front of the altar.

"Dearly beloved," began the minister, an older, balding man whose doubts were as plain as his kindness. He talked about duty and affection and "for better or worse." Standing beside his bride, Adam listened, but the words rolled over him. He'd never expected to hear them again as a participant.

Jenny, forgive me, he thought, but she wasn't real to him right now. Lynn was, although she felt more like a stranger than ever.

"To love and to cherish…"

Would love come? The very idea felt like a betrayal of the wedding vows he'd made long ago. But even they had said "till death do us part." Jenny was gone, Lynn here.

All he had to do was turn his head a fraction so that he could see the flower girls, both wide-eyed and radiant.

"You mean, Lynn will be my mommy?" Rose had asked, with such hope his heart had flipped over. "And she'll still be Shelly's mommy, too?"

"That's right," he'd said gravely. "And I'll be Shelly's daddy. You'll have to share me. Do you mind?"

She had shaken her head hard and squeezed him around the neck. "Shelly's my best friend," Rosebud whispered.

"Now she'll be your sister."

They held hands during the ceremony, looking enough alike in their white dresses, with their hair done the same and sprinkled with glitter, that he could see how they might have been mistaken for each other as infants. Closing his eyes, he could just summon the glimpse he'd had of his newborn daughter being handed to a nurse, body slick with blood and God knows what else, fuzz of brown hair damp against her head, eyes squeezed shut and mouth forming a circle as she drew air for a first sob.

If only they had banded her then...

"Do you, Lynn Marie Chanak, take this man, Adam Thomas Landry, to be your lawfully wedded husband..."

Jenny would still be dead. Was this so bad?

"I do," Lynn said clearly.

"Do you, Adam Thomas Landry, take this woman, Lynn Marie Chanak, to be your lawfully wedded wife, in sickness and in health…"

For better or worse.

He stole one last glance at his daughters and said, in a strong, confident voice, "I do."

CHAPTER TEN

LYNN STOLE A LOOK at the man sitting at the other end of the couch—the *new* couch, the one bought today, only hours after she'd let that same man slip a wedding ring onto her finger. He was her husband, she thought in disbelief that leaped to life every time she let herself realize what she'd done.

She was married.

She gave her head a small shake that failed to reorient her. This had been the strangest day of her entire life, which was saying quite a bit considering she'd also had the experience of discovering that her baby had been switched with another in the hospital. It was another strange day on top of a string of them. Her mother telling her about her father, then Adam asking her to marry him, totally out of the blue.

Her parents had urged them to take a short get-away by themselves. In a panic at the idea of being totally alone with her new husband, Lynn had made excuses. Adam had seemed relieved, which bothered her a little bit. Hadn't he been the one to talk about sex and how he wanted this marriage to last? Obviously, he wasn't consumed with lust for her.

Which should have left her feeling relieved and didn't. Lynn told herself it was natural to have her ego mildly bruised by his lack of enthusiasm. Déjà vu. She was back in the halls of her high school, invisible to popular boys.

Adam wouldn't have noticed her then, and didn't seem all that eager now to do more than legally claim his daughter.

The end result today was that instead of a romantic wedding getaway, wanted by neither party, Lynn and Adam had left the girls with Lynn's mom and stepdad and had driven to Lincoln City for lunch. Even that minor social step wasn't an overwhelming hit. Conversation was stilted. Mostly they discussed their future schedule, how to commute with the least fuss and make room in each other's homes. She felt as if she were discussing the logistics of a publisher's fall campaign with the rep.

Only, these logistics had to do with where Adam could keep his underwear and toothbrush and where she would sleep.

"Rose can have several drawers in Shelly's dresser," Lynn suggested, in her practical mode. "That way you won't have to pack each time for her. I have space in my closet for some of your things, too, if you'd like. Maybe we could add some wire shelves, or…" Momentarily she balked at picturing his shirts hanging next to hers, at the idea of him wandering bare chested into her room in the morning to search for clean clothes. Lamely she added, "Well, whatever you need."

She suspected he would look very nice bare chested. Although dark haired, he wasn't a hairy man as, strangely, her blond husband had been. She imagined smooth, tanned skin over supple muscles. Did

Adam work out regularly? There was so much she didn't know about him.

She tuned back in to see him pulling out his wallet. Lynn was embarrassed to realize she hadn't even noticed the waiter presenting the check. Had she been staring at him the entire while?

If so, Adam hadn't noticed. A slight frown suggested he was as pensive as she was. While counting out money, Adam looked at her. "There's going to be plenty to work out, isn't there?"

It boggled the mind. Astonishment washed over her with the cold force of an ocean wave. She'd never done anything so impetuous.

He cleared his throat. "I thought we could go shopping while we're here. If I'm going to be at your place half the week, we need a new sofa. It doesn't exactly count as a wedding present, considering I'm buying it for selfish reasons, but I want you to pick it out."

Selfish reasons. That meant he intended to continue sleeping in the living room. He'd give her time.

He didn't want her.

Of course, it was relief that had her nodding like an idiot. What else could it be? "I shouldn't let you spend the money, but...okay."

In the furniture store, she sucked in a breath at the first price tag she turned over.

Adam gripped her arm and moved her past a mini-showroom that featured chintz-covered furniture and an armoire so rustic you could get a splinter from opening a cabinet door.

"Don't worry about price. Let's get something decent. Preferably a sleeper."

Don't worry about price. Imagine being able to say something like that. Imagine meaning it! she marveled.

Somehow, he continued to grip her arm. Occasionally his hand moved to the small of her back as he steered her. At the hospital that first day, she'd resented his masterful attitude. Today, she was too numb. Too aware that she had just married this man. Someday, the big hand gripping her arm might unhook her bra, cup her breast, slide under the hem of her nightgown...

She gulped. He gave her an sidelong look but didn't comment.

They finally agreed on a brocade sofa that pulled out into a queen sleeper. Lynn didn't watch him write the check for such an unbelievable amount. When he joined her where she stood contemplating a cherry end table, Adam said, "I talked them into delivering it this afternoon."

And paid extra, she was willing to bet. She only nodded. "Do we need to get home, then?"

He glanced at his watch. "I suppose we should."

The salesman ushered them out the front door. "Mr. Landry, Mrs. Landry, I hope you'll come again."

Mrs. Landry. *I'm a married woman,* Lynn thought, stunned.

The couch arrived less than an hour after they got home. The two husky teenage boys carried her old one out with them.

Lynn still couldn't decide whether buying a sofa was symbolic of how far apart she and Adam were, how unreal their marriage, or whether it had been an act of intimacy: the first home furnishing they'd chosen together. Nesting.

Her discomfiture was increased when, presumably to be tactful, her mother and stepfather decided to drive up to Cannon Beach and go out to dinner, leaving Adam, Lynn and the girls to have their first evening as a family.

She had to keep telling herself nothing was different. Adam had spent the night before. She'd spent the night at his house. The only difference now was that they'd taken a legal step to clarify custody of the girls.

Annoyingly, her mind summoned words she didn't want to hear. *For better or worse. In sickness and in health. Do you take this man...*

She heard her own voice, soft and fervent, *I do.*

The traditional ceremony had not asked, *Do you take this man's daughter?*

She had known the promises she was making, as Adam had known the ones he made.

If only she'd had time to *think* before she committed herself to marriage. To forever.

But would I have refused him? she asked herself, and knew the answer. Of course not.

Silently calling herself a coward the whole time, Lynn dawdled over cleaning the kitchen after dinner, drawing out the girls' story time, the small evening rituals. She took forever to braid Rose's long curly hair, telling herself she had a right to indulge herself with the daughter whose first three years of life she'd missed. At last, even Rose began to wriggle and mumble, "Ouch."

Adam was the one who said firmly, "Bedtime, girls. Let's get those teeth brushed."

Lynn almost protested, but realized she was using their daughters as a barricade between herself and her new husband. Not fair, to them or her.

He supervised the toothbrushing and changing into nighties, Lynn tucked them into bed. When she reluctantly returned to the living room, Adam was watching CNN. She sat as far from him as she could get on the new sofa, sinking into its comfort with a sigh of involuntary bliss. She would never have spent so much for a piece of furniture, but she could enjoy it, couldn't she?

Adam snapped off the television. In the sudden silence, Lynn's heart took an uncomfortable leap. It was their wedding night. What did he have in mind?

"Your parents have been exceptionally understanding," he said.

Conversation. She could make conversation, she thought in giddy relief. "I suppose this seemed like a good solution to them, too."

"Does it to you?"

Lynn was startled into really looking at him. "I married you, didn't I?"

"Yeah, but I've been wondering if you're not belatedly getting cold feet." Tension in the set of his shoulders belied his calm tone. "Did I rush you into something you're regretting?"

"We did rush." She was still in shock; her feet were so cold she had to tuck them under her. But she couldn't let him take all the responsibility. "You're right, though. Look how happy the girls are. This really makes sense."

"Logic and emotions don't always take the same road."

"No." She struggled for honesty. "I may be sorry later. I hope not. I never thought I wanted to get married again. I wasn't very good at it the first time around." She shook her head when he started to say something. "I know you blame Brian, but I'm the one who wasn't ready to be married. I wasn't deeply in love. I guess I'm a little scared because I've just done the same thing again. But at least we're in the same boat. Our feelings aren't out of balance."

"No." His expression was odd. "Arranged marriages have worked in the past. I don't see why we can't make this one."

She wanted more than that, Lynn was astonished to realize. *Making it work* sounded so emotionless, so lacking in passion.

She forced herself to meet his eyes. "I'll try." Her voice cracked. "I can promise you that much."

Adam held out a hand to her. "I'm…not a casual man. You're my wife. That means something to me."

Yes, but what? her heart cried.

Hardly knowing what she did, Lynn laid her hand in his. His fingers tightened, and she felt his heat and strength. No, more than that: the determination and caring that made him the man he was.

It wouldn't be hard to love him, Lynn thought. She couldn't seem to look away from their hands, intertwined. The contrast made her intensely aware that they were not just parents. Not just two people dragged into a nightmare and making the best of it. They were a man and a woman.

Husband and wife.

Her heart seemed to be pounding so hard it deafened her. Slowly she dragged her gaze to meet Adam's, and saw a glint in his eyes that made her feel...peculiar. Excited, frightened, shaky.

It had been so long since she'd felt anything like this that she took a moment to realize her response was sexual. How weird that, just because he was now her husband, she felt things she hadn't yesterday or the day before.

Or had she? Lynn wondered with a fluttery sense of panic. She had always known what a sexy man he was. She'd simply figured he was out of her league. Now, all of a sudden, she owned the league.

For better or worse.

"Lynn..." His voice was rusty. "I'll give you time."

Because he didn't really want her? Or because he was a gentleman? She wished she were sure.

"I...thank you." Was that truly what she'd wanted to say?

He looked down at their hands but didn't release hers. "Your phone's ringing."

"It is?" She felt stupid the minute the words slipped out. How strange. She had once thought herself in love, but never with Brian had she felt as if everyone else in the world had faded away, like a photograph where the surroundings were misty, the focus on the two subjects. She swallowed. "I mean, I'd better answer it."

"Sure."

He was the one to release her hand. She wasn't

sure she'd have had the strength herself. How very strange.

Yet to someone else, Lynn thought, she would have looked perfectly normal as she stood and went to the kitchen. The answering machine had picked up; she heard her own voice, followed by Brian's. He hadn't called in months. Why now? Lynn hesitated with her hand just above the phone.

"Lynn? Are you there?" Pause. "Listen, I wanted to say…"

Belatedly it occurred to her that Adam might be able to hear him out in the living room.

She grabbed the receiver. "I'm here."

"Oh. Uh, hi."

"What do you want?" How cold she sounded!

The breath he drew was audible. "I've just been thinking…well, if you're really strapped for money, I mean, I could help out."

Her mouth actually dropped open. "You're offering to send me child support?"

"Well, I don't know about regular…" This awkwardness wasn't like him. "But I can send you some money when I've got extra. If you need it."

Of course she'd needed it! Her anger crystallized, and yet through it she realized that, in his own way, he was being generous.

"I miss Shelly. How's she doing?"

"She's fine." When had she last mentioned her daddy? Lynn couldn't remember. Before Adam, certainly.

"Mom and Dad were saying they'd like to see her, too."

Lynn closed her eyes. "I got married today."

"You got married?" he echoed incredulously.

"To Shelly's father."

Silence. Then he said at last, bitterness there but muted, "So everything's all wrapped up. You've got both kids and his money. You don't need me." He made a sound. "Hell, you never did."

A spark of anger incinerated her usual guilt. "That's a lucky thing, isn't it?" she flared. "You haven't exactly been here for your daughter lately, have you?"

"I said I missed her."

"Uh-huh. Well, she's probably forgotten you in all the months it took you to come to realize that. She's three-and-a-half years old, Brian. She needs parents who are here. Fortunately, she has them now."

She heard him breathing heavily. The old Brian would have had a comeback that would succeed in making her feel low. This one surprised her.

"Yeah. You're right," he said humbly. "Jeez, I'm sorry."

"Shelly loved you."

"She just never *felt* like she was mine," he explained in a tone of unwonted humility. "I guess that shouldn't have made any difference, but for me it did. But she's a great kid. And, um, I wouldn't mind meeting this Rose."

Lynn sighed. "We haven't told either of the girls what happened. That part scares me. I don't want them to feel insecure. Someday we'll have to. But in the meantime, it's awkward."

"Yeah. I understand. Maybe I could, like, just drop by and see both the girls."

"You have a legal right," she said stiffly.

"You know I wouldn't hold that over you. Just let me know when you think it might be a good time. Okay?"

"Yes, fine," Lynn said slowly.

She half expected there to be some catch, but apparently Brian had said what he intended to, and his goodbye was hasty. Bemused, she returned to the living room.

Adam hadn't turned the TV back on. His head was bent over a book she'd left sitting on the coffee table. It was an anthology of short stories and poetry about mothers and daughters.

"What do you think?" she asked, nodding at it as she sank onto the couch again.

"Jenny had cut this one out of a magazine, back when she was pregnant." His voice was strangled. "She was sure she was going to have a girl."

Lynn hesitated, not knowing what to say. What terrible luck, to have left something out that would remind him of his first wife!

At last she settled for, "I wish you'd show me more pictures of her."

"I have a photo album." Adam gently closed the book and set it on the coffee table. "Remind me. Sometime."

She sensed that the subject was closed with the same gentle finality as the book covers. *Please don't intrude, she heard in his tone.*

"Was that your mom?" Adam asked.

"On the phone? No. It was Brian. He's apparently been feeling guilty," she said dryly. "He says he misses Shelly. He was willing to send money if I needed it.''

''You told him we were married?'' Adam's gaze homed in on her face, its intensity unnerving.

''Uh-huh.'' She paused. ''He'd still like to see Shelly sometime. And meet Rose.''

Adam shifted restlessly. ''Life's getting complicated. Maybe we should tell the girls. They won't understand much of what happened anyway. I've read that adopted children are less likely to have problems later if they've always known, and the adoptive parents tell them as much as they can handle at any given age. I think we should do the same.''

Lynn nodded slowly. ''We almost have to. So your parents and in-laws can meet Shelly, and Brian and his parents Rose.''

''I wouldn't suggest it if that were the only reason.''

Had she offended him? Meeting his gaze, Lynn said quietly, ''I didn't think you had. I know how much you love Rose. And Shelly.''

''They're what matters,'' he said with intensity she took as a message.

Not you. Not us. Even if it is our wedding day.

The very thought felt selfish. She should be totally focused on the well-being of Shelly and Rose, grateful that Adam was doing the same. Not wishing he cared about her.

''Of course they are,'' she agreed.

Stroking the brocade fabric of the sofa, she closed her eyes momentarily. Thank heavens, Brian had called when he did! She had been on the verge of making herself look foolish.

Adam couldn't have made it clearer that he didn't want her, that he'd married her for her daughter. How else could she interpret the grief on his face when the poem Jennifer had loved brought back memories of her? The firm reminder that this wedding had taken place because of the girls?

"Do you know," Lynn said with what she hoped was a pleasantly apologetic smile, "I think I'll get ready for bed. If you don't mind my using the bathroom first?"

"No. Of course not," he said courteously. But when she stood and started past, his hand on her arm stopped her. His voice changed. Deepened. "Thank you. For today."

"For today?" she repeated stupidly.

"For agreeing to be my wife."

Was he flirting with her? Reassuring her? She had no idea.

This man she'd married confused her. But then, she thought, looking down at his big hand gripping her arm, they had given themselves plenty of time to untangle the mystery each represented to the other. They'd promised a lifetime. She didn't have to understand him today.

"I'm glad." She flushed. "I mean, that we did it. And that you're not sorry."

He smiled, his eyes a warm rich brown. "Good night, Lynn. Sleep well."

"Good night." Cheeks still glowing, new hope fizzing in her chest, Lynn went to peek in at their children and to brush her teeth.

TELLING THE GIRLS turned out to be absurdly easy. After lunch the next day, Adam took Rose for a walk

when the rain let up. Lynn settled down on that sub-
limely cozy new sofa with Shelly on her lap, head
against her shoulder.

They had fewer such moments these days. Having
two children was a mixed blessing. Holding this
child she'd loved from the first day, powerful emotion swelled in her chest, bringing a sting of tears to
Lynn's eyes.

"I love you, punkin," she murmured against her
daughter's silky head.

Shelly gave her a compulsive hug. "I love you,"
she whispered with unusual force.

Lynn bit her lip. "I have something I have to tell
you."

Shelly didn't move for a moment. Finally she un-
curled enough to look up with big, solemn eyes the
exact shade of her daddy's. "Are Rose and Adam
going home today?"

"Tomorrow." Lynn smiled, if shakily. "But Monday we'll go to their house. I guess it's our house
now, too. Just like this is theirs."

Her forehead puckered. "Is Rose my sister, now?"

"Yes. That's kind of what I have to tell you
about."

Shelly waited.

"A few months ago, Adam and I found out something. You and Rose were born the same night in the
same hospital. Almost at the same time."

Her frown deepened.

"What we found out is, the hospital mixed you
two up. The baby who came out of my tummy was

Rose, not you. You came out of Adam's wife, Jennifer.''

Alarm stirred. "But *you're* my mommy."

"I'll always be your mommy. I love you," Lynn said fiercely. "But haven't you noticed that Rose looks kind of like me? We have the same impossible hair and—'' she wrinkled her nose "—these freckles.''

After a long pause, Shelly nodded.

"And *you*," Lynn said, and gave her a squeeze, "look just like Adam's wife. Except for the parts that look like him. Your eyes are the same color.''

"You said he could be my daddy now. Right?''

"Right.''

"But you're still my mommy." Only the barest hint of a question imbued her declaration.

"Always and forever." Choked with emotion, Lynn still hesitated. "I just thought you should know," she explained carefully, "because you have more grandparents who want to meet you. Adam's mommy and daddy, and his wife's. I mean, his first wife's.'' *Oh, forget it,* she decided. "Rose's grandparents are yours now, and yours are hers.''

Shelly looked perplexed.

Metaphorically Lynn threw up her hands. Making a face, she said, "I guess it's a good thing your dad and I got married, huh? We're one family, so we can share all those grandparents, right?''

Shelly's expression became crafty. "If I have more grandparents, do I get more presents? When I turn four?''

"Probably," Lynn admitted. She tickled her daughter. "You greedy little thing, you!''

Shelly giggled and then burrowed back into her arms. Around the thumb she'd popped into her mouth, she asked, "How come Rose and Adam went outside? Without us?"

"So he could tell her the same thing I just told you. That really I'm her mommy, and he's your daddy."

The thumb came out. "But you're still mine, too."

Lynn wanted to make very, very sure Shelly believed her. "Forever and ever," she said strongly. "And Adam's still her daddy, no matter what."

Shelly nodded. "That's okay," she said matter-of-factly. "We can be sisters, just like you said. I *like* Rose."

"I know." Lynn hugged her and rocked gently. Shelly's eyelids grew heavy and at last her thumb fell from her mouth. Smiling and crying, just a little, Lynn carried her to bed.

Not three minutes later, she heard footsteps on the stairs and Adam appeared with Rose in his arms. With swift intensity, his gaze took in Lynn's face, and she guessed that he saw the traces of tears. But she smiled.

"Hi. Did you guys have a good walk?"

Rose looked at her with vivid blue eyes. "Daddy says you're my mommy."

She smiled tremulously. "That's right."

"I never had a mommy before."

"I know."

"Can I call you Mommy?"

"You bet." Her heart sang.

"'kay." Rose wriggled. "I want down, Daddy."

He lowered her to the ground. She came to Lynn

and said sweetly, "Daddy says I should take a nap. Do I hafta?"

Laughing, Lynn went to one knee in front of her. "Yep. Moms and Dads usually agree."

"Poop," she said succinctly.

"Come on." Lynn held out her arms. Rose climbed trustingly into them. "Shelly's already asleep. Can you be really, really quiet, or would you rather nap in my bed?"

"Can I look at books if I nap in your bed?"

"Why not?" Lynn said recklessly, not checking to see what Adam thought of the plan.

"Your bed, please." Rose sounded prim.

"Sleep tight, Zinnia," Adam said above her.

"Daddy!"

"Yeah, yeah. Rose."

Her eyes misty, Lynn smiled at him over their daughter's head as she stood. His answering smile was wry. He knew what she felt, and felt the same. Today, they had gained something and lost something. Being an exclusive parent was heady. You were the whole world to your daughter. Now, suddenly, Rose and Shelly didn't have just a mommy or daddy. They had both. They had permission to love equally.

Now Lynn had Rose's soft arms around her neck, had her whisper, "I'm glad you're my mommy." In turn, she had to live with the small hurts inflicted when Shelly was fascinated by her real daddy, wanted him instead of Mommy.

But this was the way it should be, Lynn thought as she tucked Rose under the quilt on her bed, as she tiptoed into Shelly's rooms to snitch a stack of picture books for Rose to look at under the covers, as she kissed Rose's forehead and quietly slipped out of the room.

A family.

Anchored by a mommy and daddy who had never kissed, never shared a bed, didn't know each other's birthdays. Weren't in love, never had been.

Didn't know if they could be.

But Lynn trusted Adam enough to know that she wasn't alone in hoping they would find love, in *wanting* to find it.

Today, she chose to be an optimist and believe they would.

CHAPTER ELEVEN

LYNN'S FIRST OFFICIAL ACT as Adam's wife might be the most difficult. She had to play gracious hostess to his first wife's parents. Knowing they must resent her taking their daughter's place, she had to understand and respect their grief.

Or perhaps, she thought with a small sigh as she checked the lasagna in the oven, Angela and Rob McCloskey would know perfectly well that they had no reason to resent her. She might be Mrs. Adam Landry in their daughter's place, but she hadn't replaced Jennifer in his heart and probably never would.

The girls were playing in Rose's bedroom when the doorbell rang. Suddenly flustered, Lynn pulled off her apron and hurried to the front door, meeting Adam in the foyer. On a wash of greetings, Adam waved them in. The night was wet and chilly, and even the dash from the car had left water beading on their hair and coats.

Jovial and bluff, Rob McCloskey was clearly a man's man, who looked as if he belonged out on the golf course with a foursome. His elegant wife gave Lynn an immediate pang, because Shelly might look like this when she was in her fifties. Lynn could see her in the shape of Angela McCloskey's face, the set of her eyes. Lynn heard her daughter in this stranger's musical voice.

The resemblance confirmed a truth that her heart didn't want to accept: Shelly wasn't really hers. She came from these people. Lynn's claim was emotional.

The introductions were cordial. Adam hung wet coats in the closet and ushered the McCloskeys into the living room. Lynn smiled because she didn't know what else to do.

"What can I get you?" Adam asked.

"White wine," his mother-in-law said with a pat on his arm. She then turned to study Lynn with a thoroughness that might have seemed rude under other circumstances.

"I do see Rose. My dear, you have the same hair!"

"You mean, the same impossible hair?" Lynn laughed ruefully. "And I would have known you for Shelly's grandmother anywhere."

A crack in her smiling demeanor let pathetic eagerness show. "It's true, then? Adam said she looks like Jennifer."

The men were talking a few feet away. Lynn bit her lip and asked in a low voice, "He did warn you, then? From the pictures he's shown me of your daughter, the resemblance is uncanny. I didn't want you to be taken by surprise."

"He did, and we've been so excited about meeting Shelly. With our Jenny gone, you can't imagine how we felt when Adam told us Rose wasn't hers. Not that we don't love Rose. We do, of course. But Jennifer was our only child."

Hoping she sounded more comfortable than she felt, Lynn said, "Yes, Adam's told me. I know this must be very difficult for you."

Through a shimmer of tears, Angela McCloskey smiled radiantly. "Oh, it was! But now she's home. Oh! Not that you didn't give her a home. But, oh, you know what I mean."

Lynn knew exactly what she meant. She chose her next words carefully. "I love Shelly dearly, although I admit that sometimes she's a mystery to me. Finding out she didn't carry my genes explained a few things. She's so fearless! And a chatterbox."

"So was our Jenny. She was so sunny from the moment she was born. People adored her, you know!"

Lynn kept smiling, hard as it was. "I know Adam did."

Or should she say *does?*

"Well, where's our little girl?" Rob boomed.

"Why don't we go on up there?" Adam suggested, adding deliberately, "Rose is excited that you're coming."

"Rose is such a delight," Angela said confidingly, as Adam herded them toward the stairs. "What a gentle, sweet girl. Perhaps more like you."

Kindly phrased and meant, perhaps, but Lynn had the uneasy feeling she and her daughter both had just been damned with faint praise.

Lynn hung back as they neared the girls' open bedroom door. *Please, please,* she thought, *don't scare Shelly. Don't hurt Rose.*

"Girls," Adam said quietly, "your grandparents are here."

Drawn despite herself, a pedestrian to a car accident, Lynn followed the others into the bedroom, where the girls were plumbing the new dress-up box Lynn had begun here.

Rose tried to scramble to her feet but teetered on her high heels. "Grandma. Grandpa."

Shelly had wrapped a purple feather boa around her neck. A glittery tiara tilted rakishly in her hair. She looked like a tiny, garish elf queen.

Staring up, she asked boldly, "Are you my grandma and grandpa?"

Angela McCloskey choked. Lynn couldn't see her face, but she knew tears must be streaming down it.

Lynn was startled when Adam reached out and took her hand in a bruising grip as he watched the drama unfold. She hadn't even realized he'd dropped back to her side. Or had she come to his?

Rob McCloskey started to speak and had to clear his throat. "Yes," he said at last, thickly. "Yes, your mommy was our daughter."

"But *my* mommy's right there," Shelly began, but stopped as her forehead puckered. "Oh. You mean, the mommy who had me in her tummy."

"That's right," her grandfather said. "She was once our little girl. Our Jenny."

"Did she play dress-up, too?"

"Oh, yes." Angela knelt beside the trunk and reached in. Her voice was almost steady, but tears tracked mascara down her cheeks. "She was as pretty as you are."

"I'm a princess," Shelly said with satisfaction.

Angela lifted out a filmy white shawl. "A very beautiful princess."

Quiet Rose burst out, "*I'm* a princess, too, Grandma." Her voice went very quiet. "Me, too."

Angela McCloskey won Lynn's liking and respect forever when she smiled through her tears and held out the shawl for Rose, not Shelly. "Of course you are! Our princess. And this is just what you need to finish your outfit."

Adam's fingers laced with Lynn's and he drew her out into the hall. Gently he shut the bedroom door, leaving the McCloskeys alone with their granddaughters. Both their granddaughters.

And then he brushed his knuckles across his wife's cheek. They came away wet with her tears.

ADAM PULLED INTO his driveway, laptop and briefcase on the seat beside him, and felt like a Norman Rockwell man of the house: eager to throw open the front door to the delicious scent of dinner in the oven, hear the squeal of delight as his children raced to fling themselves at him, and kiss his wife's soft, demurely presented cheek.

He gave a grunt of amusement. The picture was surprisingly accurate except for the last part. So far, the only time he'd kissed his wife's cheek was at their wedding when the pastor said, "You may kiss the bride," and somehow she'd turned at just the right time so that their lips didn't meet.

But, damn, he looked forward to getting home anyway, a pleasant change from the last difficult years. Instead of Rosebud being with him, slumped wearily in her car seat, thumb in her mouth, she was at home ready to dash to meet him with Shelly, her eyes bright, her face animated, her giggle floating behind like a vapor cloud.

Why hadn't he realized how much easier life was when you were married?

Or would be, he reflected, if theirs wasn't a commuter marriage. Today was good; tomorrow would be, too. Then he and Rose would be alone for two days, after which they'd pack up and make the too-familiar trek across the rolling Coast Range to a first glimpse of the broad Pacific Ocean, the constant throb of the surf, and the tiny apartment above the bookstore.

But, hell, that wasn't so bad, either. The trip got old, sure. He wished the apartment was bigger. But even on rainy days, Adam liked to run on the beach in the early morning. In the short months he'd known Lynn, the bookstore had come to feel homey with its dark wood, bright book covers, playroom for children and the quiet talk in the background. He'd sit at a table with the *New York Times* spread in front of him while the girls disappeared into the castle. He enjoyed watching Lynn greet people with her warm, gentle smile, guide them to a shelf, chat with them as if the conversation was the most fascinating of her day. When someone loved a book on her list of favorites, her face lit up with the joy of finding a kindred spirit. Days when she seemed unusually quiet, he was almost tempted to draw a lone shopper aside and whisper, "Tell that woman your favorite writer is E.B. White."

He had been surreptitiously reading the man's essays and had discovered the charm. They were whimsical, sharp-witted, good-hearted: everything that Lynn was and valued.

Tonight, in his lonely bed, Adam intended to start her favorite fantasy novel by an author named Robin McKinley. Reading the books Lynn admired was a backdoor way to get to know her, but worth the effort. She was passionate about reading and her children.

Adam was beginning to wish she was passionate about him.

They had been married only a few weeks, and his good intentions and patience were eroding with stunning speed. Take tonight: he parked in the garage and went straight into the kitchen.

"I'm home," he said unnecessarily, because Lynn was already turning from the stove with a welcoming smile.

"Girls!" she called. "Dad's home!"

Feet thundered from the living room and he found himself enveloped in giggling little girls. He tossed them in turn into the air and rejoiced in the squealed "Daddy!" from both.

Such a small word, to mean so much.

Satisfied, they galloped away just as quickly, and he went toward his wife who was stirring something on the stove.

"Spaghetti," he said, seeing the bubbling sauce.

"Yes, I hope that's okay."

He didn't like it when she sounded anxious.

"I've told you. I'm not picky."

"That doesn't mean there aren't foods you hate," she said with some spirit.

The sauce smelled good, but he liked even better

the clean citrus scent of her hair, caught in a ponytail today. Gorgeous as it was tumbling around her shoulders, Adam found her most irresistible when her hair was up, tiny tendrils escaping to draw his gaze to her slender neck. He wanted to kiss her nape in the worst way.

She stole a shy look at him and then ducked to clatter in the pan cupboard. "Let me get the spaghetti on," she said in a muffled voice, "and we can eat in ten minutes."

What if he just kissed her? Was she shy because she wanted him to, or because she saw his intent in his eyes and it scared her?

Nothing in his experience told him how to handle this courtship. He knew how to romance a woman he was dating, although God knows it had been a long time since he'd done so seriously. But Lynn was his *wife*. They were getting to know each other, developing a degree of comfort. What if he made an unwelcome advance and blew what progress they'd made?

Another difficulty was that he didn't want to be dishonest with her. He liked her, he found her to be sexy as hell. But he hadn't let go of his feelings for Jenny, and he didn't know if he ever could or wanted to.

Tenderness, liking, sparks between the covers—he was hoping for all those this time around. But he was afraid that if he started bringing home roses, Lynn would get the wrong idea.

Adam wasn't sure why that bothered him. He'd *married* her, for God's sake. He took the vows seriously. He wouldn't be unfaithful.

But when he took to thinking about love, he started feeling edgy, uncomfortable. Disloyal. He didn't want to be a man who slipped on a new wife to replace the old as if they were nothing more than a succession of favorite shirts. He'd *loved* his Jenny, although already memories were slipping away. He wouldn't so quickly dishonor her or his feelings.

But, damn, he wanted to have hot sex with his second wife.

Celibacy had been no more than an occasional irritation until he had a woman in his house. Now it was more like a bad back, an ever-present ache that stabbed sharply when he moved wrong.

Proximity explained it, he kept telling himself. Lynn was a pretty, shapely woman, but would he especially have noticed her if he'd happened into her bookstore? No. Love was when you were struck by lightning, when you knew this was *it*.

This was just sex. Plain and simple.

But something told him putting it that way to her wouldn't lure her down the hall to his bedroom. *Lure*. See? Even his choice of words to himself implied a lie.

"Why don't you help the girls wash their hands?" She was bustling around him as if he were an inconvenient post holding up the kitchen ceiling. If he'd been staring lustfully, she hadn't noticed or was pretending not to.

A lot of pretence going on, Adam thought grimly.

But he was still glad to be home, glad that dinner was bubbling on the stove instead of sitting in the refrigerator with a sticky note from his housekeeper telling him how to cook it. He was glad Rose hadn't had to spend ten hours at preschool today, and that Shelly had been here to hug him when he walked in the door.

And he was glad that Lynn would be there after the girls went to bed tonight, quiet company if both read, good conversation if they chose not to.

He was glad not to be alone.

"Sure," he said, "if I can't do anything here."

She cast him a mildly amused look as she dumped spaghetti and boiling water into a colander. "Nope. Just get Rose and Shelly."

At the dinner table, she said grace, something he'd never done but which seemed, if nothing else, to introduce a different note to mealtimes for the two three-year-olds. At breakfast or lunch, they'd giggle, make messes, even occasionally start food fights. At dinner they were on their best manners. He liked the change, as he liked most that Lynn had brought with her.

Tonight the girls told him about the playground and how it had started to snow—slushy rain, Lynn interjected with crinkled nose—and they got all wet but they played anyway—did Daddy know your bottom stuck to a wet slide?—and Mommy made them take a hot bath when they got home.

"We were sea lions," Shelly told him. Bouncing in her chair, she barked like the ones on the rocks offshore from Otter Beach. "Like that."

"Yeah. We were *both* sea lions!" Rose said.

Lynn laughed. "Of course, most of the bathwater washed up on the beach."

"The beach!" They thought that was hysterically funny.

He grinned at her. "Sounds like fun. I hope you had some beach towels."

"I used half the contents of your linen closet," she said, a smile shimmering in her eyes. "Thank goodness for your little elf."

"Ann? You don't see much of her, huh?"

"She pleasantly made it known she'd just as soon not 'trip over us.' I try to either take the girls someplace, or at least keep them out of her hair. She's going to be glad when we're gone Thursday."

He wasn't. He hated Thursdays. Lynn and Shelly packed up at the crack of dawn and drove away so that Lynn could open the bookstore at ten. He had to drop a sleepy Rose off at day care, where she cried. Ditto Friday, except that instead of the two of them sharing a solitary dinner, they grabbed fast food and headed for the coast and their home away from home.

Where Rose got to sleep cuddled up to her new sister, while he got the couch.

After dinner, while he and Lynn companionably cleaned the kitchen, she told him that Brian's mother had called.

Brow crinkled, she said, "I think she was ashamed of herself. And maybe ashamed of Brian. She regretted not being more supportive—quote unquote. It was a strange conversation. I haven't heard from her in months."

His basic cynicism asserted itself. "What did she want? Rose?"

Lynn paused with her hands in a soapy pan, her lips pursed. "You know, I really think she was genuine. She said that, when we think the time's right, she and Walt would like to meet Rose and see Shelly again. She said as far as she was concerned, Shelly would always be her granddaughter. It sounded a little pointed, which is what made me think she was disillusioned about Brian.''

''Her contrition is a little late,'' Adam growled.

''Isn't it better late than never?'' Lynn suggested gently.

He took one last swipe at the counter. ''Yeah. Probably. Whatever you want to do about them is okay by me. I can be nice.''

Her smile was quick, amused and approving. ''I know you can.''

Thanks to that smile, he was in a damned good mood when he started the dishwasher and watched Lynn pour two cups of coffee. He enjoyed their evening talks. To his surprise, she'd shown real interest from the beginning in what he did, how he made decisions on what companies were going to make money for his clients, what triggered his gut feelings. He'd noticed that she was reading a book on investments plucked from her bookstore shelf, which pleased him unreasonably.

Jenny had laughingly declared that his work was boring. ''You don't even see real products or real money. It's all on paper. Numbers.'' She had delicately shuddered. ''I don't know how you can make yourself care.''

Adam remembered arguing. ''It's real, all right. Think of the buying and selling of stocks as the blood running through the veins of the economy. That—'' he'd melodramatically stabbed a finger at the open page of closing stock prices "—is the report from the lab technicians who just ran tests on the blood."

She pouted prettily. "Oh, fine, but we don't have to *talk* about it, do we?"

The subject had been turned that time, and Adam found that he rarely commented on work. Personalities in the brokerage firm where he was now a senior partner, sure. Jenny liked office parties and gossip. The guts of his work, she didn't want to hear about.

The memory bothered him, but he excused her. She'd been young, good Lord, probably no more than twenty-two. A kid, she would seem to him now. He probably had been prosing on as if some rise or fall in prices was the be-all and end-all of the universe. As if the stock market wouldn't plunge up and down as often as a frisky colt out to pasture. Of course, it was relatively new to him then. Hell, he hadn't been that much older than Jenny, twenty-five when they set up housekeeping. They were newlyweds, and other topics of conversation hadn't been hard to find.

Jenny would have matured if she'd had the chance. He didn't want to compare her to Lynn. It wasn't fair. If nothing else, circumstances had been different. Jenny hadn't needed to take a crash course in her husband's interests and character. She knew him. *Except,* a disquieting voice murmured in his ear, *for the facets of him that didn't interest her.*

She never suggested he change jobs, Adam argued with himself.

She liked the money.

She just didn't want to be bored by a blow-by-blow account of his day at the dinner table every evening. So what?

Shouldn't she have loved the whole man? whispered that insidious voice.

Maybe, Adam thought, beginning to be irritated. But he didn't love her any less because she was possibly a little self-absorbed. She'd been spoiled as a kid. When he met and married his Jenny, she was young, beautiful and sexy, the center of a crowd at every party. Motherhood would have changed and enriched her, just as loving Rose had irrevocably changed him.

He'd be willing to bet Lynn had been considerably more frivolous before she'd had a child, too.

Hard to picture.

Adam shut the door on any further debate.

It figured, however, that as if to make a point tonight Lynn brought the book on investing when he and she carried their cups of coffee into the living room.

Which meant only that she wanted to know who the hell she'd married, Adam countered the voice before it could break the silence. Just as he did.

"Learning anything?" he asked, nodding at the book.

Lynn wrinkled her nose. "I think I'm getting more confused. All these formulas. P/E ratios." Sounding honestly puzzled, she asked, "Why not just stick to investing in companies whose products you like? Or stores that are well run and clearly busy? Avoid the stores you hate because merchandise is cheap or clerks are always slow or that you hear people grumbling about? I mean, doesn't common sense work?"

"Yeah, to some extent," Adam agreed. "For the individual investor, that's exactly the advice I'd give."

She looked pleased.

"However," he continued, "remember how many of the corporations on the stock market make products that are invisible to the average consumer. Operating software for computers, or a circuit board in airplane navigation systems, or whatever. Also, because a local store is well run and popular doesn't always mean the whole chain is. Haven't you had a place you really liked suddenly go out of business? Maybe go bankrupt?"

Lynn nodded thoughtfully.

"Could be the problem wasn't even with that chain of appliance stores or whatever. They might be owned by a giant retailer who has been sucking them dry to plug a drain in another branch of their empire. Maybe this other branch makes jeans, and they haven't kept up with the youth market. How are you going to know this?"

"I'm not?"

"Probably not," Adam agreed. "Our job is to know well ahead of time when problems are going to cause a corporation to retrench or go belly-up. So our clients don't take a bath. It's no different than you making informed decisions on what books to carry. Sometimes I imagine you just flat out love a book. Mostly, you've learned what your customers will buy. Or won't buy. I'll bet you carry stuff you personally despise because you know it sells."

"Sure I do." She gave a gusty sigh and with an

air of dogged resolve flipped open the book. "You've convinced me."

"Are you planning to start investing?" he asked, trying to sound careless.

"Oh, sure. As soon as I franchise." Her cheeks turned a little pink. "I just thought it might be a good idea if I knew what you were talking about when you have a good day, or a bad one."

"Ah." A sense of warm satisfaction filled him. When she had said she would give this marriage her best, she'd meant it.

The evening was typical. They read, she asked questions that spurred brief, sometimes spirited, discussions, and finally she reached for her bookmark and said in that ultracasual way she had for this particular pronouncement, "I'm off to bed. If only the girls would sleep in."

Usually he didn't try to hold her, but tonight, for reasons obscure to him, he hated the idea of her disappearing upstairs.

He set down his newspaper. "Before you go. I've been thinking. When do you go back to having the store open more than four days a week?"

"Usually April." She closed her book and looked inquiring. "Why?"

"What the hell are we going to do then?"

"Go back to weekends?" Lynn said tentatively. "And Mondays and Tuesdays? I'm always closed on Mondays and can hire someone to cover the store on Tuesdays. Or stay closed."

Two days here. Two there. Three apart.

"We were unhappy when we were doing it, and we weren't married then." He didn't give her a chance to respond. "What about when the girls start school? Does Rose go here and Shelly in Otter Beach?"

"I don't know!" Her fingers clenched the book in her lap. "Is this where you suggest again that I sell the store?"

God. He hadn't meant to walk this road at all tonight, or any time in the near future, even if he could foresee the potholes ahead. He'd only wanted to keep her from going off to bed.

But maybe they should face the problems before they arose.

"I want you to start thinking about the future," he said evenly. "That's all."

"Keeping the bookstore and my own home was part of the deal." Her eyes were huge, beautiful and dark with apprehension. "You agreed."

He tossed the newspaper aside. "Maybe at the time, neither of us was thinking about this marriage as a long-term proposition. Now I am. And I'm asking that you do, too."

She sounded tart. "And why, all of a sudden, are you planning fifteen years ahead?"

Evade, or tell the truth?

Half the truth. "The kids are happy. Things are going well. Why not?"

"Because we're still strangers."

Why did that hurt? "I thought we were getting past that."

Her tongue touched her lips. "I feel as if I still know hardly anything about your past."

"You've met my parents. What else is there to say?"

"Your marriage…"

Wariness lent a hardness to his voice. "Jennifer has been dead for three-and-a-half years. She has nothing to do with us."

Lynn was silent for a long moment. He resisted the urge to shift under her probing gaze. At last she nodded. "Maybe you're right." Her tone was pleasant but distant. He'd lost her, somehow.

"I'm not trying to pressure you." Another lie.

"I will think about the possibility of selling the store," she said, as she set her book aside and stood. "I have been already, to tell you the truth. You know I love what I do, but I also recognize that you can't practically move to Otter Beach, and I could find work over here."

"You could not work at all for a few years. I make plenty."

"But then I'd feel like a kept woman," she said gently. "I know I shouldn't. We're married, after all, but…" An almost infinitesimal pause gave away what she was thinking: *but I don't feel married.* "No," she concluded, "I need to maintain some independence."

Adam wished he could be sure her fear was rooted in the failure of her first marriage, in the knowledge that sometimes a woman had to be able to take care of herself and her child, rather than in a lack of commitment to *this* marriage. He wanted to know she was in it for the long haul, too.

When she gave herself to him, when she shared her bed, he would know.

Until then, every waking moment would be uncertain.

Was that what he wanted? Not so much her body as reassurance?

Hell, no, he thought, letting his gaze sweep once over her, from that mane of unruly hair to slender bare feet. He wanted both. Her body beneath his, and her trust held out on an open palm.

Neither could be coerced.

"Okay." Adam made his voice deliberately soothing. "You need to feel as if you're earning your way. I don't have a problem with that. And I'm really not trying to push you into anything. Until Shelly and Rose start kindergarten, we can probably go on this way. I'm just, uh, not looking forward to you and Shelly packing up Thursday. We feel like a family when we're together."

Their eyes met and she smiled with dawning warmth, although her mouth was tremulous. "We do, don't we?"

Then come to me, he thought. *Blush. Say, "I think it's time we take the next step."*

"Good night, Adam," she murmured, and left the room.

He had to grit his teeth to keep from stumbling to his feet and begging, *Don't go.*

Maybe he would have noticed her, if under completely different circumstances he'd wandered into her bookstore. Heard her soft laugh and been tempted by her hair before she turned to face him. Seen a blush turn her cheeks to wild roses as her lovely, cool eyes met his.

Groaning, Adam tried to remember Jennifer, the way she'd looked up through her lashes, the coy tilt of her head, her throaty laugh, her sultry mouth, but it was all just words, fleeting impressions. Lynn was real, vivid, *here*.

Jennifer was a long-lost dream.

Even Shelly no longer reminded him of her mother. He knew objectively that they looked alike, but his little girl had so much personality of her own that only her cheerful, endless chatter and her boldness recalled Jennifer. Perhaps when Shelly was a teenager she would bat her eyes and smile with deliberate, mysterious purpose. But for now…hell, for now she had Lynn's directness and the sweetness of a much loved child.

Not Jennifer's hunger for attention.

Now, where had that idea come from? he wondered, frowning, but knowing it was true. His Jenny had wanted always to be the center of attention. Her own company was never enough.

Adam swore aloud. He'd loved his wife, and she was dead. Why all the analysis now?

So he could justify letting Lynn walk into Jennifer's place? Not just in his home and bed, but in his heart?

No! he thought, on a shattering wave of remembrance too vivid. Suddenly he did see his Jenny, still and warm, but gone, her life an illusion given by machines.

Adam buried his face in his hands and yanked at his hair. *Remember her alive!* he told himself fiercely. Remember her generous sensuality, her quirky sense of humor, her lively mind and effortless ability to make whatever she touched beautiful. Her flower arrangements—he seized on the memory. He used to think they were like her, careless and artful at the same time.

He couldn't let her go. Not so easily. Not so quickly.

He could give Lynn everything but his heart.

CHAPTER TWELVE

EVERY TIME SHE HEARD a car engine, Lynn went to the kitchen window. No Adam.

For the first time, she'd left Shelly with Adam and Rose, coming home to open the bookstore all by herself. The quiet drive had been an unexpected pleasure. She was so rarely alone to let her thoughts drift aimlessly, to listen to Bizet's *Carmen* instead of *Sesame Street* songs. But that was two days and a night ago. Now she missed her family terribly.

She glanced at the clock for the twentieth time. Dark had come hours ago. Front and back porch lights were beacons in the night—the strong beam of a lighthouse calling them home, Lynn thought fancifully.

Thursday evening she'd read a murder mystery, not had dinner until nine o'clock and then eaten an entire pint of mint-chocolate-chip ice cream, feeling decadent the whole time. Tonight she used her energy and anxiety to clean. Floors and sinks shone, and she'd moved every piece of furniture so that not even one dust bunny escaped her.

At eight-thirty, half an hour after his usual time, she heard the deep, throaty murmur of Adam's Lexus and the crunch of gravel under the tires.

With a rush of pleasure, Lynn dropped a handful

of forks—she'd been rearranging the silverware drawer—and hurried to the door. Footsteps clattered on the outside stairs. Little-girl voices called, "Mommy! We're home!"

Opening the door, Lynn scooped to snatch first Shelly, then Rose up into her arms for huge hugs. They felt so solid, smelled so sweet, and she didn't know how she had been able to endure two days without them.

Below, the car door slammed again in the darkness, and Adam came into the circle of porch light and started up the rickety staircase, burdened by a duffel bag and...was that a hula hoop? She hadn't seen one in years.

Shelly didn't like the fact that Mommy's attention had wandered for even a moment. Tugging on Lynn's hand, she did a little dance. "Mommy, I went to school with Rose! We learned to write letters! Didn't we, Rose? And how to count in...well, the way somebody else talks. I don't remember who. You wanna hear me? *Uno, dos, tres,*" she enunciated with earnest care. "Rose knows how, too. Don't you, Rose?"

"Course I do," Rose declared with the air of a big kid. "*Uno, dos, tres.* See? And Teacher said I know my colors. My shirt is orange. Isn't it, Mommy?"

"Mine is purple," Shelly said importantly. "I know my colors, too, Mommy."

"I know you do, sweetie. And very well, too."

The hula hoop slung over Adam's shoulder rolled off and bounced down the stairs. He mumbled something not meant for three-year-old ears, dropped the duffel bag on the landing and chased after the neon-green plastic hoop.

The girls turned to watch, giggling in merriment. "Grandma gave us one a' those," Shelly explained. "A hoo…hoo…" Her lips pursed in a perfect circle. "Hoo…"

"Hula hoop," Lynn supplied.

Grinning ruefully, Adam started back up the stairs.

"Hoo-hoop. She said she played with one when *she* was a girl. She wriggled. Like this." Shelly swiveled her hips so hard she fell down laughing.

Rose, of course, had to demonstrate and tumble theatrically amid more giggles.

"Grandma must have looked very funny," Lynn said, trying to imagine the petite, elegant woman waggling her hips like a Hawaiian dancer. Now, that she would have liked to see.

A small cloud stilled Shelly's laughter. "I can't make the hoo-hoop work."

"Daddy says we don't got no hips," Rose agreed.

"Have any," Lynn corrected automatically.

Daddy rolled the hula hoop into the house. "Here it stays," he said firmly.

Losing interest in it and Mom, Shelly popped to her feet. "Let's go play," she commanded.

"Okay," Rose said happily.

They raced down the hall, rattling pictures on the wall, and flung open the door to their bedroom.

Lynn frowned, a new worry niggling. "I hope Rose doesn't get too used to going along with Shelly. Does it seem to you as if…"

Flowers appeared under her nose. "Happy anniversary," Adam said huskily.

Her wondering eyes took in roses and huge fragrant lilies and a scattering of tiny white bridal wreath. She breathed in the glorious scent and then looked up in astonishment at her husband's face. "Anniversary?"

"One month," he said gravely. "Today."

The paper cone crackled as she took the bouquet from him and cradled it. "Thank you." She sounded—and felt—absurdly shy.

"A kiss might be appropriate." He wasn't smiling, to suggest that he was kidding; he just stood there squarely less than a foot away and waited.

Did he mean it? Heat blossomed in her cheeks and her pulse sprinted. She'd known this was coming. She'd seen in his eyes that he was thinking about her that way. As a woman. She wanted him to. She'd just had no idea in the world how to hint that she wouldn't mind if he did kiss her.

But did he have to leave it up to her?

Maybe he was trying to give her an out, if she really detested the idea. He was being a gentleman.

As stuffily as Miss Manners, Lynn admitted, "A kiss would be one polite way to thank you."

"Then?"

Taking a breath and hugging the flowers to her breast, she rose on tiptoe to give him a quick peck.

It didn't work that way. He bent his head to meet her halfway. Their mouths touched and a shiver skidded down her spine. Somehow he came to be gripping her upper arms. The heavy scent of lilies rose from between them, thickening the air. His lips teased hers apart, then hardened. She heard a groan and the kiss deepened, but...

"Mommy!" Feet thundered down the short hall behind her.

Lynn jerked away, her heart hammering and her face so hot it must be the color of a lobster. "Yes? What is it?"

"Mommy, where's flower blankie?" Shelly asked with a hint of anxiety.

The faded, warn flannel crib blanket was rarely far from Shelly.

Her mind cloudy, Lynn couldn't look at Adam. "Did you take it to Adam's house?"

Shelly's brown eyes widened and her mouth formed an O. "I forgot it," she whispered, and then her face scrunched miserably as tears formed. "I want my flower blankie!" she wailed.

Lynn crouched to hug her. "It's not in the bag?"

"This is all clothes," Adam said. "I'm sorry. It's my fault. I should have checked."

"You know, your blanket is fine in your bedroom at Adam's house. It'll be waiting for you Sunday night."

"I want it now!" Shelly screamed. "Daddy can go get my blankie."

"Honey, it would take him all night." Lynn knew darn well that reason wouldn't forestall what was coming. But she had to try, didn't she? "You can do without it for three days."

Sobbing, the three-year-old flung herself onto the floor and drummed her heels. Lynn sighed, remembering last night's peace and quiet. Ah, well. She was glad Shelly was home, even if she was screaming and turning purple.

Rose never threw temper tantrums. She stood now

halfway down the hall, her thumb in her mouth and her face a study in worry and perplexity.

It took Lynn half an hour to calm her distraught daughter. Adam and Rose settled in as Shelly sobbed, hiccuped, and finally burrowed in her mother's arms for a few minutes of comfort and resignation.

"Do you feel better now?" Lynn asked. They were alone in the living room, cuddled in the depths of the new sofa.

Shelly nodded against her breast.

"Do you want to get ready for bed now?"

A sniff, and Shelly's head bumped Lynn's chest as she nodded again.

"Okay. Up we go."

On the way down the hall Lynn caught a glimpse of Adam and Rose sitting at the kitchen table sipping from mugs of cocoa with marshmallows floating atop. Fortunately, Shelly didn't see.

Teeth brushed, in her nightgown, Shelly finally remembered that she shouldn't be the only one who had to go to bed. "Where's Rose?" she demanded.

"She'll be along in a few minutes." Lynn ran the brush through her small daughter's thick mink-brown hair, so unlike her own. "I bet she took a longer nap than you did today, huh?"

"*She* slept on the way. I wasn't sleepy."

"I think she'll be ready for bed pretty soon. Now, let's tuck you in." She plopped Shelly down on the bed and kissed her. "I missed you, punkin."

Shelly's eyes watered again. "I missed you, too. I wanted *you* to kiss me g'night. Only you weren't there," she accused.

"No, but your daddy was." Lynn kissed the snub

nose. "And it sounds as if you mostly had fun staying with Rose and Daddy."

They chatted about preschool, and Lynn felt an easing inside of some tension she hardly knew had been there. The possibility of losing Shelly terrified her still. What if she hadn't been missed at all?

At Shelly's sleepy request Lynn left on the lamp beside the bed and slipped quietly out. In the kitchen, Adam smiled at her.

"Want some cocoa?"

Her gaze shied away from his. She hadn't yet let herself think about what had happened, but she'd have to soon. It changed everything. Unless he'd hated it, he would want to kiss her again.

She wanted him to.

"Please." Another blush fired her cheeks at the double meaning.

A glint in Adam's eyes told her he'd guessed at some of her thoughts, or at least that the kiss was in the forefront of his.

"You c'n have a marshmallow, too, if you want," Rose told her generously.

"Thank you. I'd like one."

"How come Shelly cried like that?"

"I think she was tired," Lynn explained. "Have you ever felt really sad, mostly because you were tired?"

Rose nodded, but doubtfully.

The kettle sang, and a moment later Adam's big hand set the mug of cocoa in front of her at the kitchen table.

"Thank you." Lynn sent a smile his way without quite meeting his eyes.

"I like cocoa." Rose sounded quietly satisfied. Perhaps she also liked having Mommy and Daddy all to herself. Neither girl was used to sharing. It was a wonder they got along so beautifully.

Lynn suggested a game, which they played. Then she ran a bath for Rose and stayed with her. Braiding her hair took time.

But bedtime couldn't be put off forever. Adam did the honors and tucked Rose in. Lynn washed mugs and wiped the table and arranged the flowers more carefully in the stoneware jar Adam had put them in. They were glorious, too fancy for anything but crystal, she thought, tilting her head, but she would enjoy them anyway.

Was it possible she and Adam had been married for a month already?

Every nerve strained for the sound of his footsteps in the hall. He would come looking for her, she knew. To take up where they'd left off?

Or would he give her breathing space by asking how business had been for her, by telling her what the market had done this week, how Shelly had liked staying over with Rose?

She felt jumpy. Where was he?

"Shelly's sound asleep."

Lynn gasped and whirled. He blocked the kitchen doorway, his expression inscrutable.

"You scared me!"

"I'm sorry." He didn't sound sorry, but rather... pleased. As if he was glad she'd been affected enough to be jumpy. "What were you thinking about?"

"I...the flowers are gorgeous."

"I'm glad you like them." He strolled toward her.

Her back to the kitchen counter, Lynn had nowhere to go. Did she want to flee? All she had to do was say, *You're crowding me. I need time.* Was he? Did she? It was hard to think with her heartbeats pounding in her ears and her knees wanting to buckle.

He stopped inches away. Lynn swallowed and stared fixedly at the buttons on his white shirt. The tie that he must have worn today was long gone, probably slung over the seat of the Lexus along with the suit jacket. He was dauntingly handsome in charcoal slacks and a dress shirt, his face dark and saturnine in contrast to the white. Several of the top buttons were undone, exposing a tanned throat. All she had to do was reach for the next button.

"I enjoyed kissing you." His voice was a soft rumble.

Lynn sneaked a peak upward, expecting to see the gleam in his eyes, but a frown was gathering on his brows. He wasn't sure of her, she realized suddenly. Did he share her same apprehensions? The possibility stunned her. He was a confident, handsome, wealthy man.

Stuck with her by circumstances. He probably didn't know what to make of her. She wasn't his usual kind of woman.

She was nothing like his beautiful, charming wife, Lynn thought, with a sinking feeling.

Okay, she argued with herself, maybe she wasn't anything like his Jennifer, but he'd kissed her. He wanted her. He seemed to like her. That was enough to build on, wasn't it?

"I enjoyed it, too," she admitted shyly, eyes still downcast. "I mean, the kiss."

"Good." He reached for her hand and placed it on his chest.

Slowly she splayed her fingers, flattening her palm. Wonderingly, she felt his heart beat, as hard and fast as hers. The knowledge that he was as affected by her as she was by him allowed her to look up.

Muttering something she couldn't make out, Adam bent his head and kissed her again. The first kiss had been the kind a man might give a woman on her doorstep before he said good-night. This one was between two lovers: urgent, needy, a promise and a demand. He drank in her breath, his tongue stroked hers. His fingers dove into her hair and cupped the back of her head.

I'm your husband, he said without words. *Our bed is right down the hall.*

It scared her, the demand, but the urgency awakened her own and the promise enticed her. *We're husband and wife. We have children and a life together.* Lovemaking would seal the bond, make Adam hers.

She uttered a soft moan and slipped her arms around his neck, rising on tiptoe so that she could be closer to him.

He strung heady kisses across her cheek, nibbled at her earlobe, tasted her throat. When he lifted his head, she saw the hot light in his eyes.

"Is this an invitation, Lynn?"

She'd hoped he would just sweep her into his arms and carry her down the hall, making a decision, not asking for one. Trust Adam to need the words. He wouldn't let her be a coward.

But she wasn't quite brave enough to say *Yes. Please.* She had to hope he would understand that her confession was also tacit permission. "I'm not very experienced. Brian was the only man…"

Adam laughed huskily. "Sweetheart, this isn't a job interview. Experience is not required."

Lynn had seen only two photos of his wife: a smiling one of her pregnant that hung in a silver frame beside Rose's bed, and the one Adam carried in his wallet and had shown her that first day at the hospital. It was that one she saw now, in a too-vivid flash—the sultry eyes and full, sexy mouth, sleek hair and confident tilt to her head. She would have known how to seduce her husband, how to please him.

Lynn wished desperately that she hadn't thought of Jennifer.

Maybe experience wasn't required, but she'd feel more sure of herself if she had it. "No, but…" she began.

Adam didn't let her finish. "What experience could prepare us for each other? We have to learn as we go. Together."

She had the dreadful feeling she was being conned, that he was too slick, too quick with his answers, but she kept coming back to the fact that he was her husband. Sooner or later, he would join her in her bed down the hall. Why not sooner?

Sooner, Lynn thought hazily, was good. Deep in her belly, desire cramped. Oh, yes. She was ready. As ready as she would ever be, considering what a failure she was with men, how little she understood her own heart.

But her heart had nothing to do with this. This was an old-fashioned marriage of convenience, and she didn't have to worry about love, did she?

"Yes," she murmured. "You're right. I just don't want you to be disappointed."

"Disappointed?" His mouth had a tender twist. "What if I disappoint you? Would you hold it against me so soon? If tonight isn't perfect, we'll get it right another time. You have to tell me what pleases you."

Brian had never asked, but she knew the lack of pleasure she'd had with him was as much her fault. It had never occurred to her to say aloud, *This pleases me. That doesn't.* She'd tried with body language to tell him, but in the midst of passion silence was what he heard.

Silence was always easier for her.

"You...you'll tell me, too?" she asked breathlessly.

"You'll please me," he said in a rough voice unlike his own. "I've wanted to touch your hair since that day at the hospital. I've been dying to see if you have freckles anywhere but here." He kissed her nose. "To hear you say my name as if you mean it."

Excitement flowed through her like a drug in her bloodstream. Every hammering beat of her heart sent a tingling thrill farther toward her fingertips and toes.

"Adam," she whispered.

"Yes." His eyes smouldered. "Like that."

She let her head fall back as he kissed the hollow at the base of her throat. A whimper escaped her when he touched her breasts, cupping, weighing, teasing.

"I think," he said hoarsely, "it's time for me to invade your bedroom."

She'd felt the same about his, as if when she explored his house an invisible force field had kept her from stepping through the doorway. This one room was a part of him too private for her to know.

"We'd better check that the girls are asleep." Her voice came out as a mere thread of its normal self.

"Mmm." He kissed her, slow, deep and hot.

Melting, she hardly knew when he flicked off the kitchen light and steered her down the hall, pausing briefly in front of the girls' room.

"Sound asleep," he murmured, and swung her into his arms.

With a muffled squeak, she stiffened and clutched at his shoulders. "What are you doing?"

"Shh. Don't want to wake the girls." With his shoulder, he turned off the hall light and carried her into her dark bedroom. "Symbolism is important. We skipped this part on our wedding day. Seems like the thing to do now."

He was carrying her across the threshold. A shiver passed through her. *My woman to carry home,* the gesture seemed to say. Their marriage wasn't that kind.

Think about it tomorrow, she decided. Worry then. Now she could be grateful he was choosing to romanticize their lovemaking.

Beside the bed, he lowered her with the care and finesse of a man with plenty of practice. He kissed her even as he reached for the lamp on her bedside table. A part of her was shy and wished he hadn't turned on a light, but she also liked the idea of being able to see him. How terribly unreal it would seem tomorrow, if they grappled in the dark, if she couldn't see his expressions, his body. She might wonder if she'd dreamed the whole thing.

Adam undressed her slowly, telling her how beautiful she was as he tossed aside her shirt, her bra, her jeans and socks. His own shirt joined hers on the floor, so that Lynn could flatten her hands on his chest as she'd imagined doing. His body heat almost burned her fingers. He had a vee of fine dark hair, and otherwise his skin was smooth over well-developed muscles. She liked the way he sucked in a breath when she grazed his nipple or when her hands ventured lower.

In the end, she was too shy to make the move. He did it for her, grasping her hands and placing them on his belt.

"You undress me," he said rawly.

She trembled as she undid his belt, unbuttoned the waistband of his trousers, inched the zipper down over the long, thick bulge. Brian's penis had rather repulsed her; she didn't like to see it, and couldn't account for why she did very much want to see Adam's.

It was smooth, hard and large, and she was dying for the moment when he would push it inside her. Lynn moaned and then was shocked that such a wanton sound had come from her.

Adam shucked the rest of his clothes in a few

quick movements. Deafened by the thunder of her own heartbeat, Lynn stared as she'd never done before. He was beautiful, and *hers*. Tall and powerful, sleekly muscled, his skin a golden hue. Her own freckled, pale skin looked so pallid in comparison, as if she lived under a rock.

But he was finding those freckles and kissing them. First her chest, then he turned her gently and trailed his lips along her spine. She quivered when he slipped her panties down, caressing her thighs and calves with long strokes of his hands.

"Beautiful," he murmured, and turned her to face him.

She tried to cover herself, an arm across her breasts—though he had already seen them—and the other hand hiding the curls as wild as those on her head.

Adam lifted her onto the bed and followed her down in a tangle of limbs.

"Your hair on my pillow," he said thickly. At least, that's what she thought he said. A dark flush ran across his cheekbones and his skin seemed taut over the angles of his face. Braced on his elbows above her, he finger-combed her hair until it was spread in every direction on the lacy white pillowcase. "Just like this."

"It's awful hair. Always in knots."

He seemed fascinated by every wild strand. "It's glorious."

"Poor Rose had to get it from me."

"Poor Rose will be driving the boys crazy in ten years or so."

"Shelly will be prettier." What an absurd conversation to be having with a man whose weight was bearing her down.

She'd distracted him and he looked surprised. "Will she? I'm not so sure."

But Rose looked so much like her, and Shelly so much like his first wife. Did that mean—could it mean?—that he really thought she, Lynn, was as pretty as his beloved Jenny?

Heartened by the very idea—at least he was letting her pretend—Lynn tugged his head down to hers. The kiss started slow and sensual, but couldn't stay that way. His thigh was between hers, and she could feel his erection butting against her belly. She wanted more than kisses, she wanted...

"Ooh," she breathed, when his hand flattened on her belly and then stole lower, exploring, teasing, stroking. "Oh!" she cried, and clutched at his hand. "Now. Please."

"Wait," he said in that voice so unlike his own. "I have something here." Leaning off the bed, he grabbed his pants and took a packet from his pocket. Adam ripped it open and, swearing at hands that had become clumsy, put on the condom.

She watched in fascination and something like disappointment. She'd wanted him, just him, inside her. She should feel lucky that he'd come prepared. It had never occurred to her that if they took this next step, birth control would have to be part of it, or else they might have another child before they knew it. Then they would be tied together forever.

She wasn't so certain she minded the idea. A child,

with Adam…little shivers rippled in her center, sexual pleasure simply because she imagined being pregnant with his child.

He might have claimed they had to learn together, but she felt as if she was in the hands of a master. He knew what to do to give her pleasure. He had her arching like a cat and whispering urgent pleas. "Do you like that?" he'd murmur, and, "Oh, yes," she would sigh.

But she explored as well, if timidly. When he groaned or she felt his muscles jerk, her own excitement escalated. He wanted her; she hadn't been wanted so often in her life.

He was the one who couldn't wait at the end, who with sudden stark need parted her thighs and pressed inside her. She felt his shuddering restraint, knew he was holding back so that he didn't hurt or frighten her.

Lynn's heart gave a squeeze. As he gritted his teeth and eased the last inches inside her, she had a fluttering moment of panic. She'd lied to herself.

Her heart *did* have something to do with this. Even if he didn't feel the same.

Adam spoke, his voice so guttural she couldn't make it out. *I love you,* she imagined, knowing she would despise herself later for the pretence but holding it to herself nonetheless. As Adam began to move steadily, surely, she clutched at him with frantic hands and let her last protective walls fall.

The cramping, exultant wave came then, tumbling her head over heels in the tsunami. She could not fall in love, she thought desperately, and was so terribly afraid she already had.

ADAM HELD HIS WIFE until her racing pulse quieted, her breathing slowed, until he felt her boneless relaxation against him. Only then did he ease away, tuck the covers around her, and sit on the edge of the bed.

He buried his face in his hands and thought, *It couldn't have been that good. I couldn't have felt so much.* The explanation was much simpler. He hadn't had sex in over three years. The triumph at claiming her, the raw, primitive exhilaration because she was his, those were natural emotions. Lynn was his wife, and he'd been driven lately by the need to make their relationship fact. Any man would have felt the same.

And, hell, he wouldn't like himself if a certain amount of tenderness wasn't added to the brew, if he hadn't given a damn whether she was pleased or not.

Anything else was in his imagination.

Swearing under his breath, Adam rose to his feet and then froze when Lynn made a soft sound and burrowed deeper in the pillow and quilts. When she settled down, he went quietly to the window.

Jennifer, forgive me.

No! There was nothing to forgive. He'd married for Rose's sake, for Shelly's, and he owed it to them, to himself, to Lynn, to make this marriage real and lasting. Jennifer would understand.

He wouldn't let himself think even for a moment that this lovemaking had been more honest than anything he'd ever shared with Jennifer.

Lynn's shyness, her obvious astonishment at her effect on him and even at her own physical response, had touched him. He was flattered, maybe, by the implication that she'd never found such pleasure with her worthless husband, that only he, Adam, had the power to awaken her sexuality.

Jennifer and he had been good in bed together. Brazen, she'd loved to flaunt her delicate, perfect body. *Shy* was a foreign word to his Jenny. That didn't make her response to him any less meaningful.

Staring out at the soft yellow glow of street lamps, able to hear the muffled beat of the surf though the window was shut, Adam wished like hell that he could be as casual about sex as men he overheard talking in the locker room of his health club. Half of them were getting it on the side even though they were married, he'd learned. It meant nothing—a little fun, an itch scratched.

Adam didn't want to have an affair. All he asked was that he be able to make love to his wife without feeling as if he was cheating on Jennifer, without this constant, tearing remembrance that she'd lost everything, that all he could do in return was prove that his love was enduring.

Maybe he hadn't been ready to test himself by bedding Lynn.

Flattening his hands on the cold glass, Adam grimaced. Too late, he reminded himself. There was no way in hell he could tell her in the morning that this had been a mistake, that maybe they should keep their relationship platonic. He owed her better than that kind of hurt.

And the truth was, he didn't want to go back. He wanted to see Lynn's eyes flutter open in the morning, see the dawning awareness, the pretty pink blush. He wanted to kiss her and make love to her in the soft light, taste her sweetness before breakfast.

He wanted to make a habit of sleeping with his wife, in every sense of the word.

Forgive me, Jenny.

CHAPTER THIRTEEN

"WHY IS DADDY SMILING at you like that?" Rose whispered loudly. She stared at her father with deep suspicion.

As a family, they were strolling the beach for goodies tossed up by this week's storm. High tide had left a string of slippery, stinking seaweed and a long curving line of smooth small stones and broken shells, among which treasures might be found. Walking ahead with Shelly, Adam was relaxed and handsome in jeans and a cream-colored Irish fisherman's sweater that added bulk to his shoulders. A breeze off the ocean ruffled his dark hair.

They were all supposed to have their heads bowed as they searched for bright bits of agate or perfect shells, although heaven knows, after living here for three years, Lynn didn't need even one more sand dollar or stone, however pretty. Adam couldn't be too serious about the hunt, either, because when Shelly crouched to poke at wet stones, he had directed a wicked and very sexy grin at Lynn.

Little girls weren't supposed to understand that the kind of smile he'd just given Mommy was something to make every smart woman wary. Rose's knowledge was apparently instinctive.

Adam and Lynn had been married for six weeks

now. The girls were only beginning to notice that something was different between their parents. Rose had looked thoughtful a few times, but was easily distracted.

Lynn figured she'd try again. "Maybe Shelly found something good," she suggested, knowing perfectly well, and with secret pleasure, that he wasn't nearly as interested in a polished agate as he was in stealing a kiss when Rose and Shelly became preoccupied.

Bouncing back up, Shelly skipped beside Adam. Her small hand was in his; every so often he swung her over a log or rock protruding from the gravelly beach, to her delight. "Daddy is *strong,*" she had declared happily, preferring him as a companion on this walk.

Her eagerness to walk with Daddy would have hurt, if immediately afterward Rose hadn't slipped her hand confidingly into Lynn's and said softly, "I don't like it when Daddy swings me like that."

Rose had a gift for such moments. Lynn couldn't quite decide whether Rose really was afraid when Daddy swung her, or whether her empathy was already developed to the point where she sensed her new mommy's distress. Surely at only three, she couldn't be mature enough to understand other people's feelings! Yet she seemed extraordinarily sensitive to mood, and despite the fact that she'd been given almost anything material she'd ever wanted, Rose was shyly grateful for small things that Shelly would have taken for granted.

Perhaps she wasn't as smart as Shelly and would never be the leader, but she knew instinctively how to be a friend. Lynn worried only that, growing up, she might hide feelings or depression or anger because she didn't want to upset anyone else. As the two girls became old enough to understand, what effect would the switch in the hospital have on them? Lynn had read about one of the best-known cases, where the child had ended up with big problems. Would the same thing happen with Shelly or Rose? Feelings of resentment or insecurity would be natural, surely.

Of course, she thought in rueful amusement, Shelly wouldn't be able to keep them to herself. Already, she talked through everything. She was utterly incapable of keeping a secret.

Rose, however, was another matter.

Lynn breathed in the salt-laden air and gazed out at the broken surf and the curve of the earth far beyond.

When she glanced back, she found Rose's gaze wide and inquiring. "How come Daddy went to bed with you last night?" she asked innocently.

Lynn gulped. Oh, dear. The kids hadn't actually caught them in bed together yet, and she hadn't been able to think of a way to casually say, *Your daddy and I are going to sleep together from now on.*

"I saw him come out in his 'jamas," Rose continued. "He only wears his bottoms, you know."

Lynn knew.

"He says the top wraps him up like a mummy 'cuz he rolls and rolls and rolls when he sleeps."

Lynn smiled down at her daughter. "That happens to my nightie sometimes, too."

Rose's forehead crinkled. "What's a mummy? Is it like you? Only, you're not all wrapped up."

Lynn explained that a long, long time ago, before her grandparents' grandparents' grandparents were born, Egyptians had wrapped dead people in linen bandages before putting them in a tomb.

Rose's face brightened. "I 'member this boy at my school! He came to the Halloween party with toilet paper around him." She gestured. "Like that. He was a big kid. Was he a mummy?"

"Well, pretending to be one," Lynn conceded. "He probably thought it would be a scary costume."

"He wasn't dead," Rose said earnestly. "Kids kept ripping his toilet paper. He got raggedy."

"That's what happens to costumes at a party, if you're having enough fun." Lynn glimpsed something bright ahead, just poking out of the sand. She steered Rose toward it.

Rose pounced. "Mommy, look!"

It was a whole bottle that Rose pried out of dried seaweed. Probably a beer bottle, but the shape was unusual, the glass roughened by sand and salt water.

Lynn squatted beside Rose, who was wiping sand and crusty seaweed from her find. "What do you think, is there a genie in it?"

Aladdin was one of Rose's favorite movies.

"No." With one eye, Rose peered inside. "It's empty. The top must've fallen off, and he got out. Maybe he doesn't have to give wishes no more."

"No more wishes?" Lynn's gaze went to her husband's broad back and dark head, bent as he listened to Shelly chatter. "What a terrible thought!"

"Genies get tired of doing wishes, you know,"

Rose continued importantly. "Sometimes they need a 'cation."

"A vacation?" Lynn pretended to think. "I suppose they do."

"Daddy said maybe we could all go on 'cation sometime. He said maybe Hawaii. It's got beaches, he says. But you got beaches here, too."

"The ones in Hawaii are made of silky, golden sand instead of rocks. And the sun shines there lots more than it does here. Everywhere there are big colorful flowers and waterfalls tumbling into pools, and whales right offshore."

And Adam wanted to take her? It could be a sort of honeymoon, to make up for the one they hadn't had.

Shelly suddenly crowed in delight. Face alight, she pointed into the foamy fingers of the waves. "Lookit! There's one a' those glass balls!" Hopping up and down with excitement, she exclaimed, "An' it's a big one!"

"Don't you have sharp eyes." Adam lifted her onto his shoulders. "Okay, punkin, let's go get it."

Rose and Lynn followed them across the wet gravel left by a receding tide. Sure enough, the Japanese float bobbed into sight and then vanished as a wave broke over it.

"Shoot, it's getting away," Adam said, pausing at the water's edge.

"Catch it, Daddy!" His daughter bounced even harder and grabbed his hair. "Don't let it get away!"

He looked ruefully down at his running shoes and jeans, then plunged into the ankle-deep foam. "Ah! It's freezing!"

Knee-deep before he could get his hands on the glass fisherman's float, Adam grabbed it, swore and dropped it back into the water.

A mother's anxiety seized Lynn, who watched with an eagle eye. He should have left Shelly behind. What if she fell off? What if an extra big breaker should knock him down?

A wave did surge in, soaking him to his thighs. Shelly seemed to have a grip on his hair as she kept bouncing and cheering him on.

"It's going away again, Daddy! Those ol' crabs won't hurt you. You better get it, 'cuz it's mine and I saw it first."

Gingerly he picked it up again and waded toward shore. One more cold wave washed up to his knees, and then he was squelching triumphantly up above the foaming edge of the surf, his teeth a flash of white as he grinned like a conqueror mounting the ramparts.

"What is it?" Rose asked dubiously, as he set it down and they all hunkered in for a look.

A foot in diameter, the green glass fisherman's float still had the twine net encasing it. Tiny pale crabs scuttled all over it.

Lynn explained that it had floated all the way from Japan, where fishermen used glass floats still instead of plastic ones to anchor their nets. She helped evict the crabs.

"I bet somebody'd buy it, huh, Mom?" Shelly asked.

"I'm sure they would, but maybe you'd like to keep it." Two months ago, she'd have been grateful for the extra cash it would have brought, Lynn thought wryly. "To remember today by."

"Can I?"

"Yep." Adam smiled at her. "If not for your sharp eyes, we never would have seen it." His gaze touched Rose as if by accident, and then he lifted a brow at Lynn. "Do you find these often?"

"Hardly ever anymore," she admitted. "But see what Rose found?" She pulled the bottle from her coat pocket. "It's empty, so we figure the genie must be taking a vacation. In Hawaii."

Shelly stared covetously at the bottle. "I bet a genie *did* live in it. Do you think he'll come back?"

"Who knows?" Lynn let it slip back into her pocket. "You both found treasures today, didn't you?"

On the way home Shelly and Rose ran ahead. Adam had to lug the big glass float. He paused once, when the girls found a tidal pool, to snatch a quick kiss, his lips cold but stirring warmth in her.

Shelly's piercing voice penetrated Lynn's euphoria. "Daddy's kissin' Mommy! Look, Rose. How come he's kissin' Mommy?"

Adam drew back. "It would seem I'm making a public demonstration of my affections."

"He kisses *me*," Rose declared.

"Not like that," Shelly said in a tone of horrified fascination. "Not on the lips!"

Facing the girls, his free arm looped around Lynn's waist, Adam said, "I like kissing Mommy, too. Mommies and Daddies do kiss on the lips."

"Eew." Shelly made a troll face.

"Trust me," Adam said with amusement, "you'll understand someday."

"What if a boy at preschool wants to kiss me on the lips?" Rose asked seriously.

"You pop him in the nose," he suggested.

The girls burst into giggles and scrambled onto a long log washed in by the sea and half-buried on the beach so that it made a perfect balance beam for three-year-olds. They could fall without hurting themselves.

"Rose already asked why you were sleeping with me," Lynn said, as she and Adam paralleled the girls' path.

"What did you say?"

"Nothing. She got distracted. You told her you don't wear pajama tops because they end up wound around you like a mummy's wrapping, and so I had to explain that a mummy is *not* like me."

He laughed, creasing his cheeks and warming the cool planes of his face. The fluttering in her chest Lynn felt at the sight of him was becoming familiar. She'd married this man in cold blood, and now she was feeling everything she had when she'd imagined herself in love with Brian.

Everything, she admitted silently, and more.

In comparison, what she'd felt for Brian had been…a crush. A girlish stage that would have passed if they hadn't rushed into marriage. If only she hadn't been so inexperienced, so socially inept, she would have known whether her feelings for him were special or not.

Was she fooling herself again, just because…well, because she so enjoyed making love with Adam?

Lynn stole a sidelong glance at the man striding beside her, looking astonishingly carefree for the buttoned-down, austere stockbroker he was. She had fallen in love awfully fast, hadn't she?

But in her heart she knew better. She had begun the tumble a long time ago. That day in the hospital, probably, when she'd seen how much he adored his Rosebud. When she realized he felt all the same conflicts she did. Every kindness he'd given her since, every smile at the girls, every willing boost onto a kitchen chair, every game played, every grave answer to a silly question, had polished the slide down which she rocketed. How could she help it? Despite his doubts, Adam was a wonderful father. Beneath his usual rigid courtesy and occasional bluntness, he was a marshmallow. Nothing was too good for Shelly and Rose. Or her, now that he felt an obligation to her. He was chivalrous, sexy and determined to do the right thing.

What's not to love? she asked herself frivolously.

Her feelings were anything but. She knew how lucky she was. Adam would be a good husband if it killed him. His moral standards wouldn't let him look at another woman, even if he didn't love his wife. But it wasn't just that. They could be happy together; these past two weeks demonstrated that. She was sure he was contented, at least.

All she had to do was keep her mouth shut. He must never, never know that this marriage was no longer one of convenience and friendship for her. He'd only feel uncomfortable, perhaps even obliged to make up some pretty lies to reciprocate. She couldn't bear that.

Be grateful for what you have, Lynn told herself. Why spoil it by wishing for more? If Adam came to love her in return, well, it would happen. Perhaps slowly, but heartfelt emotions couldn't be forced, shouldn't be pretended. She would never want that.

She had lived her entire life appreciating what she had and not hoping for too much. She could go on that way.

What she wasn't sure she could do was bear the regular separation from Adam. Although she hadn't yet said aloud, *I will sell the bookstore,* the idea had taken root and was settling in. Owning her own bookstore had been a lifelong dream, and she loved every moment of it. Working for someone else, even in a wonderful store like Powell's in Portland, would never bring her the same joy.

And oh, how she'd miss Otter Beach! The sound of the surf and the bark of sea lions out on the stack, the tangy air, the fresh breeze and the fog that rolled in off the ocean on hot days. *How shall I list the ways!* she thought. The crunch and slide of walking on the gravelly beach and the shoot of spray through the blowhole. The vendors along the boardwalk, the tourists and even the traffic on the brick streets. To her mental list she hastened to add her garden, and her new refrigerator and her rickety back steps she would decorate with potted geraniums come summer.

This was home, the first and only home she'd ever made for herself. But today was…she mentally ticked off days on her fingers…the tenth of February. Always, by the middle of April, she had gone back to her summer schedule, having the store open Tuesday through Sunday. Just over two months away.

That would mean two more days a week when she had to be here, and Adam had to be in Portland. Could she afford to hire someone to cover at least one day? Would she and Adam split the girls up? Or alternate who got to keep them? After only two weeks, she'd become accustomed to sleeping with him: to being able to tuck her cold feet beneath his calf, to the sound of him breathing beside her at night, to that exhilarating, sexy glint in his eyes when he wanted her.

Before Adam and Rose, she had loved her life here. Shelly and the bookstore were enough. Now they weren't. It was that simple.

Soon, she told herself, she had to start looking for a buyer.

Lynn wasn't quite sure why she hadn't told Adam about her plans. Some residual caution held her back. *Be sure,* her fearful inner self whispered.

But she was sure. Not that he would ever love her, but that she did love him. And both her daughters. She was spread too thin. She had a family now, a real family, and they had to come first.

She would definitely look for a buyer. But when Adam wrapped an arm around her and steered her away from the breaking surf and toward the stairs that led up to the boardwalk and the town, she didn't say, ''Adam, I have something to tell you.''

He was the one to speak instead, calling to the girls, ''Come on, munchkins. We need to get you cleaned up, so we can head out for Portland. Daddy's got to go to work tomorrow.''

As usual, they had to take two cars, one of the drawbacks of their commuter marriage. Today, the girls rode with him. She followed his Lexus all the way to Portland. When he got too far ahead, he slowed; when she missed a light, he waited on the shoulder of the road. She pulled into his driveway right behind him and helped him unbuckle the girls from their car seats and carry them, both sound asleep, into the house that was now her home, too.

Although the subject had been on her mind, she still didn't tell him while they put together a quick dinner and ate it, or even later when, without a second thought, she passed the spare bedroom that had once been hers and joined Adam in his spare, masculine bedroom dominated by a king-size bed.

In the master bathroom, she brushed her teeth at her own sink—this bathroom alone was bigger than her kitchen above the bookstore—and slipped on her nightgown. She came out to find Adam waiting, wearing only pajama bottoms that hung low on his hips. He drew her into his arms for a tender kiss that quickly became more intense.

"You won't need this," he murmured against her cheek, as his fingers gathered her nightgown at each hip preparatory to shimmying it over her head.

Purring like a contented cat, she hooked her thumbs inside the waistband of his pajamas. "Mmm. You won't need these, either."

He sucked on her earlobe, an oddly delicious sensation. "When the girls are grown—" he nipped instead, his low voice husky "—we'll sleep naked. Let's make a pact."

A thrill swelled in her chest, out of proportion to his idle words. He must be happy with her, or he wouldn't be thinking about such a distant future.

Would he? Was it possible that he was starting to feel something special, too?

Lynn couldn't have spoken to save her life. She only sighed and let her head fall back as his mouth moved softly along her throat, pausing to trace her collarbone, before continuing down to her breast.

Why couldn't he love her? she asked a nameless somebody, in hope and defiance. Was it so impossible? Was she unlovable?

Pleasure shivered through her as he suckled her breast, stroked her hips with his large hands, cupped her bottom and lifted her up so that she cradled his erection and had to wrap her legs around his waist.

"I want you," he growled, that hot light in his eyes.

Foolish words trembled on her tongue, but she swallowed them. She could not tell him. She couldn't ruin everything.

"I'm all yours," she whispered instead, and hoped he didn't know how completely that was true.

ALMOST THE BEST PART of being married was having somebody to talk to. Lynn loved the evenings, after the girls had gone to bed. She and Adam invariably cleaned the kitchen together and then took herbal tea or coffee to the living room, where they read some of the time in companionable silence, but most often talked. "Of shoes—and ships—and sealing wax—Of cabbages—and kings," to quote Lewis Carroll.

Not so far off, either. She and Adam hadn't yet discussed sealing wax, but she thought they'd covered cabbages—she detested them, he loved even such horrors as corned beef and cabbage—and kings, in the form of royal weddings. They had taken the girls shoe shopping one day, and gone to a park overlooking the Columbia River where they could see huge freighters unloading cargo from foreign climes.

She had missed such conversation dreadfully. Lynn and her mother had been good friends. Until Adam, Lynn had never been able to talk to anyone the way she could to her mother. In college, she'd had friends and roommates, of course, but all of them were so busy with finals and labs and boyfriends, and really everyone at that age was so self-centered, she realized now, that nobody listened very well. Probably including her.

Brian was a natural storyteller, but the stories were all about himself. His prowess as a high school and college sports star, his adventures mountain climbing and skiing, his starring role in campus theater productions. She had been fascinated and awestruck and grateful that he wanted to be with her, but after the first year she began to notice that he wasn't very interested in *her* dreams or successes, and he'd cut off her attempts to discuss politics or philosophy or a book she had read by reaching for the remote control or grabbing his jacket and saying casually over his shoulder, ''I promised Cranston I'd whip his butt at one-on-one. You were just going to read or something anyway, weren't you?'' He always said it that way: *just.* You're going to do something unimportant, dull.

Adam enjoyed reading as much as she did. Lynn was flattered when she discovered him reading a book she'd mentioned loving. Since then, he had read several based on her recommendations. He didn't always feel about them the same way she did, which she didn't mind. They'd had some rousing arguments.

The television was rarely on here, she'd discovered. The girls watched a couple of favorite shows and, naturally, Rose had a huge collection of videos mostly bought by Grandma McCloskey, but Adam limited how much Rose could watch a day, as Lynn had always done with Shelly. He religiously watched the news, primarily because world events had such a bearing on the next day's stock market. A revolution in some tiny country half a world away would impact the U.S. economy because a raw material for manufacturing came from there. She was impressed by Adam's instant grasp of the import of such news. Obscure political events took on meaning for her, too. She found that she read the newspapers and watched the television news with more interest now.

Only occasionally did she bump against a closed gate beyond which she wasn't welcome. A very few topics brought stinging reminders that their closeness was illusion.

Tonight, for example, Lynn curled her legs under her at one end of the sofa and said, "I forgot to tell you that your mother called today."

Adam laid down his book willingly. "What did she want?"

"Nothing special. I think she just wanted to chat." Lynn frowned, trying to remember. "She didn't leave a message."

"What did you 'chat' about?" He looked unwillingly fascinated. "I didn't know my mother knew how."

"Oh, she has an opening in a San Francisco art gallery next weekend. She asked if I'd like to come over and use her potter's wheel and kiln." As explanation, Lynn added, "I'd told her I took a couple of years of ceramics in college. I loved using a wheel."

"Ah." He sounded amused and a little bitter. "The way to her heart."

"Did you learn?"

"She tried," Adam said shortly.

"Did you?"

"Probably not." He laughed without much humor. "I felt about her studio like most kids do about a baby brother. It was my competitor for her attention, and it always won." This smile, though crooked, became more relaxed, more genuine. "Besides, I have not a grain of artistic ability. I made the ugliest damn pots you've ever seen."

"It's odd that we were both only children. I felt a little more secure than you did, though."

"Were you lonely?" He looked as if he really wanted to know.

"No." Why hadn't she been? "We were such good friends. Mom didn't seem lonely, so how could I be?" Lynn had never told this to anyone, but now she admitted, "I was terribly shocked when Mom got married. It made me wonder—oh, this sounds terrible…"

Adam finished for her, "You wondered if she'd ever really been as happy as you thought she was."

"Yes." Lynn made a face. "I suppose everyone grows up and looks at their parents and one day realizes maybe they weren't quite who you thought they were. If that isn't too muddled a sentence."

"Clear as Perrier," Adam assured her with a grin. "Except 'everyone' doesn't have to reevaluate a parent, because some of us knew ours. Mine are just who I concluded they were."

"Are they?"

He went still. "What's that mean?"

"Just that…" She hesitated. "I had the impression your mother was probing to find out whether I'd be a suitably loving wife for you. She seemed concerned."

"Concerned," he repeated flatly.

"Some people aren't very demonstrative."

He gave a short, hard laugh. "My mother is not demonstrative."

"You think she doesn't love you?" But he was so quick to hug Rose, to smooth away a tear or tickle her into laughter! He couldn't possibly have learned that from books!

"I think she feels an obligation."

"Well, I think you're wrong," Lynn said stoutly. "She was definitely suspicious of me." She thought for a moment. "I guess that's natural since she knows why we got married."

"Then she doesn't have any reason to worry about you breaking my heart, does she?"

"No." She spoke quietly, not letting him see that he had hurt her. "You're right. Maybe I misunderstood."

Say, *You* could *break my heart,* she begged him without words, her gaze lowered to the pale amber of her cinnamon apple tea. Say…

Gentler, his voice broke her pitiful thoughts. "You're not unhappy, are you?"

"Me?" Lynn made herself look up with wide eyes, as if astonished at the question. "Why would I be unhappy?" *Because I love you, and you don't love me,* she answered her own question.

"Some women are romantics." His tone was odd.

She would have sworn she wasn't one of them. *She* had never intended to remarry; *she* was incapable of the depth of passion and commitment a man would want in a wife.

She was an idiot, Lynn thought, and fully deserved the fix she'd gotten herself into.

"Not me," she claimed, and took a calm sip of her tea.

She felt his gaze resting on her and would have given almost anything to know what he was thinking. But for some peculiar reason her emotions seemed close to the surface. If she had met his eyes just then, she might not have been able to keep her secrets.

And she must. She must! She was so lucky, had so much, she wouldn't be foolish enough to let herself ache for the little that Adam couldn't give her.

"Did I tell you what Rose said today?" she asked with a smile so bright it felt brittle.

Without moving a muscle, Adam relaxed. Lynn sensed it with every fiber of her being. He had feared she would ask him something he couldn't answer, or didn't want to answer. Like, *Can I break your heart?* Or even, *Are* you *happy?*

Instead she was deliberately reminding him of what they had in common: their children.

He laughed in the right places at her story, told one of his own, then commented on the book he was reading. The evening was ordinary, pleasant; outwardly both were comfortable.

After turning off the lights and going upstairs, they even made love. No, Lynn reminded herself, tears burning her eyes as she lay sprawled atop him in the aftermath, her face hidden against his chest, not love, *they had sex.*

There was a difference, and she had been pretending there wasn't. A mistake she would try very hard not to make in the future.

Adam rolled, settling her against him, and she sighed and turned away as if already half-asleep.

They could be content, even happy, without both being deeply, passionately in love. And so she reminded herself again: enjoy what you have, be grateful for Shelly and Rose's sake, and don't grieve for what you can't have.

Hot tears, falling silently, wet her pillowcase.

CHAPTER FOURTEEN

"COFFEE, SIR?" The waiter accepted Adam's nod and refilled his cup. "Our cheesecake is excellent."

Adam skipped the dessert; Lynn decided to indulge. The three partners in Adam's firm were having dinner with their wives at a Portland restaurant. This was throwing Lynn in with a vengeance. She had never met these friends and colleagues, and both they and their wives had known Jennifer.

Now, amid general chatter as the others debated dessert, she touched Adam's thigh and murmured, "I'm going to the rest room. Will you ask if they have herbal tea? I forgot."

"Anything but peppermint." He knew her tastes.

When she rose, Jillian, another of the wives, stood as well. "I'll join you."

As Jillian passed Adam to follow Lynn, she leaned down and murmured in his ear, "I like her. You're a lucky guy."

Erica, sitting on Adam's other side, had overheard. With the other two women wending their way between tables toward the back of the elegant restaurant, she said, "I'm so glad this marriage has worked out for you, Adam. Ron told me the circumstances, I hope you don't mind. It sounded like a prescription for disaster, and instead the two of you are a pair of lovebirds!''

Lovebirds? Adam thought incredulously. Where the hell had she gotten that idea?

''You do look happy,'' agreed her husband, who had been Adam's best friend since university days. Ron Chainey was the only one here who'd met Lynn, as he'd been the best man at the wedding. ''You've been keeping Lynn tucked away.'' His grin was wicked. ''Now we know why.''

Erica, a buxom redhead who was unapologetically plump, patted his hand. ''I'm so glad, after Jennifer, that you've found someone.''

''He always was a lucky son of a gun.'' Ron aimed a mock punch at his shoulder.

When Adam failed to volunteer details about his married life, conversation drifted again. Eugene Warren, the third partner in their brokerage, wanted to complain about his clients' demands for Internet stocks, an old refrain.

''HiTech is the latest.'' He rubbed the top of his head, already balding though he was only in his mid-thirties. ''The P/E stinks!''

The price to earning ratio, a standard for judging whether a stock was overvalued, was lousy for most Internet stocks. Amazon.com stock sold for as much as companies with solid earnings, even though the Internet book mart still wasn't posting a profit.

''You know that's true of all Internet stocks,'' Ron said mildly.

Warren stuck like a tick to his grievances. ''They're going to crash one of these days. A company like Amazon.com or HiTech has no real assets.

Hell, a few phones and a warehouse are all that's behind the fancy graphics. What are we valuing?''

"Potential?'' Adam suggested.

"All in the eye of the beholder. The projections are pie in the sky! If it looks too good to be true, it is. You know that. Let's have a little healthy cynicism here, can we?''

Desserts arrived, and Ron picked up his fork. "Gene, we've talked about this before. We can't use the same standards for judging these companies. They represent something completely new, a different way of making money. They're breaking ground. Sure, prices will probably shake out at some point. But in the foreseeable future? I don't think so. HiTech has a great website, they're delivering the product fast, and customers are flocking to them. I think their market will grow.''

Gene Warren continued, his thesis something to the effect that shopping on the Internet was a novelty. People would get tired of waiting for their computers to load web pages, tired of having to return items that didn't look anything like they did in the tiny grainy picture on the computer screen.

Waiting for his wife to return, Adam couldn't keep his mind on an old discussion about business. He hadn't seen Lynn in a dress more than a time or two. She was beautiful tonight, in a simple teal-colored sheath of rough silk. That glorious hair was anchored in a French roll on the back of her head, the tiny runaway tendrils appearing intentional.

When she'd twirled for his approval, she'd smiled impishly. "This dress is courtesy of your credit card, I must warn you.''

"It's stunning." Her legs went on forever. No, not forever, as her deliciously rounded bottom suggested. "*You're* stunning," he amended, probably sounding as dazed as he felt. "Worth every penny, and a hell of a lot more."

"Why, thank you."

She sounded the tiniest bit breathless, which made him wonder whether it was so obvious that he would have liked to whip that zipper back down and strip the simple little dress right off. Or maybe just hitch it up to her waist...

Damn. Sitting here at the table, he was hardening at the idea. Whatever else you could say about their marriage, the sex was good. Better than good. Incredible. No wonder they looked happy.

They *were* happy. He was reasonably sure she felt the same.

Eugene Warren's axiom echoed in his ears. *If it looks too good to be true, it is.*

Damn Eugene Warren and his perennially pessimistic outlook, Adam thought in irritation. Just because life was good didn't mean something had to go wrong. His arrangement with Lynn was giving them both what they wanted. How could that go sour?

Sure, you're getting what you want, an inner voice jeered. *You're getting everything: a willing, passionate sexual partner, both daughters, all the trappings of a happy marriage. In return you're giving...what?*

Knowing he was being defensive, still he fired back, *The same.* Lynn wasn't suffering here.

He wasn't the only one who thought she was happy. Even these old friends had a similar impression. He and Lynn had everything going for them. The only part of a conventional marriage they'd skipped were the words *I love you,* and neither he nor Lynn needed them.

Deep in his brooding, he didn't hear her footsteps. She was already pulling out her chair and saying, "Ooh. Look at that cheesecake," when he caught her scent. Adam stood and pushed in the chair after she'd sat.

"Thank you," she murmured, and began talking to Jillian across the table. Something about an art fair for children that was being held at a school.

"Face painting," Jillian was saying, "you know the girls would love that! Oh, and there's always sand art and finger painting for the little ones, and origami. And swirl art!" She laughed. "Now, there's a mess to clean up! But the kids have a great time. Do bring Shelly and Rose."

Adam wanted to kiss Lynn's neck, right where those tiny wisps of auburn hair curled like miniature tumbleweeds. She had incredible skin, milky pale with just a hint of peach, like the redhead she wasn't quite. He'd pull out the pins securing her hair one at a time, until the thick mass of curls tumbled into his hands and over her bare shoulders. Slither that silk sheath down her slender arms, exposing the lacy bra he'd caught a glimpse of as he zipped up the dress for her. Why, he wondered idly, was undressing a woman such a turn-on, even when a man knew what he'd find under the silk?

Because he liked what he would find, he answered himself. From an erotic cloud of hair to her generous breasts, he loved her body. And it wasn't just that.

Her kisses were shy, not provocative. Sweet, as if they meant something beyond the moment. The sounds Lynn made he found especially endearing. It was as if she couldn't help herself. He liked that: knowing she was shy, and probably blushed the next day at the memory of herself sobbing with pleasure or whimpering at the touch of his hand, but that he moved her beyond inhibitions.

One of the men asked him something about the Trailblazers, Portland's pro basketball team, and Adam answered, but as briefly as possible. Impatience barely in check, he waited for Lynn to finish her cheesecake.

As she swallowed the last bite, he tossed some bills onto the table and said abruptly, "We need to get home. Grandma is baby-sitting, you know, and it's after her bedtime."

A wide, devilish smile spread across his buddy Ron's face. "Uh-huh. Sure. It's Grandma's bedtime you're worrying about."

"Shut up," Adam said amiably. He took Lynn's hand and tugged her to her feet. "We're newlyweds, aren't we? We're entitled."

They escaped only after a couple more minutes of razzing. In the lobby, Lynn shrugged into her coat when he held it for her. Neither talking, they went out into Portland's usual chilly, damp night.

"*Are* you concerned about Angela baby-sitting?" she asked, as he unlocked the passenger car door for her.

He pulled her to him for a quick, hard kiss. "Nope. I got to imagining how much I was going to enjoy unzipping your dress."

"Oh." He could hear her blush, if such a thing were possible.

On the drive home, Lynn agreed that she liked his friends, liked their wives, had indeed made plans to take Rose and Shelly to the art fair at the elementary school where Jillian served as PTA president. Yes, she thought she could be friends with Jillian in particular; did Adam know that she'd written a children's book and was seeking a publisher?

Despite her willingness to answer direct questions, Lynn was rather quiet. It seemed to Adam that her voice was constrained. Maybe she was tired, he decided. Could be she'd been nervous about meeting his friends and was relieved it was over. Or she was anxious about leaving the girls with Angela. There were any number of reasons she might be a little distracted.

But on top of his earlier brooding, it bothered him that she wasn't as open as usual, that she seemed to be doing some brooding of her own.

If it looks too good to be true... The wail of a distant siren seemed to whisper just to him.

He had too many moments like this, when he felt as if he were balancing a dozen wineglasses on his nose like the Chinese acrobats he'd taken Rose to see last fall. Any misstep and he'd see them teeter, arc in slow motion through the air, shatter on the floor. Maybe it was losing Jennifer the way he had. He knew how quickly the rug could be yanked out from under you.

Especially when the only promises given were "I'll try my best," and a more formal "I do."

At home her smile seemed forced, too, when Angela jabbered about the cute things Shelly said and how smart she was and wasn't it nice that the girls loved each other like sisters?

"Thanks for baby-sitting, Mom." Adam kissed her cheek and managed to get her heading toward the front door. He walked her out to her car, thanked her ten more times, and stood with hands in pockets watching until the brake lights winked once and her BMW disappeared into the trees. Asking her to baby-sit had been Lynn's idea; he had always waited in vain for her to volunteer. She'd agreed with such alacrity, he guessed she had *wanted* to be asked. Apparently he and she were two of a kind. Thanks to Lynn, his relationship with Angela and Rob was the best it had ever been.

More surprisingly, he'd realized recently that he was seeing more of his own parents, too. Just today, his mother had called to chat. She'd asked a few probing questions about his marriage, which made Adam wonder if Lynn hadn't been right after all. His mother might care more than he'd suspected. These past weeks, they'd come to dinner several times and had Lynn, Adam and the girls over to their place. Hell, his mother had even given Shelly and Rose a tour of her studio! Adam was coming to the unwelcome conclusion that he had shut his parents out, not the other way around. He was lucky that Lynn was around to mend fences he'd evidently damaged in his clumsiness.

Lynn. He locked the front door behind him, anticipation quickening in him. He could take his wife to bed. At last. There, at least, they were close, their moods invariably in sync. She wanted him, he had no doubt about that much.

She'd left lights on downstairs but had apparently already gone up. Disquiet touched him. Was something wrong? Had somebody said something tonight that upset her? Damn it, why wasn't she talking to him?

Irritably he asked himself why he was jumping to conclusions. Maybe she'd slipped upstairs to get ready for him. He might find her lounging in a sexy pose on the bed. He just hoped she hadn't taken the dress off. He wanted to save that pleasure for himself.

Flipping off lights as he went, Adam paused in the upstairs hall, as he knew Lynn would have done a few minutes before, to step into the girls' bedroom and assure himself they were both safely tucked into bed, healthy, their sleep untroubled. As he stood beside the bed, Rose's eyes opened and she gazed sleepily up at him.

"Daddy," she whispered.

He bent down, cupped her face and kissed her forehead. "Mommy and I are home. You sleep tight, sweetheart."

"'kay, Daddy," she murmured even as her heavy lids sank closed. After a moment of stillness, a small snore escaped her parted lips and she rolled away, nestling closer to Shelly.

Adam's smile died when he reached his bedroom and saw Lynn. Her back was to him. She'd already shinnied out of her panty hose, unclipped her earrings and let down her hair. As he watched, she massaged her scalp, then ran her fingers through the curls and shook them out. At last, she groped behind her neck for the zipper on her silk dress.

He stepped silently behind her and eased the zipper down. She started, then bowed her head to let him work. As the dress parted, he brushed his lips along her nape. The skin was so soft here. With his fingertips Adam traced her spine, ignoring the catch of her bra, slipping inside her panties. She moaned.

"Are you tired?" he asked. "You didn't wait for me."

"I am tired," Lynn admitted.

"If you want to go right to sleep…" Hoping like hell she'd say no, Adam nuzzled the curve between neck and shoulder.

She sucked in a breath. "I thought I would." Her voice was throaty, not much above a whisper.

Disappointment smacked him in the face, fear in the gut. She might just be tired. But what if it was more?

He straightened away from her. With determined civility, Adam said, "Then you'd better get right to bed. Would you rather I read downstairs for a while?"

"No." Lynn turned suddenly and wrapped her arms around his neck. "No, don't go. I'm not that tired."

"If you want to sleep, it might be best…" The translation, he thought grimly, was, *I need to put some distance between us if I can't have you.*

Her eyes were huge and dark, and he felt tension quivering through her. "You've changed my mind. If…if you're still in the mood."

The disappointment evaporated like a cold sweat;

the fear lingered. She tugged his head down to hers with a hint of desperation. Her mouth was needy, her fingers on his tie and shirt buttons clumsy. She seemed suddenly frantic for him.

He shrugged out of his shirt as she swept it from his shoulders. Her dress pooled at her feet. As he flicked the catch of her bra, she was already unbuckling his belt and unzipping his fly, taking him in her hands. She made mewling sounds as he reached inside her panties and found her hot and damp.

"Yes. Right now," she whispered, an ache in her voice. "I want you."

He stripped the panties from her as he laid her on the bed. The ceiling light was still on. There seemed nothing romantic about what they were doing right now, but he was past caring or remembering the slow seduction he'd planned.

Her urgency had communicated itself to him. He didn't even get his pants off before she tugged him down. Thrusting inside her, he drank in her cries with his mouth. She whimpered when normally she would have sighed softly. Clutching desperately at his back and shoulders, her nails bit into his flesh. When his mouth left hers, she pleaded with him.

"Harder. Faster. Oh, yes. Now! Oh, please, now!"

Ripples traveled through her belly and she cried his name. "Adam!"

Groaning, teeth gritted, he finished with a triumphant shout, emptying himself inside her. He collapsed on top of her, his mind eddying in a dark whirlpool. What in hell had happened here? Why had she been too tired one second, then too impatient to wait for him to kick off his trousers the next?

He liked being wanted. He didn't like the fact that she had seemed to need the physical release more than the intimacy of their lovemaking.

He must be crushing her, he realized. It seemed a superhuman effort to roll to one side, but he managed. When he tried to take Lynn with him, keep her wrapped in his arms, she stiffened.

"I'm cold," she said in a small voice. "I think I'll take a shower. If you don't mind."

That brought his eyes open. "Why would I mind?"

"I'll be back to bed in a few minutes." She was definitely beating a retreat. She slipped off the bed and scooped up her dress, holding it in front of her as if to hide her nakedness. A second later the bathroom door shut and he heard the shower start.

He usually felt good in the aftermath of sex. This time he felt…obscene. Sprawled on his back on the bed, ankles cuffed by his trousers.

Swearing, Adam sat up and finished undressing. He hung up his slacks and tie, draped the shirt over a chair, and pulled on his pajama bottoms. He brushed his teeth and splashed water on his face at one of the two sinks outside the bathroom. Leaving on the lamp at Lynn's side of the bed, he switched off the overhead light and climbed into bed.

Her shower wasn't a quickie. It ran and ran, as if she felt the need to scrub every inch of her body, or simply to let the hot water unknot the tension he'd felt. Guessing that she'd prefer it, Adam pretended to be asleep when she finally, quietly, came out. Water ran briefly in the sink as she too brushed her teeth. A moment later the mattress gave as she sat. The lamp went out, and she slipped in on her side of the bed, seemingly careful not to touch him.

Wide-awake, Adam wondered how Lynn really felt about him. She had entered willingly into their bargain, but he knew damn well that was for the sake of the girls. When he screwed her tonight—there was no other way to put it—did she pretend he was someone else? When she'd pulled his mouth down to his, changing her mind with such odd abruptness, did she hunger for the physical connection without it mattering who held her?

Did she think about him during the day, or in the night when they were separated? Had her feelings for him grown, or were they still two strangers who happened to share a bed?

Adam hadn't expected to feel so insecure. Not daring to move, he stared into the darkness and knew that something was missing for him in this marriage. He didn't like discovering that he wanted her to love him. She said, "I want you," and it wasn't good enough. The words and everything that went with them counted after all.

What kind of jerk did that make him, considering he didn't, couldn't, return her love?

Did she wonder if he closed his eyes and imagined he was making love to Jennifer? The idea unexpectedly jolted him. Was that what was wrong?

The possibility was particularly ironic considering his own guilt because he so seldom did think about Jennifer anymore. She was slipping away from him, Lynn's vivid presence routing the ghost. He had trouble seeing Jenny's face anymore, hearing her laugh; she no longer visited his dreams. He sure as hell didn't imagine her when he was making love to Lynn.

That guilt crushed him suddenly in its grip. He'd lied to himself, he thought in despair. He'd never intended to hold Jennifer close to his heart once he had remarried. His promises on their wedding day, the vows he'd sworn to God beside her deathbed, all meant nothing. Out of sight, out of mind.

Muscles rigid, Adam wasn't sure he could keep lying here in this bed next to his too-still wife. He needed to be away from her. Able to pace. Bang his head against a wall. He needed to find Jennifer again, if she was here at all.

Or maybe, just maybe, he needed to find a way to say goodbye. Lynn deserved better than their farce of a marriage. Could he give it to this shy, gentle woman with guts, brains and a heart?

Before he lost her?

Her breathing was regular, soft. His gaze sought the light numbers on the clock. He'd been lying here for twenty minutes now. She must be asleep.

Making slow movements only, he edged his legs over the side of the bed and sat up, then, careful not to tug at the covers, stood. He kept a bathrobe on a hook inside the bathroom door. He'd earlier turned down the thermostat, so he shrugged into the bathrobe. Lynn hadn't moved. She had to be asleep. She wouldn't even notice he was gone.

He didn't turn on a light until he reached his home office downstairs. There, Adam ignored the computer and fax machine. It was the large leather album he reached for, the one he kept on a low shelf so Rose could look at photos of her mother whenever she chose.

He sat in the large leather armchair and opened the album in his lap. On the first page were pictures taken while they were engaged. God, she looked young, was his first thought. Not so different from Shelly. A girl. She sparkled, Jenny did, even in a photograph. He traced the lines of her pixie face, alight with laughter, and remembered the first time they met, when she'd chattered so fast he didn't know half of what she said. She was beautiful, but in a different way with her eyes slanted like a cat's, her high cheekbones and pointy chin. She'd worn her brown hair short, increasing the elfin effect. Next to her, he had always felt stolid, slow moving. Even his thoughts couldn't jump from idea to idea with the lightning speed of hers. He had fallen in love with Jenny McCloskey immediately, and loved her until the day she died. Loved her even afterward, when he had been left to raise their daughter alone.

Slowly he turned the pages and watched her mature from that laughing girl to a stylish, sophisticated woman who never quite lost the mischief in her eyes. In the last photos, Jenny was pregnant, her face slightly rounder, her stomach ripe with their child. Not Rose, but Shelly.

Ah, Jenny, Adam thought, *are you really gone? Is it time to say goodbye?*

"You still miss her."

His head shot up so fast he bit his tongue. *Damn.* Lynn had sneaked up on him. She stood in the doorway, looking small and vulnerable in the thick chenille robe that had been a Christmas gift from her mother. Her eyes were fixed not on him, but on the open album.

Adam resisted the temptation to close it. He swallowed. "No. Most of the time, I don't think about her." *Because of you.* But he didn't say that. It sounded too much like an accusation.

"May I see?"

Wordlessly he turned the photo album and held it out. Lynn took it from him and gazed down at his first wife, pregnant with the child she had raised as her own.

With shock he saw her eyes brim with tears. She touched the photo, too. "She—your Jennifer—would have adored Shelly."

Adam opened his mouth to say *and Rose,* but he couldn't. Jenny had been so quick, so impatient, he thought Rose might have driven her crazy.

Lynn swiped at her tears with the back of her hand. Her voice sounded just a little hoarse. "Why tonight?"

"What?"

Now she did look at him, her gaze bravely holding his. "Why did you come down to look at her pictures tonight?"

God. He wanted to evade, but he could see that she wouldn't let him.

"I'm forgetting her. I swore I wouldn't do that."

"She's dead."

Anger flashed through him. "Do you think I don't know that?"

Her eyes were too clear, too all-seeing. "Sometimes, I'm not sure."

"What the hell does that mean?"

"She's been dead for almost four years. Shelly's lifetime. And you're still grieving as though it was only four months ago."

"Would you want to be forgotten that quickly?"

Lynn answered without hesitation. "I would not want to linger here, if some wisp of my presence crippled the people I'd loved."

He got to his feet, dumping the photo album, not looking at where it lay sprawled on the hardwood floor. "Crippled? Rose didn't know her to mourn. And look at me. I've remarried, I make love to my wife. Hell, I was so damned eager tonight, I didn't get my pants off! How is that crippled?"

Unblinking, she stared at him for the longest time. Anxiety clenched his stomach and knotted his hands at his side.

Whatever he expected, it wasn't what came.

"I love you," she said quietly.

He expelled all the air in his lungs as if a fist had driven it out.

"You love me," he said stupidly.

She loved him, Adam exulted. Her strange mood tonight meant nothing.

"Do you love me?" she asked, equally quietly.

He hadn't caught his breath yet. Not a single word presented itself. *She loves me,* tangled in his mind with one last seeking cry, *Jenny.*

Jenny was gone. Lynn was here, and his heart swelled with the startling awareness that he wouldn't want it any other way.

"See?" Lynn spoke gently. "You can't say it, can you? Or anything close."

His mouth worked.

She laughed, but sadly. "I shouldn't have even put you on the spot, should I? Love wasn't part of our deal. You warned me. I thought that wouldn't matter. I just didn't know that I was already falling in love with you."

"I...care." *God.* Even he knew that was inadequate.

"I know you do," she said with that same terrifying gentleness. "You're such a good, loving father, and you've been so kind to me. So...caring. Reading books I liked. And listening to me. I appreciate that. Really I do."

He had never felt so lumpish, even with Jennifer. He knew he needed to find the right thing to say, but he kept shying away from the obvious—*I love you.* Did he love her? Was that what he'd been feeling? Was that why he needed the words from her, the reassurance? Why he wanted her, thought about her constantly, missed her when she was on the coast? Why he'd begun imagining what a child who was his and hers together would be like?

Panic made his heart pound so hard he could hear the beats. *Think!* he told himself, his customary caution coming to his rescue. *Be sure. Don't spout off at the mouth and then be sorry.*

Lynn squeezed her hands together in front of her, looking uncomfortably as if she were praying. "I thought I could live with you and be your wife, even if you were still mourning for Jennifer. But I can't. No." She stopped him before he could speak. "It's not her. It's the fact that you don't love me. Someday you'll get over her, and you'll be ready to love again. You won't want to be married to me."

"I will never not want to be married to you." This much he knew, with unshakable certainty.

Her tiny, grateful smile ripped at his heart. "You say things like that, and it weakens my resolve. But the truth is, we're married only because I wouldn't move from Otter Beach. Well, I've decided. I'll sell the store and get a job and an apartment in this area. We can do some kind of joint custody thing. Maybe they can spend a week with me and then a week with you. Or if I can get days off during the week, I can have them then and you can have them on weekends. Or something. We'll make it work. But we will not be married just because it's the most convenient way to each have both girls."

"We *are* married."

Tears sprang into her eyes again. "It's not necessary anymore."

Anguish made his voice raw. "I don't want to lose you."

Tears ran down her cheeks now. "I'm not going far. Maybe…maybe we can be friends."

"Friends?" Adam repeated incredulously. "Goddamn it, I don't want to be friends!"

Lynn's face crumpled like a small child's. She whispered, "I'm sorry," and fled.

Adam's mouth formed the words *I love you.*

Too late.

CHAPTER FIFTEEN

EYES BLINDED BY TEARS, Lynn stumbled up the stairs. At the top she waited, listening, for a moment that stretched until a sob tore its way from her chest.

He wasn't coming after her.

She ached to crawl into bed with the girls and hold their small warm selves close, but waking them would be selfish. Instead she slipped as quietly as she could into the spare bedroom. She wanted to disappear; she wanted him not to find her, if he decided from guilt to offer awkward apologies and excuses. Closing the door behind her, she leaned back against it and let her legs collapse.

In a small ball on the floor, she cried silently so that Adam wouldn't hear her if he passed in the hall. His pity she couldn't bear. Anything but that.

I...care. She heard his stiff voice again, the faint hesitation, as if even such a tepid word required thought.

When had she decided she couldn't bear to go on living with a man who only "cared" for her, when she loved him desperately? The knowledge had crept up on her, though it terrified her. What would it mean to her daughters, who were so happy in a real family?

But they would be unhappy if their parents were,

she convinced herself. Mommy and Daddy didn't
have to be married for them to feel secure and loved.

Tonight Lynn had looked around at Adam's
friends and their wives, heard mention of Jennifer,
and thought, *They all know he doesn't love me. They
know he married me for his daughter. They feel sorry
for us. Perhaps for him especially.*

She would have felt pity for someone in the same
situation, once upon a time. Imagine, being married
to a man you didn't love! Putting up with his foibles,
sharing housekeeping and memories, friends and
family. Worse yet, accepting him into your bed.

Lynn remembered the years of rooming with other
women, the small irritations that added up to resentment despite an initial spirit of cooperation and
friendship. How would she feel when she first saw
Adam hide exasperation? When she first heard suppressed annoyance in his voice? When he didn't
reach for her at night? It was all inevitable. Even
desire didn't last, when it wasn't founded in true
emotion.

She had been determined not to make love with
him tonight. Not when during dinner she had realized
she would have to suggest a separation, have to let
him out of a bargain he couldn't have wanted to
make. But she hadn't been able to help herself. His
fingers sliding down her spine had offered unbear-
able temptation. Just once more didn't seem like too
much to ask, did it? She wouldn't let herself think
about later, about morning, about never feeling his
mouth against hers again, his big warm hands on her
breasts, his body filling hers. Just once more, they

could come together and she could know they were
a whole.

A last memory. It would be her consolation. That,
and the knowledge that at least she would never have
to hide her tears when he didn't want her anymore.

Now, curled on the floor, Lynn wiped at her wet
cheeks and longed for a tissue to blow her nose. Bed,
she thought. She would crawl into bed, and maybe
find the oblivion of sleep.

She did creep between the crisp, cold sheets of the
guest bed. As the night inched on, what fitful sleep
she found came with dreams of grief and loss. The
gray light of a rainy dawn awakened her to a pounding headache and a yawning chasm where her heart
should be. Shivering, she wished for another blanket
but made no move to get up and find one. Any other
morning, she could have scooted closer to Adam,
borrowed his warmth. But he was alone in their bed,
and she was alone here, down the hall, all because
she had followed him downstairs in the middle of the
night and found him poring over photographs of his
first wife.

Her shivers spreading, Lynn gazed sightlessly at
the rain droplets running down the window. Had she
made a terrible mistake? He did care, she knew he
did. They *were* friends, closer all the time.

But not so close, she realized with a wrench of
sadness, that he would talk about his Jenny with her.
Oh, no. That part of his life stayed behind a barred
door. She was not a real wife, who was entitled to
admittance. They had a deal, and it didn't include
letting her know the real woman he had loved.

Lynn's teeth chattered, but still she didn't move.

He had wanted her, she thought, but the comfort was too cold to help. He was a man, she was available. He found her "attractive," he had said once. "Attractive" was as chilling as the knowledge that he "cared."

She should go home, she thought. Take both girls, if Adam would let her, and heal in a place where she belonged. There she could plan the future. Advertise for a buyer, put out feelers for a job, talk to Shelly and Rose and hope she could make them understand. She needed some time before she could face Adam again.

Eventually she heard the shower down the hall. After the water stopped, she imagined him dressing. She had loved to watch the muscles in his broad, bare back flex as he bent to put on socks and shoes, as he rifled the contents of his closet in search of a favorite shirt. Then he would look so serious as he bent over to use the mirror to adjust his tie and impatiently rake a comb through his hair.

Had he slept easily? she wondered. Lynn tensed as the soft sound of his bedroom door closing came to her. Footsteps approached down the hall, paused outside her room, and finally continued downstairs. She lay shivering in the cold bed she'd made for herself until she heard the purr of his car pulling out of the driveway.

At last she dragged herself out of bed and went to their—no, *his* bedroom—where she grabbed clothes and toiletries before returning to the guest bath. His presence wasn't as strong here.

Warmer on the outside after a shower, she began

packing as she waited for Shelly and Rose to wake up.

She was making breakfast for them an hour later when she found the note Adam had left propped against the counter backsplash.

Lynn, I meant what I said last night. I don't want to lose you. We need to talk, but maybe we both have some thinking to do first. I assume you're planning to go home this morning. Take Shelly and Rose if you'd like, or drop them at preschool. Let me know. I'll be in touch.

Adam

To the point, offering her room to hope, if she'd been so inclined, and gracious. Typical of the man she loved.

Lynn crumpled the note in her hand, fought back tears, and turned to face their children.

"Girls, we're going to Otter Beach today."

How could he not have known he was in love with his wife?

Feeling like death after a sleepless night, Adam asked himself the same question over and over without getting a complete answer. Yeah, he felt guilty because Jennifer was dead and he wasn't. He'd felt like a scumbag because his love wasn't going to last for all eternity, because he could apparently transfer his affections in the blink of an eye. Maybe he'd been bothered because loving Lynn was so damned convenient he didn't believe his own feelings.

And maybe, it had just happened so gradually, he

hadn't noticed the moment he slipped from liking and lust to love and a deeper kind of passion.

Midmorning, he checked his voice mail and heard Lynn's voice say unemotionally, ''Adam, I'm taking both girls with me. I guess we do need to discuss a visitation schedule, but they'll be fine with me until this weekend. I'll call then.''

Click.

He stabbed number one on his phone and listened again. She didn't sound distressed, sad, angry, hurt. Nothing. Back to square one. He'd pick up the girls, drop them off. Lynn would be pleasant, remote, well organized. He and she would have a relationship as cozy as the one he had with Ann. Post-it notes passing in the night.

''No!'' The sound of his own voice, feral, hoarse, shocked him. He shot to his feet and paced.

He wouldn't have it.

She loved him. He'd heard her say the words *I love you.*

No, Adam had no intention of letting his wife get away. He'd go after her.

As soon as he could figure out why he had been so slow on the uptake, and why she was so ready and eager to run.

Had his determination to give her and Shelly everything left Lynn feeling bought and paid for? He tried to remember the expression on her face when she told him the silk dress had gone on his credit card, but all he could see was how glorious she looked. Hell, maybe she'd sounded a little rueful, but not resentful. He'd swear she hadn't.

Was it because he'd pressured her to sell the store

and move to Portland? But if that was the problem, why was she now agreeing to do just that? No. It didn't equate.

He stared out the window at the rhododendrons budding for spring and swore under his breath.

Who was he kidding? He'd made passionate love to Lynn and then sneaked downstairs to moon over photos of his first wife. What woman wouldn't be deeply hurt? If he'd said his goodbyes to Jennifer, not left his loss festering, Lynn wouldn't have walked out.

He hoped.

"Mr. Landry..." his secretary said behind him.

"What?" he snapped as he turned, then scrubbed a hand over his face and said repentantly, "Sorry, Lydia. I'm running on empty today."

"Your three-o'clock appointment canceled." His middle-aged secretary eyed him warily. "I could reschedule the four-o'clock appointment. I thought perhaps..."

"That the office would be better off without me?"

She smiled faintly. "That you might like to leave early."

"Yeah." Damn, his eyes felt dry and gritty. "I would. Thanks."

When she left and quietly shut the door behind her, Adam tugged his tie loose. He had the afternoon free. He could head for Otter Beach.

And what? Hand Lynn a dozen roses, say, "Gosh, the words just wouldn't come fast enough last night, but I do love you?" and expect her to invite him in?

He was still incredulous at the discovery he had made last night, long after Lynn gave him a last look so full of hurt he'd never forget it and walked out of the room with dignity.

His lips had formed the words *I love you* before his brain caught up. He *loved* her? This pretty, quiet woman he had once believed he would never have noticed if they met casually? The woman who frowned in fierce concentration as she read about investing money she didn't have, who asked earnest questions so she would be able to understand his life? The woman who loved both girls effortlessly, had endless patience with them, who could play dress-up as if she were still three years old herself?

The woman who kissed him with incredible innocence and sweetness, who could still blush though she'd been married and divorced, who made love generously and lovingly?

He groaned and squeezed his eyes shut. How could he not have known?

He left the office without any desire to go home. An hour of aimless driving brought him where he'd probably intended to go in the first place: the cemetery where Jennifer had been buried in a gleaming mahogany casket. He shuddered at the memory of the casket. He would rather be cremated, himself, than be shut into a satin-lined box for eternity, but he'd let Jennifer's parents make the decisions. They were the ones having trouble dealing with their daughter's death, he had thought. *He* knew she was gone.

Now he laughed hollowly. None of them had known she was gone. He least of all.

It was the way of her going, Adam thought, that had made goodbyes hard. Jennifer was dead, they told him, but she lay there in that hospital bed for another four weeks looking as if she'd open her eyes any moment and smile. Dead, but she was breathing, her heart beating, a life growing in her womb. He still had trouble understanding: how could she give life, when she was dead? So when had she died? When was he supposed to understand and accept that his wife was gone?

He parked on the shoulder of the asphalt drive that wound through the cemetery, and walked across the springy grass to the flat marker with Jennifer's name and dates of birth and death. He was ashamed to have to hunt. The fragrant paperwhites in a pot must have been left here by her parents. Gestures like that would be important to them. Adam didn't often come. His laughing Jenny wasn't here, only the casket that held her earthly remains.

Perhaps, Adam thought slowly, he had known she was dead. The only place she still lived was in his memory. Those memories he had edited, he saw now. His young wife was charming, funny, sexy, good-hearted, but also spoiled and a little selfish. He had made her a saint and dared anyone—Lynn—to touch her place in his heart.

He finally let himself admit what part of him had known for a long time. The truth was, his feelings for Lynn went deeper, were based on more than youthful sexual attraction. Lynn was shy but gutsy. He admired her brains, her warmth, her taste. He loved her as a mother, a woman, a friend and a lover.

Maybe what he and Jennifer felt for each other would have matured into something similar.

Maybe not. Maybe they'd be divorced, like some

of his friends. Maybe they would live in brittle silence, because she wasn't really interested in him.

He would never know. She was gone, and he
would always remember her with love and sadness
for what she'd lost. Not what he had lost.

"Goodbye, Jenny," he said softly, but she was no
more here to answer than she had ever been.

Adam turned and strode across the grass with new
energy and purpose. He had to see his wife. This
time, he'd find the right words.

If only she would listen.

SHE HAD EXPECTED HOME to be a haven. Lynn
walked through the dark bookstore, finding her way
between tall bookshelves and the dark bulk of chairs
and tables by familiarity and with the help of the
night-light left on in back.

She'd tucked the girls into bed an hour ago. Their
whispers and giggles didn't last long. Impulse had
drawn her down here, where her dream had come to
life. The dream she was about to give up.

Tonight, she found only wood furniture and books
without color and life. A business. Not very important, compared to the people she loved.

In the grip of a terrible restlessness, she gave in to
another impulse and picked up the phone behind the
counter.

"Hi, Frances," she greeted her teenage baby-
sitter's mother. "Any chance Alicia could come over
for an hour or two? Rose and Shelly are asleep. I'm
desperate to go out for a little while. Maybe just for
a walk."

"Of course she can come. All she's doing is

watching *Titanic* for the thirtieth time. Just a moment.'' Lynn heard her muffled voice; she must have covered the phone. Then, ''She's finding her shoes. She'll be over in a minute. Are you okay, Lynn? Is something wrong?''

''No, I…it's just been one of those days.''

''I can remember a few when I thought I'd scream if I didn't get away from the kids, and I had a husband to take over once in a while,'' her friend said indulgently. ''Alicia can stay all night, if you need her. But, if you're going out by yourself, be careful, won't you?''

The teenager lived only a block away. Lynn met her at the top of the back staircase. Hearing the TV go on quietly behind her, she pulled on a heavy wool sweater that had been Brian's—she would have been lost inside it if she hadn't rolled the sleeves up several times—and hurried down the stairs and across the street, toward the rhythmic boom of the sea.

She'd left the rain behind in Portland, an unusual circumstance. Here at the edge of the Pacific Ocean, torn bits of cloud drifted across the face of the full moon and a wind with the bite of winter whipped her hair back from her face.

The boardwalk was deserted, the stores dark and closed. Laughter and voices drifted from a restaurant, but nobody sat outside the way they did in midsummer. She took the concrete stairs two at a time, wanting to lose herself on the dark beach, with only the moon and the surf for company.

She wished Adam had never been part of her life here. That they hadn't raced across the beach with the girls shrieking in delight. That he hadn't gotten wet rescuing the Japanese float for Shelly. Sat at the table every Saturday in her bookstore, reading contentedly. Bought her a new couch, taught her the loneliness of her bed and the pleasures of sharing it. Cooked in her tiny kitchen, hung his toothbrush in the equally small bathroom.

Absorbed in memories, Lynn stubbed her toe on a half-buried boulder and fell painfully to her knees. Tears sprang into her eyes, but she shook them away, angry at herself.

I...care.

Couldn't he have tried? she thought pitifully. Pretended, just a little bit?

Lied? she asked herself harshly. Was that what she wanted? Give him credit. At least he was too honest for that.

She pulled herself to her feet and kept walking. White fingers of foam led her to the water's edge. Lynn walked parallel to the crashing surf, her way better lit now by moonlight. The wind bit through her wool sweater, stung her eyes, tangled her hair, but she reveled in the solitude and the cold, the white feathers and the steady throb of the surf.

Hugging herself, Lynn kept thinking, *I could be home in Portland. Debating with Adam, laughing with him, savoring the delicious anticipation of bedtime. Is this really better?*

Couldn't she have loved him in silence? He might have come to love her in turn, mightn't he? Why had she given up hope that he would?

I...care.

Couldn't that be enough? she begged herself. Was that so terrible? Didn't the greatest of passions often age into something no more exciting? So what if he still thought about Jennifer. She was gone, and Lynn was here. With time, he would think about his first wife less.

She stopped and faced the breakers as wisps of cloud raced in front of the moon. *Why wasn't I patient?* she thought miserably. *Why couldn't I...settle?*

Wasn't having something better than nothing?

How could she convince Rose and Shelly that she'd made the right choice if she didn't even believe it herself?

Lynn found a boulder to provide a windbreak and backrest. Huddled against the night and her own unhappiness, she remembered every moment of her married life, every word Adam had spoken, every touch. She tortured herself with full knowledge of what she had thrown away, and began to see that she was a coward.

She had been so terrified of losing Adam slowly, she had brought on a quick, clean break. She knew she'd be okay on her own. She'd done this before. What she had no idea how to do was coax a man into loving her, or how to endure his indifference when he made it plain.

Burying her cold face in the scratchy wool of the sweater sleeves, Lynn heard herself as clearly as if she'd spoken aloud. She'd be okay on her own. She'd done this before.

Oh, God. She had told Adam once that being a single mother came naturally to her, that it was the pattern she knew. She was comfortable as a mother, but not as a wife.

In her fear, she had made no effort to fight for Adam. Being a wife was too scary. Run and hide.

Her tears soaked the sweater sleeves, her nose dripped. If only she hadn't told him she loved him! Lynn thought wretchedly. Bitter, angry words could be taken back, but not her naked declaration.

I don't want to lose you, he'd said, but how could they go on as they had before, when neither of them would be able to forget that one of them loved and one didn't?

For the girls' sake, would he agree to live that way? Was she brave enough to try, if he would give her the chance?

The rags of clouds were knitting together into dark masses and the wind smelled of rain. Chilled to the bone, Lynn started back along the beach, the wind shoving her from behind. She was so cold! Her feet were numb and blockish in thin sneakers. Dressed so inadequately, she shouldn't have stayed as long as she had.

The first icy shards of rain came as she turned her back on the ocean and picked her way carefully between rough rocks and piles of driftwood toward the steps up to street level.

She was almost there when she saw that a man leaned against the railing only feet from the opening to the beach. With the lamplight behind him, he was dark, anonymous and imposing. She hesitated. Probably he only wanted his solitude, as she had, but it was awfully lonely out here if he were to threaten her. Still, there was no other easy way up the concrete and granite bulkhead, and she was very cold.

Taking a breath for courage, she bent her head and

hurried toward the stairs. She had set foot on the bottom one when he spoke.

"Lynn?"

"Adam?" she whispered. The wind whipped his name away, unheard.

"I've been waiting for you." He didn't move.

Slowly she climbed the few stairs. Hip against the railing, he faced her. His expression changed when he got a good look at her in the yellowish light from a sodium lamp.

"You've been crying." He sounded angry. Gruff.

"My eyes watered. The wind…" Why was he here?

He swore and stepped forward. The relief was overwhelming. Right this second, it hardly mattered why he'd come. Oh, how easy it was to let herself be enveloped in his warmth and strength.

"I'm sorry," she tried to tell him, but had no idea if he heard her.

He was swearing still, growling something against her hair. It seemed to be an echo. "God, I'm sorry. You've got to forgive me, Lynn."

"Forgive you?" What was he talking about? She tried to pull back, but his arms tightened, binding her to him.

"How did you find me?"

"The baby-sitter." At last his grip relaxed. "Can we go home, Lynn?" His hand, cold enough, caressed her frozen cheek. "You need a hot bath."

"Yes. Okay."

I…care. Of course he did. That had to be enough.

Her legs were reluctant to move. Adam had to steer her along the sidewalk, stop her with one hand from stepping out into the street in front of a lone car passing through town. Even her thoughts were sluggish now.

His Lexus was in its usual spot in the gravel lot. *Adam is here,* she thought, amazed.

The staircase seemed to go on forever. At the top, Adam bundled her inside. She stood in the kitchen, beginning to shake, and was distantly aware that he was paying Alicia and seeing her out.

When she heard water running into the tub, she shuffled down the hall to the bathroom. Still in his own heavy sweater, he was on his knees, testing the water temperature. When he saw her, his expression brought to life an ember of warmth inside her.

His jaw muscles flexed. ''Shall I help you get undressed?''

The glow spread. ''No. I'm okay. Just chilly.''

''Damn it, Lynn—'' He bit off whatever he'd been going to say. ''I'll boil water for tea. I'll get you something to put on.''

He started to brush by her, but paused, his body touching hers from thigh to chest. She felt the vibration when he spoke. ''I hope you did all the thinking you intend to do.''

She nodded dumbly.

''Good.'' He touched her cold cheek again, then left the bathroom, returning a moment later with her ugliest, most voluminous flannel nightgown and her old wool bathrobe.

He was obviously not setting the stage for seduction.

Lynn had plenty of time in the bath to worry anew as she thawed. Why was he sorry? What did she have to forgive him for? If anyone needed forgiving, it was her!

When she'd quit shivering and her skin glowed pink, she got out, toweled herself dry and put on her old gown and robe. Her hair. Lynn groaned, glimpsing the tangles in the mirror. If only she'd corralled her curls instead of letting the wind whip them into a frenzy. She took ten minutes to bring her recalcitrant hair to reasonable order and assemble it in a simple braid down her back.

Hope had thawed along with her flesh, but so had old fears. Adam might be here to talk about a divorce. Or to ask her to stay in their arrangement, while explaining gently how much he had loved his Jenny and why he would never be able to love her the same way. He might even be angry and planning to fight her for custody of the girls.

No, even terrified, she knew better. He would never do that. Not to her, not to Shelly or Rose.

He waited in the living room, sitting with his elbows resting on his knees, holding a steaming mug in one hand. Although she had made no sound, he looked up the moment Lynn appeared in the doorway. His gaze not leaving hers, he stood. "Here's your tea."

"Thank you." She held her head high as she ventured into the living room and took the mug from him. "I was cold."

"You're lucky you didn't die of hypothermia." He sounded angry again.

"I was on my way home."

"Were you trying to commit suicide?"

"I was walking on a cold night!" she fired back.

"I wanted to think! You told me to. I had to be alone."

He rotated his shoulders as if they ached. His tone was almost conversational. "What did you think about?"

Her tongue touched her lips. "You. Us," she admitted huskily.

"Your conclusion?"

She wrapped both hands around the mug, willing its heat to give her courage. "I was wrong. I..."

His expression was shuttered, just like that. "You don't love me."

"I shouldn't have told you I do," Lynn corrected him. "I was pressuring you. We had an arrangement, and it was working fine. I..." She bowed her head. "I got scared."

"Scared of what?" Adam asked, voice gritty.

"I know you like me and...and want me. At least I assume..." She stole a look at him and hurried on. "I was afraid after a while you wouldn't. That I wouldn't be able to stand it."

"You must have known I was falling in love with you," he shocked her by saying.

Afraid to grasp the hope that she had been nursing all along, Lynn looked up. "No," she said just above a whisper. "No, I had no idea." She squeezed her eyes shut. "But you don't. You couldn't make yourself say the words. 'I care.' That was the best you could get out."

He touched her at last, his hand cupping her chin. In a slow, deep voice, he said, "I love you desperately and passionately. I was just idiot enough not to know it."

"Not to know..." This felt surreal. A too-easy ending to a daydream. She didn't dare believe him.

Adam's mouth twisted. "Sit down. I need to tell you about Jennifer."

She obeyed, watching the expressions on his face, the anguish, the regret, the rueful awareness of how blind he'd been, as he talked about his young wife and their brief marriage.

"They kept saying she was dead. Wanting me to sign papers so that her organs could be harvested." He swore. "What a word. Harvested. I signed, but deep inside I didn't believe she was dead. She'd open her eyes suddenly and smile. Only she didn't. They cut Rose—no, Shelly—out of her, and then the surgeons took Jenny away. I didn't see her after they pulled the plug. I didn't want to at the funeral home. I always thought an open casket was macabre."

"You never said goodbye," she said, understanding.

"I thought I had. But I dreamed about her. I missed her like hell," he said simply. "I felt guilty when I met you and stopped missing her."

Somehow Lynn had set down the mug and was gripping Adam's hand in hers. He held on so tightly her bones ached.

"I started falling in love with you that first time we met, at the hospital. I wanted to touch your hair." With his free hand he stroked it now, and she felt as if each strand was an exquisitely sensitive nerve. "When we made love last night, you said, 'I want you,' and it wasn't enough. I felt like a bastard, but I needed you to say, 'I love you.' What didn't occur to me was *why* I needed to hear those words."

"But when I did say them…"

Their grip shifted; their fingers curled together. "Do you know what I felt?" he asked. "Triumph. Exhilaration. *She loves me,* I thought. It took me five minutes too long to realize that I love you back."

"You didn't come after me," she said painfully.

He made a sound that hurt to hear. "I had to…adjust. I'm a deliberate man. I like to be sure."

"But you are?"

"Jennifer," he said, "was my first real love. I want to believe we'd still be happily married if she had lived. But I've changed in these three, almost four, years. When I try to see her being the mother you are, I wonder. Jenny was used to having her way. A baby was a grand new toy to her, I'm afraid."

"I think," Lynn said carefully, "all women feel that way when they're pregnant for the first time. The baby seems so unreal! Of course, everything will go the way the books say it will. You don't really understand how unrelenting having a baby is until you're on your own and it's too late to chicken out. I saw that picture of her. Pregnant, I mean. She looked so proud and so happy. I can't imagine that she wouldn't have loved Rose as much as you do."

His mouth tilted into a crooked smile. "Maybe so. But she's dead. Part of me will always regret she didn't have a chance to be a mother. We had such dreams. Reality is, I'm the lucky one. I have Rose and Shelly and you. I wouldn't go back if I could. I want to wake up next to you every morning for the rest of my life, make love to you every night, use our vacations to go to Disneyland with the kids. I want to argue with you, clean the kitchen with you, and grow old with you. If—" he swallowed "—you can forgive me for hurting you like that."

Lynn tumbled into his arms. "Oh, Adam," she mumbled against his neck, "I'm the one who almost messed everything up. I think it was just like with Brian. I wasn't comfortable. I like…controlling everything. Always knowing where I stand. I got a little panicky, and I convinced myself I'd be better off the way I was before."

"Were you?" He held her away from him, his eyes dark, turbulent.

She laughed and cried at the same time. "These last months have been the best time in my life. Knowing you love me, too, is like…like…"

"Buying a thousand shares of Microsoft when it went public?"

The laughter won, though her cheeks were wet. "Something like that. I was thinking more of fireworks and Christmas in July and all those clichés."

"Fireworks," he said, his thumb teasing her lower lip, "we can manage."

His kiss proved the point. Giddy from relief and love and the onslaught of desire, Lynn whispered, "Let's go to bed."

"Mmm." Adam gripped her shoulders and set her away from him. "One last thing. I'd like to wake up next to you every morning, but I'll settle for four mornings a week if you want to keep the store here. You need to know that."

"Thank you." She pecked him on the lips. "But I hate the drive, and I want to be with you. I might take a while off and think about what to do next. Or, hey, I might decide to take on Powell's Books after all! In my own small way, of course.''

''Uh-huh. And now—'' he stood and held out a hand for hers ''—your offer is sounding better and better.''

They did, of course, pause partway down the hall to watch thankfully as their daughters slept.

''Right now,'' Adam said softly, his words tickling Lynn's ear, ''I feel blessed.''

''Triply blessed,'' she agreed, and blinked away tears that were too joyful to shed.

Adam scooped her into his arms. ''Let's go make some fireworks!''

They did that, too, neither forgetting the words that counted, after all.

**3 Stories of Holiday Romance from three
bestselling Harlequin® authors**

*Valentine
Babies*
by
ANNE STUART

TARA TAYLOR QUINN

JULE McBRIDE

Goddess in Waiting by Anne Stuart
Edward walks into Marika's funky maternity shop to pick
up some things for his sister. He doesn't expect to assist
in the delivery of a baby and fall for outrageous Marika.

Gabe's Special Delivery by Tara Taylor Quinn
On February 14, Gabe Stone finds a living, breathing
valentine on his doorstep—his daughter. Her mother
has given Gabe four hours to adjust to fatherhood,
resolve custody and win back his ex-wife?

My Man Valentine by Jule McBride
Everyone knows Eloise Hunter and C. D. Valentine
are in love. Except Eloise and C. D. Then, one of
Eloise's baby-sitting clients leaves her with a baby to
mind, and C. D. swings into protector mode.

VALENTINE BABIES

On sale January 2000 at your favorite retail outlet.

HARLEQUIN®
Makes any time special ™

Visit us at www.romance.net

PHVALB

Looking For More Romance?

Visit Romance.net

Check in daily for these and other exciting features:

Hot off the press

View all current titles, and purchase them on-line.

What do the stars have in store for you?

Horoscope

Hot deals

Exclusive offers available only at Romance.net

Plus, don't miss our interactive quizzes, contests and bonus gifts.

PWEB

Coming in January 2000
Classics for two of your favorite series.

by REBECCA YORK
&
KELSEY ROBERTS

From the best of Rebecca York's

Till Death Us Do Part

Marissa Devereaux discovered that paradise wasn't all it was cracked up to be when she was abducted by extremists on the Caribbean island of Costa Verde.... But things only got worse when Jed Prentiss showed up, claiming to be her fiancé.

From the best of Kelsey Roberts's

Unlawfully Wedded

J.D. was used to getting what he wanted from people, and he swore he'd use that skill to hunt down Tory's father's killer. But J.D. wanted much more than gratitude from his sassy blond bride—and he wasn't going to clue her in. She'd find out soon enough...if she survived to hear about it.

Available January 2000 at your favorite retail outlet.

SUPERROMANCE®

Pregnant...and on her own?

HER BEST FRIEND'S BABY by **C.J. Carmichael**
(Superromance #891)
Mallory and Drew are best friends—and then they share an
unexpected night of passion. Mallory's pregnant.... Being
"just friends" again is impossible. Which leaves being lovers—
or getting married.
On sale January 2000

EXPECTATIONS by **Brenda Novak**
(Superromance #899)
Jenna's pregnant by her abusive ex-husband. Her first love,
Adam, comes back on the scene, wanting to reconcile. Will he still
want her when he learns she's pregnant with another man's child?
On sale February 2000

BECAUSE OF THE BABY by **Anne Haven**
(Superromance #905)
They're friends and colleagues. One hot summer night, Melissa
and Kyle give in to the secret attraction they've never acknowledged.
It's changed their lives forever—because Melissa is pregnant.
On sale March 2000

Available at your favorite retail outlet.

Return to the charm of the Regency era with

GEORGETTE HEYER,

creator of the modern Regency genre.

Enjoy six romantic collector's editions with forewords by some of today's bestselling romance authors,

**Nora Roberts, Mary Jo Putney,
Jo Beverley, Mary Balogh,
Theresa Medeiros and Kasey Michaels.**

Frederica
On sale February 2000

The Nonesuch
On sale March 2000

The Convenient Marriage
On sale April 2000

Cousin Kate
On sale May 2000

The Talisman Ring
On sale June 2000

The Corinthian
On sale July 2000

Available at your favorite retail outlet.

HARLEQUIN®
Makes any time special™

Visit us at www.romance.net   PHGHGEN